WILD HEARTS

The gentle sister of Ireland's most infamous rebel, Maire O'Byrne remains ever loyal to country and clansmen—until a strange twist of fate carries her to Lord Duncan FitzWilliam, the proud Norman master of Longford Castle. And now she must feign amnesia to ensure her brother's safety—even as her yearning heart seeks the warm shelter of an enemy's arms.

WILD ROSES

A man of peace in a land seething with rage, Lord Duncan is touched by this mysterious, afflicted lady whom he believes is a pawn in a dangerous family intrigue. Yet desire is Duncan's greatest peril, for his need commands him to tear down the wall of secrets that stands between him and beautiful Maire—and to give himself fully and passionately to a love some would call treason.

Other Avon Romantic Treasures by
Miriam Minger

MY RUNAWAY HEART

If You've Enjoyed This Book,
Be Sure to Read These Other
AVON ROMANTIC TREASURES

DREAM CATCHER *by Kathleen Harrington*
THE MACKINNON'S BRIDE *by Tanya Anne Crosby*
PHANTOM IN TIME *by Eugenia Riley*
RUNAWAY MAGIC *by Deborah Gordon*
YOU AND NO OTHER *by Cathy Maxwell*

Coming Soon

LADY OF WINTER *by Emma Merritt*

MIRIAM MINGER

WILD ROSES

An Avon Romantic Treasure

AVON BOOKS NEW YORK

**For my family and friends
with all my love**

WILD ROSES is an original publication of Avon Books. This work has never before appeared in book form. This work is a novel. Any similarity to actual persons or events is purely coincidental.

AVON BOOKS
A division of
The Hearst Corporation
1350 Avenue of the Americas
New York, New York 10019

Published by arrangement with the author
Library of Congress Catalog Card Number: 96-96176
ISBN: 0-380-78302-9

First Avon Books Printing: October 1996

AVON TRADEMARK REG. U.S. PAT. OFF. AND IN OTHER COUNTRIES, MARCA REGISTRADA, HECHO EN U.S.A.

Printed in the U.S.A.

RA 10 9 8 7 6 5 4 3 2 1

Prologue

Ireland, 1212
Near the Hill of Tara, Meath

The moment he ducked his head inside the fire-blackened hut, a scream rent the air.

Terrified. Shrill. Fading into frantic whimpers as the girl, her eyes filled with stark fear, clung to her weeping mother.

Cursing again that he'd come too late, Duncan FitzWilliam could see the girl was dying. Thirteen years old, perhaps, no more, already her tear-stained cheeks bore an ominous pallor, as glaring to the eye as the brilliant red blood soaking the lower half of her gown. Forcing back the fury that threatened to engulf him, he moved slowly to the girl's pallet but stopped when she made to shriek anew.

"Woman, tell her I mean no harm," he said to the mother who stared up at him with fear in her own eyes though she hugged her child fiercely. "My men and I—we've come to help."

"Help, lord?" Her voice hoarse, breaking, the Irishwoman looked from him to her ravaged daughter's face, her work-worn fingers caressing an ashen cheek with heartrending tenderness.

"You can't help my Uta . . . not you, not the priest . . . not the angels above—ah, God!"

As the woman's sobs filled the hut, her dying daughter's whimpers become as weak as her labored breathing, Duncan felt his rage grow hot and deep once more that an innocent should so suffer.

Yet thus it had always been. The innocent suffered and the ruthless trod them like dust under their heels. But not this time. Not on his land. Not while he held breath.

"Come." He knelt and gathered the girl in his arms before the Irishwoman could protest, and so gently that she stared at him in teary-eyed astonishment. She could but hasten after him as he rose and carried his broken burden outside into a spring morning so gloriously sunny that it seemed to mock her sorrow.

Mock, too, the ring of smoldering huts, sunlight dancing upon scorched earth and slaughtered sheep and chickens. Fortunately for the Irish tenants, most had escaped into freshly sown fields of wheat and rye when the three rogue Norman knights had come upon the tiny settlement. Fled for their lives, a few panicked souls reserving enough presence of mind to alert him at Longford Castle. But it hadn't been swiftly enough for young Uta, whose slender body had borne the worst of the knights' brutal attack while her mother had been made to watch helplessly.

"Clement!"

"Yes, Baron, I come! I come!" A stout man with a wide, kindly face came running, his monk's robe held above his knees. "I've done what I can for the few wounded—"

"Good. Tend to the girl and give comfort to her mother. Take them away from here, to the stream. The girl should have some peace—"

"Bastards . . ."

Duncan glanced at the Irishwoman, her face filled with such hatred that he knew she had spied the three prisoners slumped to their knees near the horses.

"Unholy bastards! God's curse upon you! God's curse for what you've done to my Uta!"

She flew at the closest prisoner so suddenly that Duncan couldn't have stopped her, but he hadn't thought to try. Nor did he signal for any of his men to wrest her away from the bound Norman knight who bellowed in pain as she raked her nails down his face.

As the woman's enraged shrieks filled the air and the two other prisoners clamored for mercy, horses stamping their hooves and whinnying in fright at the din, Duncan cradled the girl who moaned piteously in his arms. It was more for her sake than the prisoners' that Duncan finally nodded for one of his own knights, Gerard de Barry, to stop the frenzied attack.

A moment longer and he had no doubt the woman would have scratched out the Norman's eyes which, in truth, made no difference to him. His prisoners would have no use for sight where they were bound.

"Go, Clement, take the girl," he quietly bade the friar. With a cry the mother shrugged free of Gerard's hold and ran to clutch her daughter's limp hand as Clement set out for the stream, though just before they disappeared into the trees, the Irishwoman glanced over her shoulder and met Duncan's eyes.

He saw fear no more, only a burning look of comprehension as if she sensed what lay ahead. And a flicker of gratitude. But Duncan turned away, his purpose not wholly to avenge her dying daughter. His grip tightening upon the hilt of his sword, he gave the barest nod to his men. At once the prisoners were hauled to their feet, all three swaying more from drunkenness than any rude handling.

Fools. Sotted with ale, they had raped and plundered, and so they had been captured, sleeping off their cruel deeds along the same stream where Clement had taken the girl. For such witless folly alone, they deserved no pity.

"Hang them."

Duncan's growled command might have been a dousing of ice-cold water for how sober the prisoners suddenly appeared, their expressions incredulous as thick twists of rope were yanked down over their heads.

"M-my lord, s-surely you misspoke," cried out one stricken knight, only to wheeze and cough at the noose pulled taut around his neck. In desperation another man began to fight his captors, while the third, looking the worse for the Irishwoman's attack upon his face, nonetheless drew himself up in belligerent fury.

"You cannot hang us without a trial, Fitz-William! We've rights, damn you, not like these Irish dogs you treat as if they were your own kind!"

"Rights?" Duncan's laugh was harsh. "You lost all rights, man, when you chose to take up arms two years ago against King John." Unmoved that one of the doomed knights began to retch over himself, Duncan watched grimly as the ropes were tossed over a massive oak limb. "Pity that you didn't flee to France then with the earls de Lacy and their traitorous vassals instead of remaining to wreak havoc upon my land—"

"Your land, you half-Scots bastard?" His eyes bulging in rage, the man's voice rose to a rasping scream. "Walter de Lacy's land, no matter that accursed king across the water parceled it out to the likes of you. And there's scores more like us in Ireland who'll not let you forget it!"

"Then they'll join you in hell. No one destroys what is mine, or does harm to those under my protection and lives to tell of it. *No one.*"

Duncan wasn't surprised by the vehement oaths hurled at him, nor at how quickly they ceased in stricken disbelief when he glanced at Gerard de Barry, the tall, russet-haired knight shouting an order to the men holding a trio of impatient horses. Sharp slaps on the rump were heard, then the ropes sprang taut, Duncan not taking his eyes from the three Normans as they writhed and jerked high in the air, legs kicking, tongues swelling, and faces turning blue.

A few moments, no more, and life was gone, a question in Gerard's eyes as he approached Duncan.

"No, let them rot there," he said before a word was spoken. "As a warning to both Irish and Norman. I guard well what is mine."

Duncan turned and strode for his horse so

suddenly that the Irish tenants who had circled close to watch the hanging fell back and crossed themselves as he passed by, which made him smile grimly. No matter he had come to their aid, any Norman to these stubborn, unruly people remained one of Satan's own sons, and it didn't help that he bore the dark looks of his Scots mother. But his smile faded when a wild keening carried from the direction of the stream, which meant only one thing.

The girl was dead. His throat grown tight, he muttered a terse prayer and mounted.

Chapter 1

Near the Wicklow Mountains

"Begorra, Maire O'Byrne, have you ever seen a more glorious morning?"

Doing her best to smile, Maire glanced at her older brother Niall, his broad grin tugging painfully at her heart.

"Has the air ever smelled sweeter? Fine spring sunshine, a sound breeze coming down from the mountains. It's giving me an appetite, that's what it's doing. Aye, big enough to eat one of Ronan's prize cattle!"

As laughter rumbled from the eight O'Byrne clansmen bringing up the rear, their horses trotting two by two behind her and Niall's mounts, Maire hoped Niall wouldn't sense her growing unease. Jesu, Mary, and Joseph, she couldn't tell him now. If she did, he might ride back to Ferns, and what good could come of that?

Her hand trembling slightly at the thought, she swept a midnight strand from her face and fixed her eyes upon Niall.

Nearly twenty-seven, he had never looked

more handsome or more full of life, his blue-gray eyes dancing as he rode beside her, the sunlight catching glints of red in his dark brown hair. Maire knew he was thinking of Caitlin MacMurrough.

Almost a dozen times now over the past two years they had visited the beautiful daughter of Donal MacMurrough, the most powerful chieftain of the MacMurrough clan, at her father's stronghold in Ferns. An amazing thing, too, Maire thought with fresh heartache as Niall fell back to laugh and talk with their burly clansman Fiach O'Byrne and the others, leaving her to lead the way across a vast meadow sprinkled with wildflowers. The MacMurroughs had long been enemies of the O'Byrnes, until the day the two clans had joined forces to rescue Triona, her eldest brother Ronan's spirited wife, from Dublin Castle.

Rescue? Despite her low spirits, Maire couldn't suppress a smile. *Triona?* Whenever she thought of the incredible story since told countless times in the O'Byrne feasting-hall, of a ruthless Norman baron and even his own king bested by a copper-haired slip of a woman, Maire still felt a sense of awe at her sister-in-law's brazen courage.

It amazed her even more that Triona forever insisted she, Maire O'Byrne, possessed bravery that surpassed hers . . . especially now, when she was feeling anything but courageous. In truth, she felt a coward. How could she not, when she bore news that would break Niall's heart?

A burst of infectious laughter behind her made Maire grip the reins so tightly, her fingers hurt, and she blinked against sudden tears.

These past two years had forged a bond between herself and Caitlin MacMurrough as close as sisters; it had been Triona who had insisted Maire accompany Niall on his courting visits to Ferns not only to help build her strength, but because she had believed Maire and Caitlin would become fast friends. And so they had, though Maire almost wished now that she had never made this last journey.

Caitlin's tearful revelation to her only hours ago had cut her to the quick, but how could she not want her friend to be happy? Yet Niall, poor Niall. He had waited so patiently, at Donal MacMurrough's firm behest, for Caitlin to reach eighteen years before any talk of a wedding take place, and now that date had come.

But so too, had come a change of heart for Caitlin as sudden as a summer squall, or perhaps Maire had sensed the truth several months ago but had refused to believe it. Refused to believe the radiant light in Caitlin's eyes during their last visit when she had gazed not upon Niall O'Byrne, but a strapping young Irishman of a neighboring clan, a godson of Donal MacMurrough. It had been barely sunrise when Caitlin had come to Maire's bedchamber, her lovely features as pale as her linen sleeping gown.

"Oh, Maire, what am I to do? I love Brian! I've promised to wed him, too, but we haven't spoken to my father yet because of Niall. He's been so good to me, so kind. I thought I loved him all this time, truly I did, but Brian . . . Jesu forgive me, I don't know how to tell him!"

Caitlin had sunk upon the edge of the bed in despair, her green eyes, so like Triona's, stricken with tears, her silken blond hair falling across her face as she bent her head and wept. Maire had wept, too, for her tenderhearted friend, for Niall, for something that clearly could never be . . . then for the burden that was placed upon her as Caitlin desperately took her hand.

"Maire, please, you must tell him for me. To see Niall's eyes, the hurt. I couldn't bear it."

"Oh, Caitlin, no, I can't—"

"Aye, Maire, you must, it's the only way! But not here, not until you return to Glenmalure. He'd want to find Brian, they'd fight, I know it! And if either of them were wounded, dear God, or worse—oh, please, Maire! Triona can help you. Triona will know what to say to Niall."

Caitlin's pleading voice echoing in her mind, Maire closed her eyes and prayed fervently that Triona would, indeed, know the right words to say. Niall trusted her, had thought Triona the perfect match for Ronan the moment he'd seen her and then done all he could to help bring them together—

Another burst of laughter startled Maire, and so abruptly that she jerked upon the reins, making her snow-white gelding snort and toss his head. At once it seemed Niall appeared at her side, his hand reaching out to steady the prancing animal, his handsome face grown sober with concern.

"Maire—"

"I'm fine, Niall, truly." Her cheeks hot with chagrin, she wished she'd been more careful with her mount. All it ever took was the slightest hint of difficulty to send either Niall, Ronan, or both brothers rushing to her aid, their overprotectiveness of her undiminshed despite the miraculous progress she'd made.

Or so the priest who often visited from the monastery in Glendalough claimed it to be, a miracle. Maire knew that regaining the use of legs long denied her since a childhood fever, had taken months of hard work as well as countless prayers in her bed at night that one day she might walk as gracefully as Triona or Caitlin, or any other woman. She walked, that was true, but graceful she was not, and wondered if she would ever be.

Mayhap it was that obvious flaw which kept her brothers so vigilant, her awkward gait a constant reminder that they must shield her from hurt of any kind. And after what had happened last autumn . . .

Maire sighed softly, shoving the unhappy memories away and glancing at Niall to find him studying her, his expression grown thoughtful. At once she mustered a smile, but he didn't appear convinced.

"Begorra, little sister, that's a halfhearted attempt if ever I've seen one. Out with it now. What's troubling you? You've hardly spoken since we left Ferns, not like you at all"—a slow grin lit Niall's face—"though I admit I'd be more worried if Triona ever grew silent. Aye, that's a thought now, isn't it?"

His low chuckling doing much to quell her

sense of panic, Maire tried to keep her voice light. "Things wouldn't be half as lively, to be sure. Not for Ronan, not for any of us."

"And they'll be livelier still when she hears there's soon to be a wedding. Damned if it hasn't been the longest two years of my life! Yet I'd never have met Caitlin if not for Triona, and we all know that to be true. She'll think herself a fine matchmaker now, the very finest in Wicklow . . . Maire?"

It happened so fast, tears welling in her eyes, that Maire cursed that she'd never been one to conceal her emotions. Niall sharply reined in his horse and dismounted, coming to her side.

"It's nothing to trouble yourself over, Niall O'Byrne, nothing," she said brokenly, knowing the wretched sound of her voice alone would leave him anything but certain that all was well. Within an instant she was pulled gently from her horse, Niall holding fast to her arm as he drew her away from their clansmen, who had reined in their mounts and waited silently, Fiach and several others keeping wary eyes upon the surrounding woods.

"If it's nothing, then I'm deaf and blind," Niall said so gently when he stopped and faced her that Maire felt fresh tears burn her eyes. "Now you'll tell me what's plaguing your heart . . . though I've a sense of what it might be."

Suddenly unable to breathe, Maire stared at him, wondering wildly what he might say. "Y-you do?"

"Aye, and if I could change things for you this very moment, I swear I would. I know my happiness with Caitlin makes you long for your own . . . and I'm certain it will come, in time. A fine husband, children. Ronan may hold a different view, but only because he doesn't wish to see you hurt again. Yet you can't allow what happened last year to make you think it's impossible. Will you promise me, Maire?"

So relieved that she'd been spared telling Niall the truth, at least for now, she could only nod, though the ache inside her had grown near to choking her.

To hear Niall speak of a dream which had once seemed so close to her grasp . . . only to turn to disaster and, for a time, throw such a terrible wedge between Ronan and Triona that Maire had feared for their love. Triona had never wanted but to help her, spending countless hours with her as she learned to walk again and ride a horse, forever encouraging her, and even finally convincing Ronan that he should consider finding Maire a husband.

Yet she didn't have to close her eyes to recall the look upon Colin O'Nolan's face when the chieftain's son had come from the Blackstairs Mountains in Carlow to meet her. She could still feel the thunderous beating of her heart when she had so eagerly and hopefully walked across the crowded feasting-hall toward the head table, knowing Colin had been told of her legs and yet still wished to consider her for his bride . . . only to reach him and feel all hope die.

Saints help her, how could she ever forget the dismay, even repulsion, on his face as if he wondered whether her lower limbs were made of uneven blocks of wood rather than flesh and blood?

How could she ever forget mortification and anguish so deep, the pain cut her still?

How could she ever have dreamed any man would want a wife who dragged one leg behind her and swayed like a hobbled horse when there were other young women both healthy and whole . . . ?

Gazing blindly across the sunswept meadow, Maire brushed away tears that fell as much for Niall as herself, yet she allowed herself only a moment's self-pity. With time the memories would fade, and, after all, she had much for which to be thankful. A family who truly loved her. Ronan and Triona's little Deirdre, whose sweet smile could brighten any day. And, right now, Niall deserved her only concern.

"One of Ronan's prize cattle, did you say?" she somehow managed to tease, grateful when Niall's endearing, familiar grin cut across his face. Aye, she would hold her unhappy news until they were safely home, where Triona and Ronan both could help sway Niall from doing anything rash. "I feel a wee bit of an appetite myself. Too bad we'll have to wait hours before a feast could be prepared—"

"Mayhap not." Niall looped his arm securely through hers as he drew her back toward the horses. "I thought I might ride ahead and share with our brother that a MacMurrough bride will soon be coming to Glenmalure. That is, if you wouldn't mind our clansmen escorting you home. I know Fiach is a sober sort, but every once in a while he manages a smile."

"He'll make fine company. I don't mind at all." As she was lifted back onto her mount,

Maire decided it was a good thing Niall leave them, for her heart began to ache anew that he looked so merry.

With a last squeeze of her hand, he vaulted onto his horse's back and wheeled the powerful bay stallion around, calling out to Fiach and the rest of their clansmen to guard her well and see her swiftly home as he galloped headlong across the meadow. In moments, he had disappeared into the thick trees, and only then did Maire let her cheerful facade crumble.

But not so her clansmen could see her distress, all of them riding a length behind her as they set off at a canter. Keeping her face forward, she let the tears come. The horses' thundering hooves drowned out her prayer that Niall not think Donal MacMurrough had somehow encouraged Caitlin's change of heart and swear vengeance.

That the chieftain had allowed the younger brother of the legendary rebel Ronan "Black" O'Byrne to court his much-beloved daughter had shown the truce was solid between the two clans. Yet peace was forever so fragile—

"Ah, God!"

The agonized cry had come from behind her, Maire gasping as an arrow zinged past her ear, another O'Byrne suddenly shrieking in pain. Incredulous, she jerked hard on the reins and spun her horse around as another arrow struck a third clansman in the throat, her eyes widening in horror at the blood spurting from the wound. At once Fiach O'Byrne, his bearded face stricken, spurred his mount to her side.

"Normans, Maire! The devil take them, ride with you! Ride with you after Niall!"

Chapter 2

Dear God, Normans? So close to the Wicklow Mountains?

Almost in a daze, she stared at the host of mounted knights bursting from the opposite trees, their terrifying battle cries chilling her, their mail shirts and brandished swords blinding in the sun.

"Saints preserve you, woman, ride!"

Maire cried out as Fiach slapped her gelding's flank, the startled animal lunging so suddenly into motion that she nearly lost her seat. Desperately she grabbed the horse's snowy mane and held on, her throat constricting in disbelief as the terrible clamor of sword hitting sword rang over the meadow. She was already into the trees where Niall had disappeared moments ago when she heard more screams, hideous death screams. Her flesh crawled with fear.

None of her clansmen had ridden after her. At least she thought none, until the heavy pounding of hooves made her hope wildly, giddily, that she wasn't alone. Swiping the hair from her face, she dared a glance over her shoulder, only to feel her stomach knot in terror.

Three Normans were bearing down upon her like apparitions of hell covered from head to toe in fearsome metal, their horses great lunging behemoths to her smaller mount. It was then she began to pray desperately that Niall was nowhere near, that he wouldn't hear her screams and return to harm's way. Jesu, Mary, and Joseph, protect him! Protect her!

With cramped fingers she clutched the gelding's coarse mane all the tighter, her cheek pressed to his sweaty neck, her breath tearing at her throat as the animal weaved and raced through the trees at a breakneck pace that rekindled a shred of hope that she might yet escape. As if in a blurred dream the forest flew past her, flashes of deep green melding with mottled sunlight and an occasional brilliant shaft that broke through the dense leaves. She squinted against the sudden brightness, daring once more to lift her head and look behind her . . .

It happened so fast, a violent thud and then pain so intense that Maire scarcely realized she was lying sprawled upon the ground, a low-hanging branch wavering and shimmering above her. And again came the piercing sunlight through the leaves, blinding her as she fought to drag air into her lungs, fought to fend off the strange darkness threatening to overwhelm her as the terrible throbbing in her head grew stronger, more fierce. Dazedly she heard horses snorting and blowing, and men's voices growing near.

"God's breath, does she live?"

"Barely, I'd wager, after that blow. Hit the branch square on, she did, foolish little bitch."

"Ah, Henry, you're only grousing because you'll have to wait now to spread her legs. A pretty bit, too, for an Irish wench, though too thin for my taste."

"Anything would be too thin compared to the big-breasted sows you take to your bed, man! Gather her up and let's get back to the others. Lady Adele should be well pleased with today's sport, wouldn't you say?"

Coarse male laughter ringing deafeningly in her ears, Maire groaned as she felt herself being lifted, the pain in her head grown so acute she was aware of little else. Nor did she think to fight her captor, her limbs useless and limp, the world become no more than a hazy blur. Within what seemed an instant, the shadow of trees and leaves was gone, only open sky above her, and more blinding sun.

"You ran her down! Delightful!" came a feminine voice. A cool palm slipped across the left side of her head, which throbbed and thundered. "A terrible lump, though, big as a chestnut. Did you strike her, FitzHugh?"

"Ha! A branch felling her was hardly the surrender I had envisioned—"

"And you'll leave her be, too, Henry, if she's to recover. Since Gwyneth died aboard ship, you know I need another maid. This wench will do nicely . . . an Irish savage to amuse me. Then again, she might amuse my dear brother, too. She's surely lovely enough. And what better way to show the man I want only the best for him, yes? A humble gift to herald my surprise visit!"

Gay laughter piercing her skull, Maire blinked in agony as she was jostled once more, nearly retching when she was flopped onto her stomach over a saddle. But she did vomit when she spied the bloody carnage upon the ground, Fiach O'Byrne's severed head staring up at her with sightless eyes.

"God's nightgown, my lady, now I'll stink like Irish puke!"

It was the last thing Maire heard as numbing darkness claimed her, mercifully silencing the uproarious laughter that rang all around.

"What do you mean, *visitors?*" As Duncan dismounted heavily, his gaze grim as he surveyed the unexpected commotion in the torchlit bailey, his balding steward Faustis wrung his hands.

"Important visitors, my lord! They're in the great hall—have been for an hour. And they've already eaten everything the cooks prepared, a full carcass of salted beef, half a pig, eight legs of mutton, and still they clamor for more!"

Duncan wasn't surprised, one dark glance at the horses filling the stable—leaving barely room for those of his own men—telling him the entourage that had descended upon his household was indeed large. Destriers, pack animals, a magnificent dappled gray gelding that any man would consider a prize, though a sidesaddle of finely polished leather was propped upon a nearby stall—

"Sidesaddle . . ." Intuition gripping his gut,

Duncan looked back at Faustis to find the squat little man counting aloud on his plump fingers and shaking his head.

"And twelve casks of wine, my lord, twelve in an hour! Heaven help us, we'll be drained dry at this rate—"

"Faustis, God's teeth, enough! *Who* are my damned visitors?"

His outburst clearly rattling the man, Duncan almost regretted his harsh tone when sweat broke out upon Faustis's jutting brow.

"She said . . . I-I mean, they said I mustn't tell you, my lord. It's a surprise."

"A surprise."

"Y-yes, my lord."

For a moment Duncan couldn't say another word for the tightness in his jaw, only Gerard coming up beside him and casting him a quizzical look, prodding him once more to speak to Faustis. "So whoever is in the hall eating my food and drinking my wine—"

"Ten knights, my lord, twenty-six men-at-arms, maidservants, a band of minstrels—"

"Ah, so my surprise visitors brought their own players. Jugglers? Acrobats?"

When Faustis gave a weak nod, stammering something about a dwarf court jester, too, Duncan had heard enough. Swearing under his breath, he didn't wait for Gerard or his other knights but strode across the castle courtyard, his bone weariness forgotten, the marauding Irish rebels he and his men had chased half the length of Meath pushed from his mind as well, at least for now. He swept off his mailed coif, the drunken carnival in the great hall something he was compelled at once to see.

God's teeth, were some days fashioned simply to plague him? First word had come that a farming settlement had been attacked, may Walter de Lacy's men rot in hell. He imagined the tenants who worked those fields—and the poor woman who'd lost her daughter—had exhausted themselves abusing the three Norman corpses he'd left hanging from that tree. Then a rider from his westernmost castle had brought news of Irish rebels stealing cattle, and now surprise visitors . . .

Duncan scowled to himself as the revelry grew louder and more boisterous; a stranger to Longford Castle would have no difficulty finding the great hall for the noise. And considering it was so late, dusk long hours ago, no wonder the servants had a haggard look about them, especially the ones bearing more steaming platters of food from the kitchen.

But what caught his eye were the two Irish serving wenches huddled near the great arched entrance to the hall, one of them clearly much distressed and weeping. Duncan came up so suddenly behind them that both young women gasped and spun around, their faces stunned and pale in the torchlight.

"Are you ill?" he demanded, cursing the need to speak so loudly for the raucous laughter echoing from the hall when one serving wench, a comely redhead, again burst into tears. Her plump companion hastily threw her arm around the smaller woman's shoulders, her voice shaky yet indignant.

"Not ill, lord. The wee thing's terrified, she is. One of your guests, forgive me for speaking so boldly, has demanded she come to his bed this night! And she's a new bride, a fine husband—one of your own blacksmiths, lord, waiting for her at home in the village—"

"Go to your husband, then. Now."

The young woman didn't hesitate, murmuring a hoarse thanks as she fled past Duncan and disappeared down the steps to the kitchen. The other wench picked up an empty wine jug and made to leave too, but not before casting Duncan a weary yet grateful smile. Yet he scarcely noticed it, his jaw clenched tight as he entered the hall.

"Duncan!"

The beautiful blond woman hastening from the high table in a flutter of sapphire silk made his gut knot all the harder, his suspicion proving correct. As the carousing continued around him unabated, minstrels playing their lutes feverishly, servants scurrying to keep cups and trenchers full while drunken knights grabbed and pawed at any hapless female and kicked at the hunting dogs fighting for scraps, Duncan found himself enveloped in a perfumed embrace of jasmine and musk.

"Oh, Duncan, how delightful! I was beginning to wonder if you'd ever arrive!"

She immediately stepped back smiling to sweep her gaze over him from head to toe, which allowed Duncan to assess his half sister as well. Older than him by eight years, Adele de Londres nonetheless carried her thirty-six winters well, bearing the face and form of a woman a decade younger. She was lovely. There was no denying it. Perhaps one of the fairest women in Britain. But what the devil was she doing in Ireland?

"You haven't changed at all in two years, Duncan. Still as handsome as ever, no—more so! But I suppose power does that to a man, yes?"

Tensing at the sudden brittle glint in her blue eyes, Duncan gave a slight nod. "I've done well, thanks to King John—"

"*Well?* One of the largest estates in Meath, three castles, countless manors? Why, you put the rest of the family to shame, dear brother. Who would have ever thought—ah, but I always knew you were destined for great things, glorious things! And when I heard just how well you were doing, I decided to come and see for myself." Adele waved her hand with a flourish at the sumptuously appointed great hall, her smile brilliant. "Truly, my lord, I haven't been disappointed."

Duncan didn't reply, her words grating upon him as much as her unexpected presence, bitter memories rushing to the fore.

Who would have ever thought . . . Yes, he could well imagine the profound delight his three half brothers found in the prosperity he had finally attained after long, loyal years of service to King John. He could almost hear them toasting him now, no doubt wishing him an early grave like the one that had claimed his Scots mother—

"Oh, Duncan, must you scowl so? I see that, too, hasn't changed. And I won't stand for it, not tonight, not after I've traveled all this way to see you. Come and sit with me and tell me everything!"

Again the cloying smell of Adele's perfume assailed him as she playfully looped her arm through his and urged him toward the high table. But they hadn't gone far before she slowed her pace, glancing with unabashed interest over her shoulder.

"One of your knights, brother?"

Following her gaze, Duncan felt his ill humor mounting as Gerard de Barry entered the hall with several other men, his longtime comrade in arms surveying the pandemonium with a mix of incredulity and dry amusement.

"Yes, and a friend as well. I take it the men"—Duncan looked with derision upon the drunken sots carousing at the high table—"who accompany you serve your husband?"

"Alas, yes, they did, but I bear heavy news, Duncan. My dear lord husband took ill and died during the winter. I'm a widow these past five months."

And looking none the worse for her mourning, Duncan thought darkly, if his stunning half sister had grieved at all.

Her marriage to Reginald de Londres had been no love match, but she had rushed headlong into wedding the aging baron for the comforts his wealth could bring her and doubtless the sexual freedom his failing eyesight could afford her. It had been rumored long before Duncan had come to Ireland that she had not once slept with the old fool, substituting her maidservants instead while she enjoyed the attentions of many lovers. But if she thought the man who was as close to him as a brother . . .

"No condolences, Duncan?"

Adele wasn't looking at him but at Gerard, her airy comment clearly no more than an afterthought and not worthy of an answer as she stared boldly at the handsome, russet-haired knight.

"Gerard de Barry has spoken for a maid, Adele. She comes from Sussex to marry him in two months' time."

"Really? How wonderful for him."

"So he has often said. I've not seen a man more in love."

She caught Duncan's gaze, and he swore he saw more than a hint of feminine challenge in those disarming blue eyes before she gave him an archly appraising look. "And what of you? Have you decided upon a wife yet?"

His jaw tightening, Duncan shook his head, which made her squeeze his arm in a poor attempt at sympathy.

"So I thought. You know, brother, mourning for a woman long dead won't give you heirs to protect so grand an estate. How many years has it been since Gisele . . . ?"

"Six." Glad that they had come to the high table, Duncan disengaged his arm. "It's late, Adele, and the day has been a taxing one—"

"Oh, Duncan, surely you're not thinking of retiring so soon! And if I've distressed you—dear heavens, I promise I won't mention her name again. Yet it only proves further that a wife is just what you need, and I insist you allow me to help. If we can't find a young woman of suitable rank among our kind here in Ireland, we could always send a messenger to London and request that the Court arrange—"

"By the blood of God, woman, is that why you've come to Meath?"

His roar silencing the bedlam in the hall, Duncan felt all eyes suddenly upon him, minstrels, servants, and drunken knights alike staring in surprise. But his own men didn't appear unduly concerned, Gerard calmly sampling a cup of wine, while Adele seemed less than startled, though two bright spots of color had touched her cheeks.

"Indeed, Duncan, I see your temper remains in high form. Perhaps it would be best if we talked tomorrow . . . after you've had a chance to rest. As you said, your day was a taxing one. I only hope you find the night passes more pleasantly . . ."

She didn't say more, a cryptic smile upon her generously curved lips, but turned to rejoin her knights at the high table. Yet Duncan caught her arm, firmly drawing her back to face him.

"One thing, Adele. If your retainers are indeed under your command, given Reginald's demise, then warn them well that I'll not have my servingwomen suffer any abuse during your short visit. Have your own maidservants see to their lusty amusements, not mine. Are we understood?"

Just as firmly easing her arm from his grasp, Adele gave a regal nod. "Of course, brother. We are simply guests here, for however long our stay. Not marauders. Oh, and as for your own lusty amusements, I've met—now, what was her name? Ah, yes, Flanna. Pretty enough for an Irish wench, though I've seen prettier. I enjoy some comfort that your longheld grief hasn't kept you from taking women to your bed. Sleep soundly."

Again she gave a curious smile, but Duncan didn't tarry to wonder at its meaning, her words alone a none-too-subtle taunt. That Adele had met his mistress Flanna—damn his sister! She was already sniffing into matters that were none of her concern, and after a stay of only a few hours' time!

So it appeared, an interminable day that had merely plagued him before now become a blight of epic proportions. Striding past Gerard, he thought to stop and warn him of the beautiful yet voracious fox now in their midst, but a sharp tug at his cloak distracted him.

He spun around yet saw no one, until an amused cackle made him look down. No higher than his knees stood a misshapen little man wearing a bright red cloak and a matching cap, Adele's court jester, who grinned at him from ear to ear and made a lewd gesture jabbing a stubby finger into a circle formed by his other thumb and forefinger.

"Sweet dreams, Baron. Sweet dreams!"

Before Duncan could utter an oath, the dwarf scuttled away and took refuge under a nearby table, which was a very good thing. Harboring dark fantasies of throwing Adele's entire entourage into the moat, the time-honored tradition of hospitality to one's guests be damned, Duncan was only too glad to leave the hall. That the sanctity of his home had been so shattered was almost more than he could bear.

"My lord! My lord, wait!"

He didn't wait. Faustis was puffing with exertion as the steward caught up with him at the tower stairs leading to his private apartment.

"My lord, there is something I must tell—"

"Not now, Faustis!"

"But my lord—"

"Not now!" And he meant it, Duncan taking the stone steps three at a time, his fury only mildly abating as the noise from the great hall began to recede. He didn't stop until he had slammed the door to his bedchamber behind him and thrown the bolt, the quiet which greeted him making him swear with relief.

Chapter 3

Peace.

If there was any refuge for him at Longford Castle, it was this place, a group of well-appointed rooms including the outer chamber, where he now flung off his cloak and began to strip from his armor, a huge bedchamber, and a smaller side room that held his precious collection of books and an oaken table, where he would sit and work often late into the night. But this evening he thought only of sleep, the bone weariness he'd felt earlier returning like a heavy blow and making him feel a man older than his twenty-eight winters.

Long bloody years of fighting in King John's armies had made it so. His body bore the marks of many battles, the worst one a deep, ugly scar across his chest that had nearly cost him his life. Yet it had won him, too, a king's gratitude, his reward the very land upon which Longford Castle stood.

A fierce sense of possession gripping him, Duncan dropped his hauberk upon a bench, the chain mail thunking heavily. Again the calming silence was broken as his stockings and shoes of mail, made of one piece, followed, and he wondered then why Flanna hadn't come from the bedchamber to greet him. Not so tired that he didn't feel a jolt of desire at the thought of her soft lips and willing body, Duncan felt renewed irritation, too, that Adele had found his Irish mistress somehow lacking.

"Dammit, man, you'll think of that blasted woman no more this night!" he vowed angrily to himself, though he knew that forcing his half sister from his mind would be impossible. That she was under his roof, her very presence an unwelcome reminder of all in his life he wanted to forget, permeated his thoughts as the offensively sweet smell of her perfume had the great hall.

With an emphatic curse, Duncan stripped off his padded gambeson and then hauled his sweaty undertunic over his head, the air in the chamber suddenly cool against his bare skin. Flexing sore muscles, he knew he could use a bath, the long day's stink upon him, but he couldn't stomach summoning servants for the commotion they would bring with the hot water. Instead he strode into the next room, a spacious chamber bathed in dim light from the low guttering fire in the hearth.

As quiet as the anteroom, Duncan's gaze went at once to the massive canopied bed, Flanna snuggled so deeply under the covers that he could barely see the top of her dark head.

Strange, that she could be too tired to greet him. Usually wine would be poured, a sensual welcome in her teasing green eyes. Wondering if

Adele had said something to distress her, he decided against waking her, afraid of the flood of tears that might provoke. If there was anything that wearied him about Flanna, it was her petulant nature; any small slight on the part of the servants was sure to bring on a bout of pouting or weeping. At first it had amused him, but now . . .

Sighing heavily, Duncan poured his own goblet of wine from the pitcher placed near the bed, then settled into a carved chair in front of the hearth. He stretched out his legs, kneading a stiff muscle in his thigh, the fire warming his flesh if not his mood. He lifted the goblet and drank deeply, then leaned his head back against the chair and closed his eyes.

It wasn't Flanna's petulance that wearied him. In truth, no woman amused him for long. It was an impossible thing, a cold fact to which he'd grown accustomed. None could ever compare . . . would ever compare, to Gisele.

He really hadn't thought of her for weeks, tried not to think of her at all, but now her image seemed to drift in front of him—her long honey hair rivaling the brightness of the sun, her smile, the love shining in her eyes, as radiant—making his stomach knot and his heart thunder. Any tears had been shed long ago, but the piercing ache inside him remained as surely as he breathed.

She was to have been his bride. But he had lost her. Only days before the secret wedding they had planned, fate dealt the cruelest of blows. And now Adele had come to Ireland to help him find a wife . . .

A laugh as grim as Duncan felt echoed around the chamber, his throat grown so painfully tight that he could barely finish his wine. Settle for another after he had known perfection? The sound of the empty goblet, too, scraping upon the stone floor when he set it down, seemed as bleak, and he scowled when a soft sigh came from the bed.

God's teeth, he was in no fit temper to contend with Flanna's complaints! Hoping that he hadn't woken her, he rose and moved silently to the bed, relieved to see that she still lay almost completely covered by blankets, her back to him. Which was odd, too, considering how she preferred to sleep cuddled against him, but tonight he was more than thankful for the respite.

Just as quietly he stripped out of his braies and climbed in naked beside her, turning his back as well. He heard another small sigh, and felt her shift ever so slightly, but he ignored her and shut his eyes.

So quiet. So dark. Fearing she might be in her own grave, Maire couldn't move for long moments, didn't dare move, only the dull throbbing in her head convincing her finally that she was yet alive. But why then, did she feel as if she were smothering . . . ?

She blinked several times, something warm and soft over her face that slow recognition told her was no grave at all, but a woolen blanket that smelled of fresh air as if recently hung to dry in the sun—

Jesu, Mary, and Joseph, the sun! Desperately

she squeezed her eyes closed, but she could not shut out the horrible memories rushing in upon her. Pain, such dreadful pain, and blinding sunlight, and shrill feminine laughter that pounded within her skull like a thousand hammers. And Fiach, oh God, poor Fiach and the others . . . all slaughtered. Dead.

Again she couldn't move, her fear so sharp that she tasted blood from biting her lips. Where was she? Where were the Normans who had attacked them?

More memories assaulted her, making her begin to tremble, making her remember the horror of being pursued, of lying helpless upon the ground, of a cool hand gliding like a mythic serpent across the side of her head. Words came to her, too, in a foreign tongue known to her only because Ronan had insisted his people learn well the language of their hated enemies, yet in her mind they were more sounds than sense. She had been in such fierce pain . . .

Maire slowly, cautiously, lifted shaking fingers to just above her left temple, wincing at the sizable lump that ached dreadfully at her touch. She wondered then if she could sit up, even walk, for the wave of dizziness that assailed her when she lifted her head slightly and lowered the blanket to her chin, noticing out of the corner of her eye a low flicker of flames.

Relief swept her, dulling some of her fear. She wasn't completely in the dark. Yet the next moment she was stricken by confusion at her surroundings when she dared once more to lift her head.

She had never seen such a place before, the

dying fire in the hearth revealing a room of massive proportions enclosed by somber stone walls, a high, timbered ceiling, and a trio of narrow, arched windows. The furnishings puzzled her, too, sparse but heavy and richly carved, and the bed in which she lay with its vermilion canopy was as large as any she'd ever—

Saints preserve her, a bed? She almost laughed nervously at herself in the next instant, though her heart had begun to pound. Of course she lay in a bed if she were smothered in blankets, her head upon a soft pillow, a sturdy mattress beneath her—oh, God, where was she?

Panic clawing at her, Maire gave no heed to her dizziness and lifted herself onto her elbow, her hair falling across her bare breasts. Bare . . . ? Incredulous, she stared at her nakedness, her heart nearly leaping from her chest at the sudden shifting beside her.

"Dammit, Flanna, lie down. Go back to sleep."

Maire froze, a heavy masculine hand covering her shoulder.

"Anything that's troubling you, we'll talk of tomorrow. Now lie down."

She couldn't blink, couldn't breathe, crying out when she was pushed gently but insistently back onto the pillow.

"Woman, it's too late for tears— Ah, God's teeth, come here."

Maire was enveloped so suddenly in a powerful embrace, hard, muscular arms drawing her close, that she had no chance to fend off her captor. Stricken, she felt a warm nuzzling at her neck. Her heart pounded furiously as a callused palm covered a breast and squeezed gently, arousing shivers unlike anything she'd known. Yet when she felt his other splayed hand glide down her belly, his fingers slipping into the softness between her thighs while something rigid and wholly foreign to her nudged between her bottom—

Maire's shriek filled the air, her elbow grinding into her captor's ribs with all her might as he swore in surprise and released her. Her only thought to flee, she lunged from the bed with such desperation that she forgot wholly her dizziness, forgot the limitations of her legs and went tumbling to the floor, tears of fright burning her eyes.

"By the blood of God, what in blazes—?"

Through her tangled hair she saw him come around the bed toward her, the Norman a hulking silhouette in the faint light and, Jesu help her, as naked as she! For she knew him to be an enemy, his marked accent one she could not forget.

Terror filling her, she scooted away from him across the cold stone floor, knowing in her heart there was no escape, sobbing wretchedly that she had not legs with which to run, to save herself . . .

Maire shrieked again when he caught her, fighting him and screeching as she'd never done before in her life as she was lifted into the air and carried back to the bed. But to her surprise the Norman merely wrenched a blanket from the mattress and then strode with her still struggling and flailing her arms to a chair in front of the hearth, where he plopped her down, his voice stern.

"Here, wrap this around you. And don't move, woman, do you understand me?"

Dimly she felt herself nod, clutching the blanket to her breasts as he left her and went again to the bed, Maire so stunned she could but watch him grab a strange sort of breeches from the floor and don them. But he might as well still be naked for how snugly they fit his thighs, and her face grew hot as she thought of how he'd held her in the bed, the hardness of his body pressing against her . . .

Maire swallowed and closed her eyes, shocked at herself, horrified that she would recall such a thing when her circumstances were so dire. Yet when she looked again, she was astonished anew that the Norman held out a brimming goblet to her, his expression grim but not unkind in the firelight.

"Here, drink this wine. It will calm you."

Again she could but stare at him, his husky voice now more concerned than forbidding. Which made no sense. Not from everything she knew about Normans, everything she'd heard from Ronan and Niall over the years about their enemies' vicious bloodlust and cruelty. And especially not from what she'd seen in the meadow, the bodies of her clansmen ruthlessly hacked to pieces.

She must have paled, for the Norman took one of her trembling hands and gave her the goblet, then covering her hand with his own, brought the wine to her lips.

"Drink."

Somehow she did, her face burning at how closely he leaned toward her, the jolt of red wine to her senses making her notice suddenly the striking cast of his features, his dark hair long to the neck much like Ronan's, yet not wholly brown or black, and the deep, vicious scar across a chest of powerful breadth that was matted with hair just as dusky.

His nearness made her notice, too, the smell of him, not clean like the blanket but sweaty and blatantly masculine, the scent of saddle and horses clinging to him. Flushing, she noticed as well the hard pressure of his fingers upon hers, and she suddenly began to choke.

"Easy . . ." Duncan set down the goblet and moved to rub her back, but she recoiled from him so fearfully, still coughing, that he sat back on his haunches instead and waited until she recovered herself. That gave him a chance to study her, and to wonder again how the devil she had come to be in his bed.

The wench was Irish, of that he had no doubt. She hadn't needed to utter a word for him to discern her ancestry, her terrified reaction to him alone telling him much. She was no more comfortable with Normans, a plight shared by clans loyal to King John as well as not, than he had a clue to her presence in his chambers. Unless . . .

Cold anger swept him, intuition once more gripping his gut.

Damn the woman! Adele's enigmatic smiles, her odd wish for him to have a pleasant night. Her criticism of Flanna that she'd seen prettier Irish women. And this wench was certainly lovely, beautiful in fact, her tangled midnight hair and eyes reddened from sobbing hardly marring her looks.

Such exquisite gray eyes too, soft as a doe's. He found himself staring into them, which was safer than at the tempting whiteness of her breasts, the blanket having drifted down when she began to choke on the wine. Unconsciously, he moved to lift the covering for her, but once more she drew away from him as if she thought him Satan reaching out to beckon her to hell.

Duncan smiled grimly. As no doubt she did. He lifted the goblet and held it out to her. "More?"

She shook her head, then grimaced so painfully that he wondered if she'd been hurt when she tumbled from the bed. Only then did he notice the swelling above her left temple, and he tensed. He hadn't seen her strike her head. Then how . . . ?

Dark questions filling him, Duncan rose so suddenly that she cried out, grabbing the blanket beneath her chin like a shield as she looked up at him wide-eyed. Her stunning gaze held such distress, such fear, and such confusion too, that he could only wonder at what harsh events had brought her to Longford Castle.

Duncan cursed at that thought and strode for the outer chamber, any hope now for a peaceful night shattered.

Was this some form of trickery on Adele's part, the wench a chieftain's daughter who'd been wrested from her home and brought to his bed as a ploy to force him to wed her? That his half sister might have contrived such a thing just to secure him a wife—indeed, if he'd taken the wench as he'd damned well come very close to doing, believing she was Flanna . . .

Pulling open the door, Duncan felt a hard stirring in his loins that did nothing but further stoke his fury, the memory of the wench's silken, heated flesh parting beneath his fingers foremost on his mind as he roared down the stairs.

"Faustis!"

Chapter 4

Duncan wasn't surprised at how quickly the squat steward came running, and he realized then that what Faustis had tried to tell him earlier must have something to do with the strange woman he had found in his bed.

"Forgive me . . . my lord." Out of breath as he neared the top of the stairs, Faustis leaned on a wall and mopped his brow. "I wanted to tell—"

"Where is Flanna?"

"In the serving women's quarters, my lord, and in a terrible temper. Lady Adele forbade her to leave until morning."

So Adele was at the heart of this mess as he had suspected. Glancing over his shoulder into his apartment to see the wench standing and more securely wrapping the blanket around herself, Duncan was wondering again what ill treatment she had endured when she staggered and sank back into the chair. He met Faustis's eyes, the man clearly paling at his expression.

"Summon Lady Adele. Tell her I want to see her at once."

"Y-yes, my lord, of course. At once." The

steward turned to oblige him, but Duncan wasn't done with him yet.

"The wench, Faustis. Did she kick and struggle as they brought her to my apartment?"

"No, my lord, not at all. She was senseless. I asked after her, thinking to call Clement to tend to the poor girl, but Lady Adele would have none of it. Forgive me, my lord, but she said rest, and your attentions, would rouse the wench quickly enough. And that I wasn't to say a word to you—yet when I saw you ready to retire . . . Ah, such a night. Such a night!"

Dismissing his overwhelmed steward with a nod, Duncan couldn't have agreed more. And this latest news didn't please him. If the wench hadn't injured herself under his roof, then she must have done so during her abduction and hopefully she had suffered no worse from that lecherous rabble of knights Adele had brought with her. And if she wasn't returned to her father a virgin, then he might very well find himself shackled to an unwanted bride . . .

Duncan strode back into his bedchamber, the wench twisting around in the chair to watch him anxiously. And this time he cared not if she recoiled from him. He would have some answers. Surely she had a tongue to speak, rather than just lungs to scream. He took only a brief moment to stoke the fire, light flooding the bedchamber as dying logs crackled and sprang to life. Then he sank to his haunches in front of her and braced his hands on the arms of the chair, his voice low but stern.

"Who is your father, woman? I can imagine well that you'd like nothing more than to be returned to your home, but I can't help you unless you tell me his name."

Her father? Maire's confusion as intense as the renewed pounding in her head, she felt as if she were trapped in a nightmare and could not wake. Yet one thing was becoming clear, that the Norman had been as surprised as she to find her in his bed—in truth, had thought her another woman altogether. Now that she'd had a few moments to think, he had called her Flanna—

"Woman, have you no tongue? Answer me!"

She jumped when he pounded a fist upon the chair, tears leaping to her eyes. She had never cried so much or so often as that day, but it seemed she could not stop. Yet almost at once she could see he regretted his action, for he sighed heavily and ran his hand through his dark hair as if exasperated with himself.

"Forgive me, but you must speak if I'm to help—"

"I-I've no father."

He stared at her mouth, the soft words she'd uttered clearly confounding him. Growing uncomfortable at his scrutiny, she licked her bottom lip, an action she promptly regretted for the way in which he continued to study her, a deep frown forming between his brows.

"No father?"

Maire shook her head, more slowly this time than the last, but even that made her temple ache.

"Your godfather, then. You must have some protector, a chieftain surely. Adele is too damned conscious of rank for it to be otherwise—"

"Truly, Duncan, do you always speak of me in such a complimentary tone?"

Maire gasped and rose from the chair so suddenly that she almost fell over the Norman, who stood as well; he caught her around the waist just before she toppled. Yet she scarcely noticed the weight of his hands supporting her as she twisted around, her heart beating so fiercely that the blood seemed to roar in her ears.

That voice! She knew at once that the imperious-looking blonde who glided into the bedchamber was the woman from the meadow, the woman whose cool hand had slid across her brow, the woman whose laughter she could not forget. Stricken, she stared into blue eyes as beautiful yet as chilling as a winter's day. The woman flicked her with an amused look, then glanced above her head to the Norman.

"Ah, such a delightful pose. I take it she pleases you, brother?"

Brother? Maire glanced in panic at the man looming so tall just behind her, noticing for the first time how closely he held her against him, his strong hands encircling her waist. But he didn't spare her a look, his expression grimly furious, so much so that she could feel his mounting tension in the splayed fingers digging into her flesh.

"I shall tell you how pleased I am this night. You've gone too far, Adele. Damn you, from what clan did you abduct this woman? Answer me now!"

The vehemence of his words clearly startling the stunning blonde, a winged brow raised in affront, Maire was astonished that Adele could answer so coolly.

"Abduct, Duncan? I brought you a gift, is all. My men and I enjoyed a bit of sport—some Irish strayed into our path on our journey north from Wexford. A motley bunch, they attacked us actually. So of course we had to defend ourselves—"

"No!"

Maire's hoarse cry filled the room, and she almost regretted her outburst when the icy force of Adele's gaze settled upon her.

"The wench still suffers from that nasty bump on her head, I see. Poor thing. She fell from her horse in the fray."

"Either that or one of your knights roughly handled her when you stole her from her home," came the Norman's equally cold voice behind Maire. "Dammit, Adele, if you used such a ploy to secure me a wife—"

"A wife? *Her?*"

Adele's voice was so full of scorn that Maire flinched, in the next moment she almost felt sick as the woman's laughter echoed in the lofty chamber.

"Good God, Duncan—oh, my, yes, this is rare. You thought I had the wench abducted to be your bride? An Irish chit? If I've any say in the matter, and I hope you allow me as much, your wife will be Norman-born as is only fitting for the astonishing rank you've achieved—"

"So you've already said tonight, Adele, remember? *Who would have thought?*"

As the room suddenly fell silent, the Norman scowled and his sister stared back at him with her lips pressed together. Maire sensed they were no longer talking about her plight but another matter altogether—something that clearly held such bitterness for the man named Duncan that his grip around her waist tightened to the point of pain, and she cried out, trying to twist free.

"She doesn't seem very fond of you, brother. No matter. I had meant her as a maid for myself, but thought her comely enough that she might amuse you. Yet I can see . . ." Adele didn't finish but reached out and clamped her hand around Maire's wrist. "Come, girl. You can sleep with my maidservants—"

"No, leave me be! Leave me be!"

Never having struck a soul in her life, Maire lashed out now in terror, scratching Adele's arm so wildly that the woman cried out in shock and pain. Maire didn't stop there, but flung her elbow once more into the Norman's ribs with such desperation that, in his surprise, he released her.

Her eyes riveted upon the door, she lunged away from him, her heart hammering in her throat, one hand clasping the blanket to her body while she prayed with all her might for her legs to run. Run! Yet in her haste she lost her balance almost at once, her stiff right leg dragging behind her, no aid to keep her from falling. She hit the floor with a terrible thud, her anguished sobs nearly choking her as incredulous laughter filled the room.

"Oh, this is truly rare! Irish, a bump on the head, and a useless cripple as well. If you think I would have chosen such as *that* to be your bride, Duncan FitzWilliam—"

"By the blood of God, woman, enough!"

His roar thankfully silencing his half sister, Duncan was at the wench's side before he even realized he had moved, her heart-wrenching weeping touching him even more than had her ungainly flight for the door. That so lovely a young woman would suffer such an affliction . . .

"Easy. Let me help you," he said as he made to lift her. Duncan was not surprised when she tried to struggle away from him, her ink-black hair damp with the tears streaking her ashen face. But she didn't fight him long, her sobs growing still as well, as if sheer exhaustion had overtaken her.

And he had no doubt she was exhausted, despite what little Adele had told him. As he carried the wench back to the chair and gently set her down, he could only wonder at the horrors with which her day had been filled, his scowl deep indeed as he met Adele's gaze.

"This *attack* you claimed—"

"So it was, but my men triumphed, I'm delighted to say."

Her tone more than slightly defensive, Duncan imagined it was anything but an attack, again given what he'd seen of her debauched retainers. Yet there was no purpose to exploring that now. "Where did the battle take place?"

"Where, brother?" Adele's grimace marred her lovely features as she massaged her injured arm. "How am I to say? I know little of this country."

"But you said you were heading north. Did you come across these Irish on the plains? Near Dublin? God's teeth, Adele, where?"

She started at his harsh tone but answered him, her voice grown twice as affronted. "South of Dublin. I believe there were some mountains to the west."

Mountains? That could only mean Wicklow. Perhaps they had been attacked after all, Duncan considered grimly. But what of the wench's impassioned protest when Adele had said her knights had been made to defend themselves? No Irish clan loyal to King John would have wantonly raised their weapons against Normans.

"Why did you stray from the coast?" he persisted, glancing at the wench. He saw that she sat huddled, with her eyes closed, her chin slumped to her chest. "Did no one tell you when you landed your ship in Wexford that the mountains are filled with rebel clans and to stay clear?"

"Of course they warned us, but we weren't so close that I considered it any danger."

"No danger?" Duncan gave a harsh laugh. "To stray anywhere near those mountains is pure folly. There are clans, Adele, the O'Byrnes and O'Tooles, who would have relished skewering each of your knights with a hundred arrows, then left their corpses to rot under the sun. Two years ago when we were fighting the de Lacys and their vassals in the north, there were so many raids by those bastards in south Leinster that King John has since tripled the reward for Black O'Byrne, a rebel I long to capture and hang myself."

Her throat suddenly gone dry, Maire tried not to move, tried not to make a sign that she had paid any heed to what was said. Adele gave a snort of disgust.

"Those Irish today were no vicious rebels, or if they were, they made a poor showing for themselves. We cut them down in barely a few moments' time—after they attacked us, of course. Fools."

"And how many were there to your ten knights and twenty-six men-at-arms?"

"Five, after my crossbowmen downed three—"

Adele abruptly fell silent while Maire heard Duncan utter a curse that would have blistered a priest's ears. Yet she did not dare move though their discussion sickened her. Poor Fiach. He and her clansmen hadn't stood the slightest chance . . .

"An attack, Adele? Sounds more like a slaughter, and yet somehow the wench survived . . . though if any of your men dared to have touched her—"

"And what is it to you?" came an indignant reply, Adele fairly sputtering. "You don't even want her! Go on, then, content yourself with that insolent little Irish whore Flanna, who seems to think she has some claim upon you."

"I asked if your men touched her, Adele? Answer me!"

"No, they didn't touch her, though Henry FitzHugh complained enough—"

"And you'll tell him to keep his accursed hands from her or risk losing them, am I understood? At least this way I can return her to her family unharmed—other than the terror she was made to suffer for your callous bit of sport!"

Maire jumped as Duncan's voice rang from the rafters and Adele's rose as well.

"Do what you will, brother; you were always one to champion those well beneath you! A curse from your Scots mother that I fear one day you will sadly rue!"

Maire didn't have to open her eyes to know that Adele had stormed from the room, though she did lift her head when Duncan slammed his fist against the mantel. The blood drained from her face. He looked so furious, as broodingly dark as Satan, his eyes upon the door where his sister had just disappeared. But when he saw her looking at him, he muttered something under his breath and sank to his haunches beside her.

"What am I to do with you? Dammit, woman, you haven't even told me your name."

Maire didn't know what to say, feared saying anything after what he'd threatened about Ronan . . . that he wanted to see her beloved brother captured and hung. Jesu, Mary, and Joseph, she had already told him that she had no father!

"Enough, I'll not press you further. In the morning we will talk again. You need rest, I need rest . . ."

He moved to lift her, but Maire tensed, her eyes darting in panic to the bed and then back to his face.

"Don't fear. You may sleep in here tonight, I've a cot in the other room."

His voice as huskily gentle as it had been enraged only moments ago, Maire did not fight him as he lifted her and carried her to the bed. Something told her that he meant his words and had no intention of touching her. He laid her down, but did not go so far as to cover her, his eyes strangely lingering upon her face before he turned and left her.

He even closed the door to the next room, leaving her alone, in that huge Norman bed where he had nearly . . .

Forcing away the disturbing memory of his hands upon her body, Maire shut her eyes, so exhausted she had no more tears.

Chapter 5

Glenmalure
Wicklow Mountains, Leinster

"By God, Niall, how could you have left her?"

Ronan's fury ringing like thunder in the feasting-hall, Triona glanced from her husband's incensed face to Niall, who stared back at his elder brother as angrily.

Jesu, Mary, and Joseph, this wasn't going well at all. Yet how could such a terrible situation go well? she asked herself an instant later, pain and worry hanging so great in the air that it felt like a live presence among them.

She had never seen Ronan so upset . . . no, there had been one other time, last autumn. And then his wrath had been directed at her; it still hurt to think of it. Maire had been at its heart then just as now—oh, God, poor Maire . . .

"Ronan and Niall O'Byrne, shouting at each other isn't going to help matters and well the both of you know it!" Triona spoke up, doing her best to keep her own concern for Maire from overwhelming her. "Aye, and it isn't right, not when we've others among us grieving for their loved ones . . ."

Her throat growing tight at the thought of Fiach O'Byrne's widow and four children, at the other slain clansmen's wives and families mourning around the stronghold, she was relieved to see a bit of the tension easing from the two men she loved so dearly. But only a wee bit. Cursing vehemently, Ronan turned to stare at the blazing fire, his broad back to Niall and Triona.

Yet she reasoned that was better than glaring and blustering at Niall and blaming him for a tragedy for which Triona knew her brother-in-law would never forgive himself, not if Maire wasn't found soon and brought unharmed back to Glenmalure. Her heart aching for him, she nonetheless did not go near, sensing there wasn't anything she could say that would lessen his pain. Instead she rose and began to pace around the table, needing to do something, anything, to ease her own.

"We have to send men out, Ronan, to keep watch and ask questions after Maire like you did two years ago with Maurice de Roche—"

"Dammit, *where,* Triona? Over the entire breadth of Eire?"

Stunned that he'd spun around to roar at her so harshly, Triona could see the immediate regret in Ronan's gray eyes as he came to fold her in his arms. She knew his unexpected outburst only masked his fear for Maire. She hugged him fiercely, burying her face against his chest while he stroked her hair, every rhythmic beat of his heart making her thank God for the day she'd left her home with this extraordinary man and come to Glenmalure. Of course, she hadn't thought so highly of him at the time . . .

"I think Triona's is a sound plan, Ronan. We have to do something, and quickly."

Niall's ravaged voice bringing her back sharply to the present, Triona wasn't surprised when Ronan released her to face his younger brother. And though he still sounded angry, at least he was calm.

"You said the attack had to have happened only moments after you rode west for Glenmalure."

"Aye." Niall nearly choked on the word. Triona had never seen him look so distressed. "But I must have been so far away already—God forgive me, I didn't hear a thing! And I was only thinking of getting back to tell you the news . . ."

He didn't finish, hanging his head and falling wretchedly silent while Ronan swore under his breath and went back to the fire. Triona muttered an oath, too, something she rarely did since she'd become a mother.

She might want Deirdre to ride and shoot a bow as well as any man one day, but she also wished for her young daughter a gentler temperament than her own, if only to spare Ronan two headstrong women in his home. Aye, and right now she felt like grabbing her bowcase and owl-fletched arrows and setting out herself in search of the Normans who'd slain her clansmen and taken Maire, the damnable spawn!

It should have been a happy day. Ronan had called a feast to celebrate Niall's news about

Caitlin MacMurrough soon becoming his bride. The stronghold had been alive with merriment and preparations until Maire's snow-white gelding had appeared riderless at the outer gates . . .

Triona forced away the vivid memory of Ronan's stricken face, of Niall's, both men as shaken in that moment as she'd ever seen them. Then the terrible commotion as every able O'Byrne ran for his weapons and his horse, only a reluctant handful remaining behind to guard the stronghold while Ronan led his clansmen in a thundering din across the glen.

Sighing heavily as she recalled the long hours spent not knowing, waiting, praying, every fiber of her being wishing she had ridden out with them, too, Triona did not want to think at all of the eight horribly mutilated bodies borne back to Glenmalure. Her heart-stopping relief that Maire's was not among them had been short-lived, Ronan's grim news that her gentle, courageous sister-in-law must have been abducted by Normans a moment she would not forget.

"I say we ride to Ferns, now, this very night."

Pulled from her roiling thoughts, Triona glanced at Niall, holding her breath as Ronan turned from the fire.

"Donal MacMurrough should know what has happened," Niall continued, his words coming faster. "He would help us—aye, he's an ally to the Normans, a trusted vassal of King John. He could send word among them that Maire is not to be harmed—"

"And have our enemies know her connection

to a hated rebel that could put her life in added danger?" Ronan broke in harshly. "Think, Niall, by God, think! That you'll wed the MacMurrough's daughter does not lessen the price upon our heads. And you, as my Tanist and the chieftain of the Glenmalure O'Byrnes if any ill should come to me bear a weight of Norman gold nearly as great as mine! If you believe the murdering spawn who've overrun our isle would not use such knowledge against us, dammit, man, then you're far more besotted—"

"Ronan, enough, please!"

Sensing Niall's renewed anger at the ominous clenching of his fists, Triona moved at once between the two men, determined that this tragedy would not forge a breach deeper than it had already become. She looked at Ronan, impassioned pleading in her voice.

"Let us think, husband, just as you said. Railing at Niall will not bring Maire back to us, aye, and don't forget he might have been murdered as well if he hadn't left that meadow. Then you would have lost both a brother and a sister. Now, what of my plan? Is it sound?"

He didn't readily answer, but his slow nod told her that her words had struck home. And Niall seemed to have relaxed some as well, his blue-gray eyes riveted upon his elder brother.

"The tracks were heading south to north, Ronan, at least for the three miles we followed them before it grew too dark."

"Aye, which would mean Dublin."

At the somber silence that fell, Triona knew her husband was thinking of the Norman-held city and its bay filled with foreign ships traveling to and from Eire. And if Maire's captors were bound for England . . .

"No, Ronan, that's only one course they might have taken," Triona interjected, unable not to when she saw his expression hardening again. "How large a force did you say must have formed the attack?"

"Thirty men from the tracks, mayhap more. Fiach and the others could never have fought off so many."

"Aye, and it makes no sense that such a large force would have come so close to our mountains . . . unless they were new to our country and hadn't heard of the O'Byrnes or O'Tooles. So let's think no more of Dublin or ships but farther north. Surely that's where Maire's captors must have been bound."

Touched by the warmth in Ronan's eyes at her fervent words of reassurance, Triona stepped from between him and Niall, hoping that the two would talk now and not shout at each other. She was much heartened when Niall's grim yet level voice once more broke the silence.

"That could mean Kildare, Meath, even Ulster."

"Aye, but we'll find her. By God, when we do, I vow those Normans will die."

Chills struck Triona at the look Ronan exchanged with Niall, the man she loved so completely appearing more a harbinger of vengeance with his midnight hair and ominous expression than ever she'd seen him. Niall, too, looked as forbidding, not as dark as Ronan but as strikingly handsome. At once the two fell into an intense discussion of how many men would be sent where to ask questions about Maire of Irish tenants working Norman land—who might have seen her, who might have noticed a stunning young woman with hair as black as night, eyes of softest gray, and the fine-boned features of an angel.

Indeed, Deirdre favored her aunt more than Triona; the only trait she shared with her wee daughter was her unruly curls. Aye, that, and a nature that bordered on stubborn no matter Triona's hopes to spare Ronan, though Deirdre could melt any heart with her smile. Longing suddenly to hold her one-year-old babe in her arms, to forget if only for a short while the horror of that day, Triona turned to leave, but Ronan reached out and drew her to him.

"Hug Deirdre for me."

Staring into his eyes, Triona wasn't surprised that he'd guessed her destination, their child a constant joy to them. And losing their unborn son only four months ago had heightened Ronan's attachment, making Triona often wonder if he would prove as overprotective of their beloved daughter as he had always been of Maire.

Aye, probably, Triona thought with loving resignation as Ronan pulled her into his arms, his lips hard and warm as he kissed her. But she could tell by the concern etching his face when he drew away that he was once more thinking of Maire, his powerful body tense as if he were already riding across northern Eire in search of her. Needing to say something to comfort him, her words came in barely a whisper.

"Ronan, Maire is as brave and stouthearted as any woman I've known. If she could teach herself to walk again—"

"Aye, but you helped her, Triona. You were with her nearly every step of the way. God protect her, who is with my sister now?"

A hard lump in her throat, Triona couldn't answer. She turned away before Ronan could see the tears burning her eyes.

A useless thing, crying. But right now it made her feel somewhat better as she fled from the feasting-hall. Ronan and Niall resumed talking, expressions of their determination that none but the O'Byrnes of Glenmalure know Maire was missing, for the safety of all, the last words she heard.

Chapter 6

It wasn't the bright sunlight pouring into the room that awakened Maire, but the smell of food.

Bleary-eyed, she stared in confusion at the young serving maid placing a pewter tray on a table pulled near the bed . . .

Bed! Recognition flooding her, Maire's gaze darted from the vermilion canopy overhead to the 'servant, more a girl truly, all freckles and gawky limbs, who studied her for a moment with open curiousity before turning to leave.

"No, wait!" Raising herself on her elbows, Maire glanced nervously at the closed door leading to the adjoining room, the girl's wide blue eyes following hers. "The lord of this place—"

"Longford Castle, miss."

A castle. Taking in the somber granite walls as if seeing them for the first time, Maire had heard of such massive dwellings from Ronan, and her spirits sank. Impenetrable. Accursed fortresses. So they had been described. Ronan grimly called them, too, the devil's own blight upon Irish land. How, then, would she ever escape—

"You asked after Lord FitzWilliam, miss?"

Almost forgetting that she wasn't alone, Maire was not surprised that the serving girl was as Irish as the usurped soil upon which Longford Castle stood. She imagined most of the servants were native-born. Slaves? Freemen? Her mind overrun with a thousand questions, she nodded. "Aye, the lord. Does he sleep still?"

"At midday?" As if Maire had asked whether the moon was made of ewe's cheese, the serving girl looked at her oddly. "Lord FitzWilliam's about his business, aye, and well I should be back to mine in the kitchen. Enjoy your meal, miss."

Before Maire could utter a word the serving girl was halfway to the door, only glancing back once to say something about hot water soon to be brought for a bath before she disappeared into the outer room. It was then that Maire noticed a large wooden tub with a stool at its center set before the hearth, which blazed with a freshly stoked fire, amazement filling her at the amenities being provided for her.

She was a captive, wasn't she? Yet all the startling things that Duncan FitzWilliam had said last night suddenly came flooding back to her, about wanting to help her, about returning her to her family and home— Oh, God, Ronan.

Her heart pounding, Maire sank back upon the pillow to stare blindly at the bright red canopy.

The Norman had said, too, he wanted to hang

her brother. He knew of the notorious rebel chieftain Black O'Byrne. Had Ronan and her clansmen raided upon his land, then? Stolen his cattle? Burned his fields? It must be so, given the harshness she'd heard in Duncan's voice. Jesu, Mary, and Joseph, if he should discover that she was Ronan O'Byrne's own sister . . .

Her stomach growling noisily jarred Maire from her stricken thoughts, the hollow ache more painful than the tender bump on her head. Feeling almost a traitor for wanting to partake of food provided to her by a Norman, she nonetheless drew the tray toward her, deciding it was better she eat.

If she was to escape from this unholy place, she would need her strength and wits about her. She had no idea if Longford Castle lay in Leinster or farther north in Ulster, yet it must be Leinster, surely. According to what she'd heard last night, it had taken less than a day's ride from the Wicklow meadow where her clansmen had been slaughtered for Duncan's sister Adele and her entourage to have arrived here the same evening. God help her, just thinking of that woman's laughter . . .

Sickened by horrible memories, Maire had to force herself to bite into a slab of white wheaten bread topped with a thin slice of roasted mutton; it was all she could do to swallow as she made herself think only of the dilemma at hand. Yet tasting food for the first time since leaving the MacMurrough stronghold in Ferns, well-prepared food at that, her hunger soon overcame her, and she made short work of the bread and a delicious apple tart studded with sugared almonds and raisins, which she washed down with a cup of watered wine.

She hadn't savored a like confection since Ronan's hapless cook, Seamus, who had long toiled as a slave in Norman kitchens before being rescued during a raid, died so suddenly two years ago, God rest him. Poor Triona! The cook's demise hadn't been her fault, but Ronan had blamed her nonetheless . . .

Maire dropped the last morsel of tart forgotten upon the tray, her anxiety mounting as she thought again of her family. And Niall, dear God, what of him? Adele had told Duncan of attacking eight Irishmen, so Niall had surely made it safely home to Glenmalure. Yet he still knew nothing of Caitlin. What if he should ride to Ferns thinking to see his MacMurrough bride-to-be only to discover she had married another?

Beset with panic, Maire shoved away the tray so suddenly that it tumbled from the bed and clattered to the floor, the last of the wine splattering the blankets. But she gave no heed, her only thought that she must find a way out of Longford Castle for Niall's sake, for Ronan's, and as soon as she could. Yet she'd scarcely flung aside the covers when an outraged screech rent the air, Maire's startled gaze flying to the door.

"Aye, you black-haired witch, out of Lord FitzWilliam's bed! Out or I'll—"

The comely young Irishwoman with flushed cheeks and blazing green eyes didn't finish but ran to the bed, her dark brown mane flying behind her. Maire could but gasp and scoot to the other side of the mattress even as Flanna screamed and flung a pillow to the floor; Maire had no doubt her attacker was the woman Duncan had mistaken her for.

"Out of that bed, didn't you hear me? That's my place, mine and Duncan's—"

"And you can have it, truly!" Clutching to her breasts the blanket that she had slept wrapped in all night, Maire half fell from the bed and spun around awkwardly to face Flanna. "I want nothing to do with your lord—had nothing to do with him. It was his sister Adele who brought me here—"

"Half sister, aye, and a witch, too!" Grabbing another pillow, Flanna threw it to the floor and stomped upon it, goose feathers swirling around the hem of her bright yellow gown as tears jumped to her eyes. "Forced me to sleep in the servingwomen's quarters, she did, when I should have been here. Instead you a-and Duncan—"

"No, no, Lord FitzWilliam slept in the other room, I swear it, and he didn't touch me!" Wincing inwardly at her lie, Maire nonetheless decided it was for the best when the young woman, who appeared very close to her own age of twenty-one years, sank onto the bed and began to weep noisily. Stricken that she could have caused such heartache, no matter it was a misunderstanding, Maire moved cautiously toward her. "Truly, Flanna, please don't cry—"

"And why shouldn't I cry?" the woman interrupted with an indignant wail, not appearing surprised at all that Maire knew her name. "I've never eaten so well, or had such fine clothes to wear, or slept on such a bed and now it's over!"

Staring in confusion, Maire ventured no closer when Flanna pounded her clenched fists into the mattress and hiccuped through her tears.

"The d-devil take it, I knew this day would come, aye, t-they all warned me."

"They?"

"The servants, damned gossipy lot! Said five mistresses had gone before me since Lord Fitz-William came to Longford Castle, all married out to his tenants when he grew tired of them. And now that will happen to me because he's found another for his bed. You!"

Flanna appearing more resigned than truly angry even though she had shouted, Maire didn't know what to say. Yet she ventured the first thing that sprang to mind. "I thought . . . I thought you were weeping because you love Lord Fitz—"

"Me? Love a Norman?" Looking at Maire as if she were mad, Flanna gave a snort and swiped at her tears with the back of her hand. "I've been bedded by the bastards since I was fourteen, aye, and I'll not say Lord FitzWilliam hasn't been the best among them. But I'd rather they take themselves straightaway from Eire and never return! Murdered my parents they did, the spawn who last ruled this place, but what's a girl alone to do? I had to eat, and none of my clansmen would look at me since I'd lain with Normans . . ."

Flanna fell silent, her somber, faraway expression hinting at hardship Maire could not begin to imagine. She had always been so protected at Glenmalure, knowing of the devastation and suffering brought to Eire by the Normans, but never feeling its brutal sting firsthand . . . at least until yesterday. Despair overwhelming her, she sank onto the bed next to Flanna, shaking her head.

"Saints help me, how will I ever leave this place?"

"You want to leave?" Studying Maire almost as incredulously, Flanna truly seemed surprised. "But they only brought you here last night—"

"Not by my will." Maire didn't dare say more about what had happened for Ronan's sake, but took heart at the sudden glimmer in Flanna's eyes. "I told you I want nothing to do with your lord. If you would help me leave Longford Castle, all would be as before, truly. And you're far too pretty for Lord FitzWilliam to send you away; aye, I'm certain you've nothing to fear."

Such a snort of disbelief greeted Maire's words that she was startled, Flanna once more appearing bleakly resigned.

"Mayhap if I had the face of an angel I'd not worry, but even one as lovely as you is no match for a ghost." Crossing herself, Flanna rose abruptly from the bed. "If you wish to leave, you've only to ask Duncan. He's a harsh man when vexed, no doubt of it, but fairer than any Norman I've known."

"No, no, it's not Lord FitzWilliam but Lady Adele who might not be pleased to see me go," Maire said hastily, not knowing how else to explain herself. "She wants me for a maid-servant—please, Flanna, will you help me? If I could leave tonight when it's dark, none would be the wiser."

Maire held her breath, but she felt another

burst of hope when Flanna jutted her chin, her green eyes flaring.

"Damned Norman witch. A maidservant, did you say?"

When Maire nodded, that seemed to decide the matter as Flanna gave a sharp nod, too.

"Aye, I'll help you, and it'll be a fine pleasure to thwart that harpy after what she did to me last night. Yet it will be late—"

Flanna didn't say more at the sudden commotion at the door, the same serving girl hastening inside the room bearing a blue silk gown and matching cloak and slippers that Maire recognized at once as hers, followed by four other female servants toting steaming buckets of water. Yet the girl stopped cold when she saw Flanna, her eyes widening as she glanced at Maire and back again.

"You silly freckled goose, what are you staring at?" Flanna demanded, fisting her hands at her waist. "I'm still Lord FitzWilliam's mistress no matter how things may look, and you can tell as much to the rest of that nosy lot in the kitchen—no, no, better yet, I'll tell them myself!"

Maire watched speechless as Flanna flew from the bedchamber as suddenly as she had come; her heart sank that she had no idea how the young woman planned to help her leave the castle. Yet given Flanna's defiant pronouncement, Maire doubted Duncan's mistress would fail her. All she had to do now was remain calm and wait for dark. Flanna had said it would be late—

"Miss, will you need me to stay for your bath?"

Maire flushed warmly as the serving girl glanced at her legs draped by the blanket; it was clear she must have heard something of last night and imagined her a helpless cripple. Adele's cruel words ringing in her ears, Maire gave a small sigh and rose from the bed, saying with quiet dignity as she walked a few steps to prove she wouldn't topple, "I can manage, truly."

Now the serving girl's face grew red. She lingered only to mumble something about a seamstress having mended a small tear in the gown and to point out that a latrine could be found in the short passageway leading from the bedchamber to the next room, and then she was gone, the other women hastening with their empty buckets after her.

Maire hurried too, to close the door, but glanced first with wary curiosity into the small outer chamber. Her face grew twice as hot as she spied a gleaming mail shirt lying on a bench, and she thought at once of Duncan, recalling all too well the powerful span of his chest and the potently masculine smell of him as he'd leaned close to her—

"Jesu, Mary, and Joseph, Maire O'Byrne, have you lost your wits altogether?" she scolded herself, discomfited that she would even harbor such memories. She closed the door firmly and went to the bed to gather her clothes, the familiar things making her heart begin to ache. She so wanted to be home in Glenmalure!

Ignoring any thought of a bath no matter how tempting the steamy water, Maire dropped the blanket she'd worn like a shield and dressed quickly, the soft linen camise and cool blue silk a comfort against her skin. Eating a Norman's food was one thing, she had to do so for nourishment. But she would not indulge in any needless luxuries; she couldn't. No matter any kindnesses, Duncan FitzWilliam was her enemy, Ronan's enemy, Eire's enemy, the blood of countless slain Irishmen, women, and children an eternal blight upon his kind.

Chilled by the thought, Maire went to the nearest window and looked out upon a bustling courtyard, but her gaze went at once to the towering castle walls and a massive drawbridge flanked by mailed guards. Her heart began to pound.

Surely Flanna didn't intend for her to leave by that route, as Maire couldn't imagine that they wouldn't be stopped and questioned. No, there had to be another way, or mayhap Duncan's mistress planned some disguise—

"A pity that hot water must go to waste. You don't wish to bathe?"

Chapter 7

Maire spun around, her heart slamming in her throat as Duncan came into the room. She knew she was staring like a fool but she couldn't help herself. The brilliant daylight added breadth and heightened proportion to a man she had thought formidable enough last night. How could he possibly seem taller or more powerfully built? Yet his shoulders were immense beneath a dark green long-sleeved tunic. Every masculine inch of Duncan FitzWilliam was as physically impressive as any man she'd ever seen, including her own brothers.

Unconsciously her eyes swept him, from the rich mahogany of his hair to strong, sinewed legs honed from much riding, legs that were snugly accentuated by black hose and leather boots worn to the knee. And his features, so brooding to her in the evening firelight, made her think now that she had never seen a man more fiercely handsome, with his dark slashing brows and straight nose framed by cheekbones and a square jawline cut as if from granite.

But what truly struck her were his eyes, a

deep, penetrating brown, both warm and intense. Or mayhap that he was staring at her so intently too, his gaze moving over her . . . sweet Jesu, Mary, and Joseph!

Flushing to her toes, Maire looked down at the floor, at her tightly clenched hands, cleared her throat, and then glanced up again to find him still studying her, no hint of emotion upon his face although his eyes only appeared warmer. With growing panic, she looked over at the tub, and he followed her gaze, which made her wonder crazily if he might imagine her bathing, as naked as last night in the bed when he had pulled her into his arms—

"If it's not enough water, I could have the servants bring you more."

He might have uttered pure gibberish for how stupidly she stared at him, and she could only shake her head no, that wasn't what she wanted at all. She wanted not to be thinking such disturbing thoughts! She wanted to be outside the castle walls and far, far away from this place! Glancing around her desperately for some way to put more distance between herself and Duncan, Maire retreated to the bed and took refuge behind a massive corner post, peering around it warily.

To her surprise she heard a heavy sigh, Duncan now looking at the floor and shaking his head.

"Dammit, woman, I've no intention of hurting you. I only came here to see how you fared—God's teeth, as a guest at Longford Castle, not a prisoner! Now, will you speak with me or not?"

Maire swallowed, his tone not so angry as exasperated. He didn't appear angry either, while here she cowered like a timid mouse behind the post. And Triona thought her courageous! Praying for even a wee bit of the plucky boldness possessed by her sister-in-law, Maire shoved a loose strand of hair from her face and ventured a step from the bed.

"F-forgive me. Truly, you've been more than hospitable . . ."

Maire fell silent, finding it as disconcerting to speak to a Norman as if he were merely a gracious host as that he looked at her as if relieved she bore a coherent tongue in her head. She followed his gaze to the tray lying overturned on the floor and the empty wine goblet atop the bed, shrugging apologetically. "I arose too quickly, and the tray—"

"Actually, I was wondering about the feathers."

Maire reddened at the snowy goose down drifting like gossamer across the floor, not knowing if she dare mention Flanna visiting her or not . . .

"My mistress has never been one to mask her feelings. I'll speak to her—"

"No, no, please don't trouble yourself," Maire blurted out, stunned that Duncan had guessed the cause of the mess. "She was angry, at first—seeing me in your bed . . . b-but I—" A blush racing to her scalp, she focused on the middle of Duncan's chest, unable to meet his eyes, and forced herself to continue. "I told her nothing had happened, that you hadn't touched me . . ."

Again Maire faltered, remembering all too

well the heaviness of Duncan's hands upon her, his fingers slipping into her body, and wishing wildly in the next instant that she could forget as her heart began to thunder and a strange warmth filled her belly. Suddenly weak in the knees, she made for the refuge of the bed again and sank down upon the mattress. This time it was Duncan who roughly cleared his throat.

"Now you must forgive me. I didn't know . . . By the blood of God, I could throttle that woman!"

He had strode to stare grimly out a window, affording to Maire a view of his broad back, as imposing as the rest of the man, when she briefly lifted her head. But she glanced down at once when he spun on his heel with a low curse and came toward her.

"Enough, woman, I need your name. It is past time that you were escorted home."

Maire froze. She couldn't look at him, feared to look at him for the panic in her eyes, her mind racing.

Saints help her, what was she to say? She couldn't give her name, for then Duncan would know she was an O'Byrne and she already knew what he wanted to do to Ronan. She would not be used as a pawn to capture her brother!

"Woman, we spoke of this last night, don't you remember? I can't help you unless I know your clan—"

"I-I don't know," Maire mumbled almost to herself, his words giving her a desperate idea. "I . . . I don't remember, nothing is clear— Oh!"

He had sunk to his haunches in front of her so suddenly and lifted her chin to meet his eyes that Maire was stunned, staring at him open-mouthed.

"What do you mean you don't remember?"

His tone so low and grim that she felt all breath had left her body, Maire didn't know if she could even speak. But as he searched her eyes, her face, somehow she made herself, sharp realization hitting her that she had found the perfect way to protect Ronan until she was free of Longford Castle.

"N-nothing is clear. I recall waking last night"—she blushed furiously and gave up trying not to—"but nothing before. I don't know what to tell you . . . it's terrible, like a fog."

Terrible, too, was the hardening of his expression, his fury clearly mounting as he muttered another low oath and Adele's name in the same breath. But somehow his fingers holding Maire's chin remained gentle, though his voice had grown harsh.

"Try to think, woman. You must! You were with your clansmen, eight of them, and there was an attack. You struck your head. Do you remember any of that at all?"

Aye, so vividly that Maire once more felt her breath snag in her throat, and tears rushed unbidden to her eyes. Fearing he might think she did remember, she jerked her chin from his grasp and dropped her head in her hands, a sob escaping her.

"I recall pain . . . it hurt so horribly, but nothing else! And I want to! I know I don't belong here, that somewhere I've a home, a family—"

"Yet you told me last night that you've no father. And you cried out in protest when my half sister Adele spoke of what had happened, did you not?"

Aye, she had, Maire choking back her tears and falling so still that it seemed the silence was a charged thing between them. What was she to say now? If she'd only thought then not to utter a word! She knew he was waiting for an answer, an explanation . . .

"God's teeth, was it your own father struck down in the attack?" he said suddenly, his voice grown even more ominous. "And a chieftain I've no doubt from the silk of your gown. I've seen none finer on many a Norman lady."

Maire gulped, saying nothing for she couldn't. Ronan had brought a bolt of the shimmery stuff home from a raid on a Norman merchant, seven bolts, in fact, in a rainbow of colors. She had more gowns than she could count; her brothers had always given her more lovely things than she needed . . . rich furnishings and hangings of painted cloth for her dwelling-house, exquisite jewels to wear, though in truth she preferred none, and more bouquets of wild roses, her favorite bloom, than could fill a dozen vases.

"Woman, that you haven't answered me does not bode well for the days to come. If not that you blush like a virgin, I would fear you had lost a husband yesterday as well. Damn Adele!"

Duncan stood so abruptly that Maire gasped, as startled by his words as that he grabbed her none too gently by the shoulders and drew her up in front of him. He looked so furious that she feared he was going to shake her to discover what he sought, but she sensed, too, when his grip eased and he once more searched her face that his anger thankfully wasn't directed at her but someone else altogether.

"If my half sister's senseless folly brings a battle cry of vengeance upon my house, then so I must bear it. But dammit, woman! Do you even remember your Christian name that I have a hope of making amends to your father's clan by your safe return?"

Maire stared into his eyes, Duncan's gaze so strangely ravaged that she was stunned a Norman would seem stricken over the deaths of any Irishmen. She told herself she should remain silent even as she heard herself speak, something inside her making her want to give this perplexing man an answer even if it wasn't the truth.

"Rose . . . aye, at least I think. I-I'm not sure—"

"Rose." Relief filling him that at last he knew something of her, Duncan wasn't surprised she bore such a name. That he'd seen few women as lovely was the sole thought that had come to mind when he had first entered the room, and she'd turned from the window in a flurry of blue silk and midnight hair, the sunshine enhancing what firelight had already promised. His gaze fell to her lips, as red as the wild roses climbing the ancient ruins at the Hill of Tara.

And sweetly curved, he found himself thinking, now that he held her so closely to note, too, how flawless was her milk-white skin, more proof of a gentle rearing. Reminded like a jolt of her father, who must have been slain by Adele's knights, Duncan tore his gaze from delicate features as exquisitely fashioned and met her eyes, a soft luminous gray he remembered all too clearly from last night, when he had opted to focus upon them rather than the tempting beauty of her breasts. He almost wished he wasn't so eager to return her to her family!

That unexpected thought made Duncan swear under his breath, and he swept her from her feet so suddenly that she cried out in alarm, stiffening in his arms.

"You've nothing to fear," he said to soothe her as he strode to the door. "I want Clement the friar to see you. He's more gifted a healer than any man I've known."

"B-but I can walk, truly."

She still sounded frightened, but how could he blame her after all that had happened whether she remembered every brutal detail or not? Yet he shook his head as they left his private apartment, watching her eyes widen as she saw the circular stone steps wending downward.

"It would task you too much. This way will be quicker."

She protested no further, and Duncan's thoughts went to the damnable circumstances at hand, though holding her in his arms was proving more a distraction than he would have imagined. He did not recall bearing a woman so lithely feminine, not since Gisele . . .

Duncan swore again but this time to himself, stunned that he had favorably compared any woman to his lost love. He had never done so before. Angrily he told himself that this woman with her unfortunate gait and Gisele were as different as night and day, Gisele as graceful and flawless as Rose would never be, as no woman could ever be—

"Please, Lord FitzWilliam, you're hurting me."

Realizing with some chagrin how tightly he held her, Duncan muttered an apology and loosened his grip, elated finally to reach the bottom of the stairs. Here he should have been thinking of his immediate plans, not the strange musings that had seized him!

He ignored the servants stopping cold in their tracks to stare as he made his way through the silent great hall to an opposite tower, Duncan deciding he would send messengers to other ruling barons as far south as Wexford and north into Ulster as well, to ask if they had word of any attack on an Irish clan loyal to King John and to give them the woman's name. That, at least, would be a place to start, and if Clement devised a potent healing brew that might aid Rose in remembering more about her family, he might yet avert an outright war. He contended already with enough accursed strife—

"Duncan, wait, word has come from the west! Those rebels have attacked again—this time not stealing but slaughtering an entire herd of cattle, the bastards."

Maire grew as tense as the Norman holding her; she was grateful at least as they were approached by a grim-faced knight with reddish hair, who was nearly as tall but mayhap a few years younger than Duncan, that he wasn't squeezing the breath from her like moments before. She could tell he wasn't pleased at the news, his expression grown forbidding indeed. She shivered, glad again for Ronan's sake that Duncan had accepted her ruse as his reply came low and ominous.

"They will pay for such waste; we've only to capture them. Take twenty men, Gerard, that's all I can spare. If this woman's clan attacks Longford Castle before I know enough to return her home—"

"Know enough?"

Confusion in the handsome knight's hazel eyes, Maire held her breath as Duncan nodded and glanced at her.

"All I've gleaned thus far is her Christian name—Rose. She remembers little else thanks to the injury she suffered . . . and thanks to Adele. Have you seen anything yet of my sister or her retainers?"

Gerard gave a derisive snort. "Still abed, I'd warrant. I saw Faustis after we spoke earlier. Poor man's still numb over Lady Adele's knights draining thirteen casks of wine. But one of your sister's maidservants did come looking for me—sent to ask if I might join her for luncheon."

"Watch her, Gerard; don't forget—you've already been warned. Adele devours men as ravenously as a glutton his meat. Your fair bride-to-be would not be well pleased."

"God's breath, man, you know I'd do nothing to grieve her. My heart is Melicent's—and all else of me. It's only Irish rebels I live to hunt down, damn their kind to hell."

The two men had been conversing so easily that Maire could sense they'd long known each other, yet she was struck by how harsh Gerard's voice had suddenly grown. She heard Duncan sigh heavily.

"I'll join you when I can." Duncan met her eyes but Maire looked away, realizing with a start that her hand was splayed upon his chest. Her face flaring hot, she balled her fingers against her waist as he added, "Just remember, Gerard, hang no one without me."

The knight's only answer a darkening expression as Duncan carried her past the man, Maire felt suddenly ill and more grateful than before that she had been wise enough to keep her true identity to herself.

Eternally grateful, too, that Flanna was coming to help her tonight. Maire's only thought was to protect Ronan from Duncan. He didn't stop until he had reached another spiral staircase leading up a second tower, but instead of ascending he went to a nearby door, rapping only once before stepping inside.

"Clement!"

Chapter 8

Maire had to blink. The large room she and Duncan entered was dark and dusty, the overpowering yet pleasant smell of fresh and drying herbs serving somewhat to settle her stomach. Basil, camomile, sweet fennel, mint, and so many others hung from the rafters, while she could see in the flickering light of a single oil lamp that crocks and colorful glass vessels of every shape and size filled trestle tables shoved against the walls.

"Clement, are you here?"

"I am, Baron, but a moment, please. Just one moment . . ."

The calm voice had come from an adjoining room, but Maire was distracted as Duncan set her down gently, his arm remaining firmly around her waist as if he thought she might fall.

In truth she was no stranger to being carried; before she'd regained the use of her legs either one of her brothers or a clansman had taken her wherever she needed to go about the stronghold, or helped her to stand or sit. Yet that had been so commonplace, while with Duncan . . . Warmed in spite of herself by his protectiveness, she decided that was all the more reason to step slightly away.

"Truly, Lord FitzWilliam, I can stand well enough—oh!"

A cat's pained yowl filled the room, Maire almost toppling backward as the startled feline jumped onto a table. Suddenly Maire found herself once more enveloped in Duncan's strong arms, and oddly enough he was chuckling, which caught her as much by surprise as the cat, whose switching tail she had just stepped upon. Duncan had been so grim only moments ago, and now to hear him laughing, a low, rich sound that seemed to rumble from his chest and even more strangely, make her want to smile, too . . .

"I thought that might happen. Clement loves cats as much as mixing his potions. He has eleven of them, usually underfoot. Look over there."

As Duncan eased his hold so she could turn around although he kept his hands at her waist, Maire saw that indeed, a sleek pair of half-grown kittens swatted at a frayed twist of rope beneath one table while more cats were dozing throughout the room, some curled on the floor, others atop casks and barrels. Even the snow-white beauty that she'd unknowingly affronted had settled into a fluffy ball of fur behind a huge mortar and pestle. Maire thought how much the feline reminded her of Triona's beloved Maeve, named after the legendary warrior-queen of Eire.

"Do you like cats?"

She started, meeting Duncan's eyes yet unable to fathom his expression, the lighting was so dim. It seemed so curious for such a formidable-looking man to be asking her such an ordinary thing, but she supposed his mind wasn't always filled with fighting and rebel clans and all the responsibilities his rank must entail. Yet she didn't have a chance to answer as a stout fellow with a shaven crown, wearing a somber gray monk's robe, hustled into the room, his voice humbly apologetic as he lit a second lamp.

"Forgive me, Baron, but the Greek text I was reading begged for me to finish the page—ah, now!" Clement twisted around his girth to study Maire. "Is this the young woman who last night so worried our Faustis?"

"Her name is Rose. I know little else about her." Duncan's voice had grown as grim as before as the friar drew closer to Maire. "She remembers little else, in fact. The injury to her head—"

"Oh, yes, those can be very bad. Very bad," Clement seemed to say more to himself, his broad, kindly face full of concern as he gently shooed a yellow cat from a stool and gestured for Maire to come and sit.

She did, very conscious of Duncan dropping his hands from around her waist, her skin still feeling warm where he'd held her. Yet she made herself focus upon the friar; he seemed to note well her awkward gait as she moved to oblige him, but she felt only compassion emanating from the man. Nonetheless it did little to soothe her sudden nervousness.

Jesu, Mary, and Joseph, would he guess her ruse? Her face grew flushed as she sat, and Clement's hand went at once gingerly to examine the bump on the left side of her head. Maire didn't have to feign her grimace or her sharp intake of breath.

"Ah, forgive me; of course it is still tender, terribly so." Patting her cheek as a father would do a child, Clement gave a sigh and then stepped back, still studying her thoughtfully while Maire's disquiet only grew.

"So what is your judgement?" Duncan said finally to break the stillness, his voice low and impatient. "Have you some potion that might help her?"

"Time will heal her best, Baron, but yes, I believe I've something to ease the soreness . . ."

As Clement turned to a nearby table and began searching rather noisily among vessels and bowls, Maire's gaze went to Duncan. She wasn't surprised he studied her, too. He did not appear angry at the friar's conclusion, but the hard set of his jaw told her that he wasn't altogether pleased.

"How much time, Clement? A few days? A week or more? By the blood of God, if her clan doesn't know soon that she is safe—"

"Such an injury has no rhyme or reason, Baron; I cannot say how long it may be. The shock of the attack upon her clansmen too, may be more at the heart of her malady. She must be treated most gently while she is among us—ah, here it is."

Maire's eyes widened as Clement drew a plum-colored vial from the clutter on the table, the friar clucking his tongue with satisfaction.

"I've some wine to mix with this powder if you'll both give me a moment—"

"I'll get it."

Duncan was gone before Maire could blink, several cats meowing loudly and skittering out of the way of his boots as he disappeared into the other room with a vehement curse. Clement sighed again, looking at Maire with some resignation.

"He is a hard man, Rose, bred from a hard life. But you've no reason to fear that you won't be treated well here. I've known no others as honorable as Lord FitzWilliam, nor a man who longs more to tame this unruly land and live in peace. That Lady Adele's knights struck down your clansmen has sorely troubled him—he's never slain anyone for less than just cause. Only yesterday he hanged three of his own kind for defiling an Irish girl. Poor child. She died in her mother's arms—"

"The wine, Clement. Mix your potion and let's be done. I've a long ride ahead of me."

Maire shifted nervously upon the stool, unsettled as much that her heart had begun to pound when Duncan strode back into the room as by what the friar had revealed to her. A Norman hanging his own kind . . . for an Irish girl? She had never heard of such a thing, would scarcely have believed it if anyone else than a friar had told her.

"So you will be journeying far, Baron?" Clement's voice broke into her thoughts, Maire watching with some apprehension as he poured a good dose of stark, white powder into a goblet and then a slow stream of red wine, swirling the two together. "Out of Meath?"

"South of Dublin to the place where the attack occured—if I must, I'll drag some of Adele's worthless band out of bed to lead the way. I want to see if the slain are still there"—Duncan glanced with somber apology at Maire—"or if anyone might have come to look for them. I hope not wolves . . ."

He didn't say more but Maire's heart was thundering so fiercely, her mind racing, that she doubted she would have heard him. Even knowing now that Longford Castle lay in Meath and not farther north, as she had feared, did little to ease her.

Duncan planned to visit the meadow? What if Ronan and his men were there? Niall? Aye, there would be a terrible battle, surely. And if her brothers weren't at that wretched place, and the bodies of her clansmen were gone, would Duncan find tracks that might point him deep into the Wicklow Mountains? Saints help her, he would know then that her clan was no more loyal to King John than Adele had thought her a fit bride—

"Here, child. Drink it down, now, all of it."

Maire's hand was shaking as she accepted the goblet and did as she was bidden, paying as little heed to the strangely sweet taste as that Clement was watching her with silent approval. He didn't speak until she had drained the goblet and he took it from her quickly, as if seeing that she trembled.

"You've nothing to fear, Rose. When you wake, your head will plague you less, I vow it."

"Wake?" Realization as to what she'd just

done hitting her like a blow, she glanced incredulously at Duncan and then back to the friar. "You . . . you gave me a sleeping draught?"

"Rest is the second-best cure, and after everything you've suffered, I can think of no better. Here." Clement scooped up a kitten winding itself around his sandaled feet and laid the purring creature in Maire's lap. "Ease yourself, child. All will be well." Then to Duncan he added while Maire watched numbly, a peculiar sensation of drowsiness overtaking her, "It won't be long, Baron. A moment or two, no more."

A moment or two? Her eyelids growing heavy, Maire unconsciously stroked the silky kitten with sluggish fingers, her chin beginning to sink like a weight to her chest though her mind still raced in desperation.

Jesu, Mary, and Joseph, what of Flanna? What of their plans for her to leave Longford Castle that very night? What of Ronan and Niall . . . and . . . ?

Maire would have burst into tears, but she had no strength left to cry, no strength even to speak as her head slumped farther and the kitten was taken from her lap. Then she felt herself being lifted, Duncan's voice grown oddly distant as the room spun around her and began to grow black . . .

"How long will she sleep?"

"'Til midday tomorrow at least. It was as strong an opiate as a healing one, Baron. And you must treat her very gently when she wakes, just as I said, to help ease the mists from her mind. I fear it may still take some time but—

ah, me, such a pity that one so young and lovely should witness such senseless horror. May God grant her heart peace."

Yes, it was a pity, Duncan thought grimly, Clement's remedy not being entirely what he had expected. Nor could he argue its merits as the deed was done, the woman already appearing fast asleep, her head lolling against his shoulder, her slender arms dangling limply.

Yet he had so much to do, messengers to be sent, the castle and his men to be made ready for any potentiality—preparations he had already been hard at since dawn—and then a journey that might keep him away until tomorrow night, if not longer, as he planned, also, to meet Gerard in West Meath, that perhaps it was best she slept away the hours. At least he would know her to be safe in his chambers.

"I trust that you'll check on her often in my absence," he said to Clement, who nodded solemnly. "I fear it was her father among those killed yesterday. The remembering of the slaughter may be as much of a shock—" Duncan didn't finish, his jaw grown so tight at the thought of Adele's blood sport that he did not trust himself to speak further. Holding his unconscious charge close to his chest, he went to the door, Clement's sober voice following after him.

"May God's peace go with you as well, Baron. It is a trying time and I will pray for us all. Irish rebels, Walter de Lacy's men attacking your tenants, and now this poor innocent brought to your house . . ."

Duncan heard no more, the door swinging

shut behind him. He wasn't surprised to see that several knights stood waiting for him, no doubt for orders, as well as Faustis, the squat steward wringing his plump hands and looking as worried as usual. Yet Duncan ignored them all and kept walking, his only thought to see the woman safely tucked in bed. There would be time enough when that task was done for other matters—

"My lord, please, a moment!"

"Not now, Faustis." Scowling, Duncan heard the steward scurrying after him, which only made him walk faster through the still empty great hall. "We'll talk later."

"B-but Lady Adele has ordered me to have food prepared, my lord, food enough for several days, as she plans to ride with her knights after Sir Gerard in search of Irish rebels. Yet you told me I must do nothing else until the storerooms are stocked to the rafters with provisions in case of a siege—my lord? My lord, what am I to do?"

"Do as I ordered, man! I will tend to Lady Adele," Duncan said without stopping, his tone so furious that a pair of serving girls spun from sweeping the floors to stare at him wide-eyed. He strode from the great hall and took the tower steps to his private chambers three at a time, no matter his burden, thunderous thoughts roiling in his mind.

Damn Adele to hell's fire! Did she think Ireland had been fashioned purely for her amusement? Follow Gerard to West Meath to make a worse mess of things? That blasted woman and her retainers had already brought enough trouble upon his house, and they would cause no more!

Duncan kicked in the door, but he stopped short as a shocked gasp filled the outer room, Flanna springing up from the bench where she must have been waiting for him. Her gaze flew from his face to the woman he carried and back again. Duncan swore to himself as his Irish mistress burst into noisy tears and stamped her foot.

"Lying witch, the devil take her! She told me you hadn't touched her but . . . but now you hold her in your arms like a lover! You've found another for your bed, haven't you? You're going to send me away!"

Flanna's petulant wail grating upon him as never before, Duncan decided in that moment as he strode past her that yes, he was going to send her away—God's teeth, that very day! First Fautis with his news and now his mistress lying in wait for him to screech and clamor. Must a man endure a trial by fire to accomplish a simple task?

Relieved to see that Flanna hadn't followed him crying into the main chamber, her exaggerated sobs in fact receding, as she must have run down the stairs, Duncan laid his unconscious burden upon the bed and tucked her beneath the covers. She didn't stir an eyelash as he took care to brush tangled midnight hair from her face, her fine-boned features as innocently peaceful in sleep as a child's.

Rose.

His turbulent thoughts amazingly ebbing just

in looking at her, Duncan allowed his gaze to drift to her lips, so red, so gently curved. Had she ever been kissed? Something told him she had not, her every anxious response to his nearness as much a sign she was unused to men as Normans. But she wasn't anxious now . . .

Duncan barely realized he had leaned over her before he felt the silken softness of her mouth against his own, her breath no more than a gentle stirring that strangely moved him. He did not recall so sweet a sensation since Gisele . . .

His gut knotting painfully, Duncan straightened.

Dammit, this woman was not Gisele! He left the bed without a backward glance, so overwhelmed by bleak memories that he didn't see the flutter of fingers or hear a tiny sigh, no more than a whisper, as he stormed from the room.

Chapter 9

Maire knew she was going to be sick the moment she opened her eyes.

The sunlit room appearing to float and shimmer around her, she dug her fingers into the mattress, hoping desperately that the nauseating sensation would subside. She even closed her eyes, praying, but that only made her feel worse. She threw aside the covers, and, her hand pressed to her mouth, she rose shakily from the bed and looked for a chamber pot but spied none. Then she remembered as if from a fog that the serving girl had said a latrine . . .

"Jesu, help me." Her gait twice as ungainly, Maire somehow half stumbled on legs she scarcely felt to the door across the room and pushed it open, panic filling her when she saw only a short dark passageway. But a faint bit of light to the left caught her eye and she rushed forward, nearly falling, and threw herself against another door, barely making it inside the narrow latrine fitted with a tiny, slitted window before she began to retch violently.

She had never felt so ill. Nor could she say

how much time had passed when she finally staggered back into the passageway, the darkness a momentary balm to her stinging eyes. She cried out at the brightness which greeted her when she reentered the bedchamber, so blinded for an instant that she didn't see she wasn't alone until Clement came up beside her, the somber-faced friar taking her arm at once to support her.

"Let me help you, child. I was hoping to be here when you awoke—I knew it would be soon. The opiate has made you ill, but the feeling will pass soon, I vow it."

Maire could only nod as he assisted her to the bed, her mouth dry as wool, her legs even more uncertain than before. With a moan of relief she sank onto the mattress and she was immediately tucked back under the covers, Clement shaking his tonsured head with concern.

"Forgive me, Rose, forgive me. Clearly I made the potion too strong. Yet your head feels better, does it not?"

Maire gave a weak laugh at the friar's words. Aye, strange as it seemed, she felt no pain as she lifted trembling fingers to the bump on her head; in fact, the swelling had receded. And her thoughts seemed so much clearer of a sudden, making her realize that if she truly had no remembrance of past events, drinking Clement's potent brew might indeed, have aided her—

Maire froze, recalling like a jolt what Duncan had said to the friar about returning to the place where her clansmen had been slaughtered just before she'd been given the potion. Her gaze jumped to Clement's. "How . . . how long have I slept?"

"A full day, child, and a good while longer. The sun sinks already—it will be dusk soon. You stirred an hour past, which made me guess then that it wouldn't be long 'til you awoke. You spoke too, so I knew—"

"I spoke?" Stricken at the thought of what she might have revealed, Maire felt a now familiar growing sense of panic though she forced herself to remain calm as Clement nodded.

"Names, mostly. Caitlin, Niall . . . and I believe, Fiach. Your family?"

Maire didn't readily answer, never having lied to a cleric, in truth, never lying at all before she'd come to Longford Castle. Yet she made herself, knowing she didn't dare trust the man no matter how kind. "I don't know . . . everything is still so confused. Did I say more that might help me to remember?"

"Only Lord FitzWilliam's name. I fear the rest was too low to understand—ah, child, don't trouble yourself. It will come back to you, in time. Now you must rest while I fetch some broth from the kitchen."

She must have paled at the mention of food because Clement patted her hand, his light brown eyes full of understanding.

"I know, to eat after what you've just suffered. But you must take nourishment, even if it's only a little. And the cooks have already prepared a savory beef broth especially for you. Lord FitzWilliam will not be pleased if you've wasted to nothing while he's been away."

"You expect his return soon, then?" Maire asked, as Clement turned his girth from the bed, her heart beginning to race as she thought again of what Duncan might have found at the meadow. The friar gave a somber shrug.

"Who can say? If he had to chase those rebels as the other day, it might be longer. He stopped here late last night to leave behind Lady Adele's men and say only that your clansmen were gone from the place where—" Clement fell abruptly silent as Maire felt the blood draining from her face, the friar studying her with fresh concern. "Ah, child, I've no wish to distress you. There's time enough to talk further. Rest now. Be at peace."

Be at peace? Maire thought incredulously, as Clement left the room. At least now she knew there had been no battle, but had Duncan guessed that the Wicklow Mountains . . . ?

Maire made herself lie still in the bed for an interminable moment, just in case Clement might unexpectedly return, but finally she was convinced he had gone to the kitchen. Only one urgent thought dominated her mind as she threw aside the covers and rose, grateful that her legs no longer felt so unsteady.

She had to find Flanna. Surely Duncan's mistress had come for her last night only to find her sleeping as if dead . . .

A faint memory suddenly stirred Maire as she moved through the outer chamber to the door, left ajar by Clement, and her gaze flew to the bench where she'd last seen Duncan's mail shirt.

A memory of a woman shouting and crying, yet try as she may, Maire could not place the voice or discern if she might have instead dreamed the strange clamor . . . aye, surely she had dreamed it. Just as she was certain she had dreamed that Duncan had kissed her—

Her face grown hot as flame, Maire could not believe as she peeked out the door how fast her heart had begun to beat. Jesu, Mary, and Joseph, nor could she believe that she would conjure such an impossible vision in an opiate-induced dream or waking!

Yet Clement had claimed she said Duncan's name while she slept, another strange thing she had no desire to contemplate further. Telling herself that she would have mentioned him only because the Norman was so perplexing, Maire began to move cautiously down the stone steps, one hand braced on the wall while she lifted her silk gown clear of her feet with the other.

In truth the descent was taxing. Duncan's words from yesterday, when he had carried her to see Clement, came back to her. It was taking so long that Maire wished for the thousandth time she could walk as effortlessly as other women, and she began to fear that the friar would return before she reached the bottom.

She had to find Flanna! She had to be gone from Longford Castle before Duncan arrived home with potential knowledge that might see her next bound in chains and dragged to a dungeon while plans were made to use her to capture her brother.

She had heard of such terrifying places from Ronan, and of how he and her O'Byrne clansmen had once come upon a ruined and near-deserted castle laid waste during the campaign two years past by the Norman King John against his traitorous vassals. The few knights left to guard the place had been subdued, she believed one or two even cut down when they had foolishly tried to resist, but there had been little left of worth for Ronan and his men to take.

And he had left soon after, sickened and made enraged by the stinking corpses found rotting in the dungeon, hapless Irish tenants he had judged who had failed to make their rent to their ruthless Norman overlords. Saints help her, did Duncan have prisoners shackled to walls somewhere deep in the bowels of Longford Castle? It seemed an incongruous thought with what she had seen thus far of the man, yet what did she truly know of him? Mayhap even now he was stretching the necks of rebels as fiercely determined to harry the Normans from Irish soil as her brother, the legendary Black O'Byrne . . .

Shuddering, Maire forced such grisly thoughts from her mind as she reached the bottom of the stairs, yet her sickened feeling lingered and gave her impetus to make haste. But which way? The castle was alive with commotion, servants rushing here and there and so focused upon their tasks that none scarcely paid her any heed as she tried to stay in the shadows.

It appeared a meal was being served, platters heaped with steaming food being carried through a great arched entrance into a room that Maire at once judged to be huge from the way laughter seemed to echo and resonate as if from soaring rafters. A feasting-hall? It must be, from the raucous sound of merriment, which made her all the more wary.

Hadn't Clement said that Duncan had returned last night with some of Adele's men? Surely his half sister's entourage must be among those carousing in the hall, and that made Maire choose at once the opposite direction and move as swiftly as she could manage, her gaze focused upon the downward steps, which she guessed from the servants bearing more food and brimming pitchers led from the kitchen.

She didn't want to run into Clement. Past the steps was another arched entrance opening into what manner of rooms, she didn't know, Longford Castle was so vast. Like nothing she had ever seen before. Yet the farther she was from the feasting-hall, the better—

"Miss, are you lost?"

Maire spun around, the freckled serving girl who had waited upon her yesterday looking at her with wide round eyes. "No, no, I was looking for Flanna, is all—oh!"

She nearly toppled at the stunted arms suddenly gripping her like a vise around the knees while the serving girl only gasped, her eyes growing wider.

"I've got her, my lady, she'll not escape from Rufus the Fool! Oh, no, I've got her good!"

Maire looked down in astonished horror at the red-garbed dwarf who held her so tightly, the little man burying his nose against her legs and chortling with glee.

"Ah, and she smells so sweet! Since Lord FitzWilliam doesn't want her, can she come and play with me? A dwarf and a cripple, what a perfect match we would be!"

As chilled by Rufus's coarse singsong rhyme

as the feminine laughter that sounded behind her, Maire didn't have to turn around to recognize Lady Adele. The nightmare mounting as the dwarf began to thrust his hips against her calves, Maire flinched at the sharp sound of a slap.

"Enough, you randy fellow! If you want to rut, go find a goat to please you."

Rufus only laughed merrily, as if Adele's admonishment had amused him, and Maire wondered in shock if the dwarf might be half-mad. But when Adele laughed too, a swarthy, curly-haired knight standing beside the beautiful blonde joining in their mirth as well, Maire began to fear that she might be that evening's amusement and wished desperately that she had never left Duncan's rooms.

"Please, ask him to release me," she said over her shoulder, her voice so low and stricken that Adele snapped at her.

"If you're going to address me, chit, then say it well enough so I can hear you!"

Swallowing hard, Maire found herself praying again for some of the boldness Triona possessed, repeating more audibly, "Please ask your man . . . Rufus, to release me. He's hurting me, my legs—"

"Really? Like you hurt me the other night, scratching me like a spitting cat?" scoffed Adele, her blue eyes glittering coldly as she came around in an angry flash of amber silk to face Maire. "Yet my dear brother seemed more concerned for your welfare than mine—how utterly usual for him. Duncan's never cared for his family, you know, at least not the better half that's Norman. Despises us, is more the truth of it—ah, but what is that to you?"

Maire didn't know what to say, other than asking again to be released, a growing group of servants now watching nervously near the steps to the kitchen. Adele didn't answer, instead looking Maire up and down, a winged brow arched as if she were noting for the first time the fine blue silk of Maire's gown. Maire decided to attempt another tact.

"Please, I was looking for Flanna—"

"Flanna? Duncan's common little tart of a mistress?"

Nodding hesitantly, Maire felt a chill as a strange smile curved Adele's lips. "I've only to speak to her, then I should return to bed. Clement the friar has said I need rest—"

"Oh, yes, I'm sure you do after you've been so sorely mistreated," came Adele's sarcastically hostile response, while Rufus only snickered, hugging Maire's knees all the tighter. "Flanna is no longer here. Duncan sent her away yesterday and I'm elated. Dreadful Irish bitch. Off to wed one of his tenants, I imagine, though a far better use would have been to give her to my men. FitzHugh, you would have enjoyed that, wouldn't you?"

"Not as much as this one here would have pleased me," said the stocky knight at Adele's side, fresh chills washing over Maire as she recognized his gruff voice from the meadow. Wholly stunned to hear that Flanna had left Longford Castle, she was gripped by growing despair as the man raked her with leering eyes while Adele clucked her tongue.

"Oh, no, that wouldn't make my tender-hearted brother happy at all, I fear. He wants to return her home as if it mattered what happened to an Irish chit . . . though with this one, I'm growing more convinced with each moment that it does. A pity I didn't let you have her in the woods, Henry, then we could have left her there and none of this damnable mess—"

"Lady Adele!"

Maire jumped, Clement's voice filling her with such relief that she felt tears sting her eyes. At once the dwarf released her legs as the friar, his expression grave, gave the tray he carried to a servant and swiftly approached. But Adele clasped a hand upon her arm, her icy stare forbidding Maire to move or even speak.

"Lady Adele, I must insist on escorting Rose back to her room—"

"*Her* room, friar?" Adele's slim fingers tightened like talons around Maire's arm. "My brother's apartment, surely, unless some new arrangement has been agreed upon? Pray don't tell me he's considering her for his new mistress—"

"Ah, no, my lady, you've misunderstood," Clement blurted out, only to be waved to sudden silence.

"No, you don't understand," Adele said haughtily. "Rose will be supping with me this evening. It had been my thought to send one of my maidservants to see after her welfare and ask her to join us, and lo and behold! Here she was, looking none the worse for the healing potion Duncan told me you gave her—just as I was on my way to the great hall. Delightful! So come, Rose dear. I believe my other knights have rudely started without us."

Chapter 10

Adele's grip on her flesh was so tight that Maire bit her bottom lip to keep from crying out. She wondered dazedly if Adele's retinue might outnumber Duncan's, now that he was away with so many of his men, and what that could mean if poor Clement resisted. Truly, she didn't want to see the friar hurt, didn't want to see anyone hurt. Mayhap if she simply played along . . .

"Rose, if you do not wish this . . ." Clement started to say to her as she passed by with Adele, the woman still holding fast to her arm, yet the stout friar fell silent when Maire summoned a shaky smile.

"Truly, I'm fine. It was the smell of food that brought me downstairs—"

"There! You see, friar?" Adele exulted, no matter that a frown came to Clement's brow. "She is much on the mend already. Wonderful! Just what I had hoped."

Adele walked so fast into the massive hall that Maire had to struggle to keep up, her awkward gait only exaggerated by such a pace. She heard sniggering behind her, and glanced over her shoulder to see Rufus cruelly mimicking her, one short leg dragging behind him as he rocked from side to side with a broad grin on his face.

Maire doubted she had ever felt such humiliation. The entire hall seemed to erupt into laughter from the knights seated on a dais and the lesser soldiers dining at long trestle tables to the buxom maidservants waiting upon them. Adele's entourage? Maire guessed as much at the many grim expressions, too, on the faces of Duncan's knights who had remained behind as well as men-at-arms and Irish servants, all no doubt having heard by now of the calamity that had brought her to Longford Castle and clearly sharing Lord FitzWilliam's sentiments, which heartened her.

She could see at their greater number that she had misjudged her fear for Clement, but the decision was made and she doubted that Adele would release her. Lifting her chin, she bore the escalating noise bravely as Adele's knights roared with laughter and pointed, though Maire could not help remembering another time when her face had burned as hot with mortification. But then it had been the look of repulsion by only one man, Colin O'Nolan, that had shattered her most precious dream.

"What a somber lot, Duncan's men," Adele said with clear disdain as they approached the steps to the dais. "Especially that one there, Reginald Montfort."

She followed Adele's gaze to a strapping older knight with graying hair and as grave an expression as any she'd seen. He was seated at the opposite end of the high table. Maire winced when Adele's grip grew tighter.

"Wretched fellow, testy as a bull. Duncan's left him in charge while he's away—with strict orders that my retainers and I are not to leave Longford Castle. Ridiculous!"

Maire didn't know what to make of such a revelation, but Adele clearly didn't expect a comment as she finally released Maire and climbed the five steps with elegant grace, indicating that Maire should follow. She did, though walking up stairs had always been difficult for her, and once more Rufus the Fool parroted her movements while fresh guffaws greeted his antics.

He even went so far as to take a tumble to the floor when Maire nearly lost her balance, her hand catching the edge of the table, which was the only thing that saved her. Her face burning, her courage faltering, she sank gratefully into an empty chair between Adele and Henry FitzHugh, not seeing that Reginald Montfort had risen from his place.

"God's breath, Lady Adele, enough of this pathetic folly! Call off your fool, or I'll see him from the hall myself!"

"Really, Sir Reginald, Rufus means no harm, his only joy in life to amuse and entertain," Adele answered with a brittle smile that only made Duncan's knight swear and retake his seat.

"You see?" she said in a low aside to Maire as if Adele had made no note that the dwarf's mimicry had been done at Maire's expense. "Damned wretched fellow. Nearly as foul-tempered as my brother. All I had wanted was to follow Gerard de Barry to West Meath to join the hunt for Irish rebels—what a delightful outing it could have been, too. But Duncan wouldn't hear of it. Said I'd caused him enough trouble already, among other things, roared at me, shouted, blustered, and was gone."

A vexed wave of Adele's white, bejeweled hand sent servants rushing to wait upon the high table. Maire's plate was heaped with food and her goblet filled with golden wine in only a few moments' time. Yet her stomach flip-flopped at the glistening meat and varied side dishes; a simple bowl of Clement's beef broth would have been far preferable in coaxing her appetite.

It didn't help, either, that Adele again gripped her arm cruelly after taking a long sip of wine, the stunning blonde's eyes grown icy cold.

"I want you gone from here. Do you understand? Gone!"

Maire was so startled she couldn't speak, although Adele rushed on before she had a chance to while the noisy din of the hall rang around them.

"You're the one who's causing the trouble here, not me. Duncan's taken too much of an interest in you—he's wasting his time over you! Riding back to that place where we came upon your wretched clansmen, dragging poor FitzHugh and three other knights of mine with him. And for what? I told him that the bodies would be gone. That I'd seen a man riding into the trees just before my crossbowmen were close enough to . . ."

Adele didn't finish, but lifted her goblet once more to drink while Maire could only stare, aghast.

Adele had seen Niall riding away? He had come that close to falling victim, as had Fiach and the others?

"I even suggested that Duncan should take you back to that meadow and leave you there with plenty of food and water," Adele continued of a sudden, her tone growing more agitated though she kept her voice low. "Surely your clansmen might return again if they came once before, and they would find you and this whole mess would be settled! But my dear brother wouldn't hear of it. Called me callous not to think of the wolves that might find you first—so you see? Until you remember more than your Christian name, it might be days, even weeks, and after what I heard Flanna screeching about Duncan kissing you—"

"He . . . he kissed me?" Her fingers flying to her lips, Maire stared incredulously at Adele, who appeared so galled that two bright spots of color dotted her alabaster cheeks.

"After he carried you back to his rooms, so Flanna claimed, and my brother didn't deny it. She had run down the stairs, then gone back and saw him—God's blood, what does that matter? For a man saying he wants you returned safely to your family to kiss you while you sleep? Stupid girl, that tells me much if not you! I wish I'd never brought you here!"

Adele's voice having sunk to a hiss, Maire could barely hear the woman's next words for how clamorous the hall had grown, many of the knights seated on the dais clearly becoming drunk.

"Duncan is growing ever more consumed by your plight, and I'll not have it! Until you're gone, I've no hope that he'll take time to consider a bride, and he needs no mistress as fair as you, I see that now. And with Flanna sent away, he'll have no vent for his lust—oh, yes, I see that concerns you, good! Perhaps the thought of my brother giving you more than a kiss might jar your memory, yes?"

Maire had paled, she knew it. Try as she might, she could not forget the sensation of Duncan's hand cupping her breast, her flesh tingling even now as Adele speculatively studied her face.

"An accursed virgin, too, I would swear it, which is all the more reason to be rid of you. Impudent mistresses are one thing with which to contend, and a ghost entirely another, but a chieftain's daughter whose clan might not rest until she's made a baron's bride in retribution if her chastity has been lost . . . ah, no."

Maire gasped as Adele dug her fingernails into her wrist and drew closer, her blue eyes narrowed dangerously.

"Ah, no, Rose, I'll allow no Irish chit to become my dear brother's bride. Never. It was bad enough that a common Scots bitch falsely claimed herself a second wife to our father and bore a son he loved above three others. Duncan FitzWilliam will have a Norman wife to thin his tainted blood and give him heirs of which his family in England can be proud."

"But I . . . I don't want to be Lord FitzWilliam's wife," Maire began, only to be sharply cut off.

"As if he would have you, flawed as you are." Adele's gaze fell to Maire's legs, her eyes grown as vexed as her expression as she then lifted them to Maire's face and spoke almost to herself. "Yet Duncan has always been one to let compassion sway him, not so wise a trait in a man who lives by the sword. If he has kissed you, who can say how your crippled state will further move him?"

Adele's clenched fist came down upon the table at the same moment a half dozen jugglers and acrobats began to whoop and tumble at the center of the hall, Maire not sure which had startled her more. Yet she was already so alarmed by everything the woman had told her, her heart pounding, her lips burning as if Duncan had only just kissed her . . . Jesu, Mary, and Joseph!

That her impossible imagining hadn't been a dream was not half as disturbing as that she found herself wishing she'd been awake to feel his mouth touch hers. Maire felt more anxious than ever before to leave Longford Castle. But without Flanna, how . . . ?

Maire glanced at Adele to find the woman still glaring at her, as if by sheer will she could make Maire disappear. Suddenly Maire realized she sat beside the one person who would gladly aid her. Desperately shoving away all thoughts of her slaughtered clansmen and the fact that she couldn't possibly trust Adele or her men, Maire had no choice but to speak.

"Please, the meadow . . . the meadow where

my clansmen—" She faltered, grisly memories assailing her no matter her resolve, but already Adele was leaning toward her, the woman's eyes narrowing. Maire swallowed and rushed on. "If there was a way for you, your men—someone to get me there. I could wait, like you said. I'm sure it would only be a matter of time before my family—"

"FitzHugh!"

Adele had risen from her chair, her knight tossing back the last of his wine and rising, too. As the two conferred in low voices, Maire was grateful for the commotion in the hall as none seemed to pay much attention. Even Reginald Montfort, who appeared well occupied by the comely servingwoman refilling his goblet. The next thing she knew Adele had gripped her shoulder and bent low to whisper in her ear.

"Look as if you're ill, damn you. It's the only way."

Look as if she were ill? In truth, Maire felt nearly sick from nervousness and she shoved away her plate, the smell of the various foods nauseating her indeed. Adele looked pleased as Maire then rose shakily, the woman looping an arm around her waist as if she were truly concerned while she raised her voice so at least those on the dais would hear.

"You don't look well at all, dear girl! Fitz-Hugh, help me support Rose on the other side."

As the swarthy knight hastened to oblige, the clamor in the great hall seemed to dim, many turning to watch as Maire was assisted down the steps. And this time Adele gave Rufus a sharp look that made the dwarf merely shrug and go back to prancing around the minstrels who had begun to play a lively tune, Adele's voice once more rising above the din.

"Don't mind us, please, enjoy your meal. Lord FitzWilliam's lovely guest merely wishes to retire—not feeling well, I fear."

A few glances of concern were thrown their way, but Maire exhaled with relief as Duncan's retainers fell back to eating and drinking while Adele's knights on the dais caroused with even greater abandon, Adele's maidservants shrieking with laughter as they were caught and fondled. The only man who approached was Clement, his eyes greatly worried, but Adele seemed to have been ready for him.

"Friar, go at once and prepare calming herbs for Rose's stomach. We'll follow you."

"Ah, me, I knew bringing her to the hall would be too taxing after that potion," Clement began, but a convincing moan from Maire sent him bustling away. Adele raised a trim brow.

"You did that quite well, Rose. Playing a part seems to come naturally to you. Now, we must hurry."

Maire didn't say a word, she couldn't, she felt so tense, that she might soon be free of Longford Castle almost too much for her to hope. As Adele and Henry FitzHugh helped her walk from the great hall toward the tower where Clement resided with his many cats, Maire wondered with every step how they might elude the good friar.

It proved most simple. Adele merely guided Maire with her knight's assistance past the door where Clement had disappeared, then through a wide passage, and into what Maire saw at once was an immense stable. The pungent smell of horse manure, polished leather, and fragrant hay made her hope and nervousness soar wildly.

"Quickly, FitzHugh, saddle our horses!"

Adele's anxious command was quickly obeyed. Within moments the woman herself gave a leg up to Maire, as Henry FitzHugh hoisted her behind him onto his massive black steed. The same snorting animal, Maire realized as she tried to still her hands from shaking, that had run her down in the woods only two days before; in spite of herself, she felt sickened as Adele mounted a fine dappled gray gelding.

"We've only moments before Clement will come looking for us—no time to fetch food or water. Ride, FitzHugh, and when we get to the drawbridge, let me speak to the guards. Say nothing!"

They burst from the stable into a gray dusk, Maire breathing cool evening air for the first time in what seemed an eternity. She kept her arms clasped tightly around FitzHugh as they rode across a vast courtyard, although the offensive smell of the man, sweat mixed with soured wine, made her wonder if he bathed in the stuff as well as drank it, or bathed at all for that matter. And she had entrusted herself to his care . . .

Trying not to think of the crude things Henry FitzHugh had said about her, Maire was stunned that it seemed they'd reached the drawbridge before she could blink. Yet her heart sank when grim-faced sentinels raced from their posts to stand in the way.

"No one leaves Longford Castle, Lord FitzWilliam's orders!" came a shout from a great burly fellow in chain mail and helmet who appeared to be in command. "Forgive me, my lady, but—"

"This young woman is ill, man, and Friar Clement cannot help her!" cried Adele in feigned desperation, cutting him off. "He told me another healer resides in the village—we must find him!"

"I'm sorry, my lady, but I cannot allow it. Strict orders and I'm bound—"

"And I ask will you say the same, man, if this poor woman dies and Lord FitzWilliam demands to know why we could not obtain help for her? Lower the drawbridge now, or I fear—*I know*—there will be the devil to pay . . ."

As the commander looked doubtfully at his men, then back to Adele, Maire doubled over behind Henry FitzHugh and began to moan piteously, her blood pounding in her ears for fear she wouldn't be convincing enough . . . only to hear the man utter a vehement oath.

"Very well, lower the drawbridge! But hold your weapons at the ready, men. Those Irish Lord FitzWilliam warned us about may be lurking near!"

A great creaking and the heavy scraping sound of chains turning massive winches filled the gathering darkness, followed moments later by a telling thunk. Maire closed her eyes for fear it was all a dream. Yet as the horse beneath her lurched forward and clattered across the drawbridge, she dared to believe she would soon be free, left to fend for herself in the woods near the meadow, aye, but surely Ronan and Niall would come back to that place and find her—

"Men approaching from the west!"

A sentry's cry from high atop a tower shattered the night's stillness. But it was Henry FitzHugh's fierce curse that made Maire lift her head to look, while Adele signaled wildly for her knight to turn his mount around. Yet there was no time to go back, as a host of armor-clad riders carrying blazing torches came thundering toward them. An infuriated voice rose above the din of hooves and the commotion now coming from the castle.

"By the blood of God, Adele, FitzHugh, where in blazes are you bound?"

Chapter 11

Maire gasped and tried to hide herself behind Henry Fitzhugh, while Duncan couldn't believe his eyes as he brought his lathered horse closer.

"Rose? God's teeth, what . . . ?" His fury mounting, Duncan barely saw the man he'd left in charge of the drawbridge rush forward, his gaze jumping back to Adele.

"Woman—"

"Rose is ill, Duncan, and we thought—hoped, that a healer in the village might do better for her than Friar Clement."

"That is so, my lord. I wouldn't have let them pass at all if it hadn't been so urgent," interjected the stricken-faced commander. "The young woman was moaning so—"

"The devil take it, then why is she out in the night and not abed, the healer called to come to her?" His roar making his dark bay stallion snort and toss its head, Duncan fixed his eyes back upon Adele, his half sister looking suspiciously pale. "Did Clement have a chance to look at her?"

"No . . . yes, I mean I changed my mind so

suddenly, Duncan. I'd sent him to his room for herbs, saying we'd follow, but his healing potion failed to bring Rose a cure. She still remembers nothing more of her family—"

"Dammit, woman, you were taking her back to where her clansmen were slain, weren't you?" Adele clamped her mouth shut, shaking her head, but that only confirmed Duncan's intuition. "After I told you that wolves . . ."

He couldn't go on, he was so angry he didn't dare. Gerard de Barry reined in his horse beside Duncan's.

"It's growing darker. We should be inside, the guards on the battlements alerted, especially now."

"Especially now?" said Adele, bringing her mount closer as well.

Clearly to draw Gerard's attention, Duncan thought grimly, though he was pleased his knight had scarcely given Adele a glance. Nodding at Gerard, Duncan's reply to his sister was low and brusque.

"We've prisoners, three Irish rebels. Clan O'Melaghlin."

"Oh, my, how delightful, Duncan! Where are they? Can I see them?"

Duncan ignored her and brought his horse side by side with Henry FitzHugh's, disgusted as much that Adele would look upon his prisoners as if they'd been brought back to fan her amusement as he was furious she had breached his orders.

Even in the deepening darkness he could see that the young woman who'd scarcely left his mind was trembling, having no warm cloak to protect her; a swift glance at both FitzHugh's and Adele's saddles showed that no provisions of food or drink had been made, either, and even Adele wore no cloak against the damp evening chill. Damn his half sister, did her penchant for folly have no bounds?

Cursing under his breath, Duncan swept the woman from FitzHugh's horse so suddenly that she gasped, stiffening in his arms as he settled her in front of him and tugged his heavy cloak around her shoulders.

"Ease yourself, Rose. I do not blame you for this night's events."

Maire said nothing, could say nothing, nor could she stop her shaking as Duncan kicked his horse into a gallop and rode across the drawbridge into the courtyard, which had come alive with people rushing from the castle, great sputtering torches held high. She saw Clement, his kindly face full of disbelief, and Reginald Montfort, too. The older knight appeared to blanch with chagrin when he spied Adele and Henry FitzHugh stop their horses not far behind Duncan.

Within moments the courtyard was filled with the whinnying, snorting mounts of at least forty men, the noise and confusion a blur to Maire as stableboys leapt forward to lead exhausted animals to their stalls while the metallic clatter of knights in battle garb seemed to ring around her. She scarcely noticed that Duncan had dismounted until he raised his arms to lift her down, yet her feet no sooner touched the ground than he had swept her up once more. His embrace was fearsome, made so by chain mail that covered him from the coif on his head to his feet.

"Gerard, see to the prisoners. I'll join you when I can."

Amazed that Duncan's commanding voice could carry so well above the clamor, Maire heard its harshness, too, which made her tremble all the more. She had heard such a grim tone from Ronan whenever he spoke of Normans or those clans who had traitorously submitted to their yoke, and it was clear Duncan felt the same about the Irish rebels. Maire watched with pity as they were dragged from their horses.

Jesu, Mary, and Joseph, two appeared no more than smooth-faced youths and must have ridden the long way together, while the third was an old man with graying beard and wild flowing hair who bore himself proudly even as he was shoved into motion by the knights surrounding him with drawn swords. Sickened, she closed her eyes, imagining the dank dungeon where the prisoners were no doubt bound, imagining the iron shackles and fiendish instruments of torture—

"Ah, Baron, I feel such a fool! Such a fool!"

Clement caught up to Duncan as he strode with Maire across the courtyard. The friar had to nearly run alongside them when Duncan didn't slow his pace.

"I went to fetch calming herbs—Lady Adele said Rose was ill. I'd told her the great hall would be too much for the poor child, and then the torment Rose was made to suffer—"

"Torment?"

Duncan had stopped to face the friar, Maire's heart pounding at the tension in his voice.

"Ah, Baron, it was a wretched thing to watch. That dwarf of Lady Adele's—Rufus the Fool. He followed after Rose, making sport of her as she walked . . ." The friar's eyes moved with fervent apology to Maire. "I should have insisted then that Rose be allowed to return to your rooms, to bed where she might rest. The next I knew, Lady Adele insisted Rose was ill yet she never came for the herbs . . . Baron?"

Duncan had set out again, his strides so furious that Maire could not help but feel the power of them, his arms tightening around her, which only made her fear she would surely share in some of the brunt of his anger. He had said he didn't blame her, yet he must have seen she was not held atop FitzHugh's horse by force. Saints help her. The only thought that gave her comfort as Duncan strode through an open door into the castle was that she had not been made to join the prisoners. Was it possible he had not guessed the truth about her clan . . . ?

"Bring hot water for a bath," he commanded a small cluster of servingwomen huddled near the entrance to the great hall, who scattered to obey. Then to Clement, who still hustled after them, "Fetch your herbs, friar, and come quickly, so you might tend to Rose. She shakes as with fever."

Maire swallowed, no fever making her tremble so wretchedly. With every step that Duncan took round the tower to his rooms, her dismay only grew.

To come so close to leaving Longford Castle, and now to find herself being carried back to the bedchamber she had thought never to see again, the same bedchamber where Duncan had kissed her . . .

Her cheeks flaring hot, Maire didn't allow herself to look at him as they entered his apartment, Duncan not stopping until he reached the hearth, where he set her down upon a chair and dragged her closer to a freshly stoked fire.

"Stay there."

She hadn't thought to move, his actions as he went to the bed and grabbed up a blanket reminding her so much of that first night when he had mistaken her for Flanna. Had it only been two days past? But this time she did not cringe from him when he swiftly returned and wrapped the blanket around her, then sank to his haunches in front of the chair.

In truth she had scarcely looked at his face until that moment, and now she found herself staring just as he searched her eyes, Duncan FitzWilliam appearing more intensely handsome in the firelight than she dared remember. If she hadn't already been trembling, she would have begun to, her gaze falling in disbelief to the masculine beauty of his lips. He had kissed her. *He had kissed her!* No man had ever done such a thing before.

"Woman, what has happened this night? Had Adele harmed you? Her man, FitzHugh? Threatened you somehow to make you leave with them? Dammit, what? You must tell me!"

Maire had started at his vehement demand, however low, which only made him draw closer, his mailed knees pressing against her legs as he wrapped the blanket more snugly around her. She sucked in her breath, everything Adele had told her in the hall rushing back to her, the vivid concern in Duncan's deep brown eyes alarming her all the more.

She knew he must pity her, especially after what Clement had revealed about Rufus's cruel mimicry, but she didn't want such sympathy . . . in truth, she wanted that from no man! Mayhap if he knew she had played a part, if he knew that she'd made up her own mind to leave, he would see that she could manage well enough and didn't need his pity.

"Rose, please, you must tell me—"

"Aye, very well, I asked her to take me!"

Her outcry echoing in the room, Maire saw Duncan's eyes darken to almost black, but she paid no heed and rushed on.

"I-it made sense . . . that my clansmen might come back to that place, whoever they might be. I still don't remember, but it made sense just as I said, so I asked your sister to take me there and she agreed—"

"God's teeth, woman, of course she agreed! Why wouldn't she? If the wolves found you first, all the better. Then there would be no witness left to what might be deemed a punishable crime if your slain father proves a chieftain loyal to King John, and she knows it! I've sent messengers throughout Leinster and Ulster, Rose, to every ruling baron. It will take only days—perhaps two weeks but no more, before I'll have found your family for you, then you'll be safely home! Dammit, woman, is it so horrible for you here that you would flee headlong into danger? Can you not see I'm doing all I can to help you?"

Maire could only stare at him, Duncan appearing as affronted as she was filled with sudden panic. Days? Mayhap two weeks at most before the truth would be known? When no loyal clan claimed her, then what would Duncan do?

Her thoughts flying to the three rebels who might even now be shackled to a dungeon wall, Maire dropped her gaze at the same moment a light knock came at the door, a female voice calling out that she'd come from the kitchen. Duncan rose and shouted "Enter!" so forcefully that Maire jumped, her eyes widening as he went and dragged the wooden tub from against an opposite wall to the hearth.

"Choose if you wish to avail yourself of the courtesies of my home, I care not," came his disgruntled voice, while Maire's gaze flew to the host of servingwomen bearing steaming buckets of water. The next thing she knew Duncan had stormed from the bedchamber, but not before commanding that a screen be brought from the next room to give her privacy while she bathed—*if* she chose to bathe—in case he must return before she was done.

Wholly stunned, Maire sat still as a stone as the tub was filled, the quiet servingwomen casting her sidelong glances that she scarcely noted. That Duncan had become so furious . . . because she seemed ungrateful for his kindnesses?

Truly, he had treated her as if she were an honored guest, given her the use of his private rooms, no less, even his bed. Were she the daughter of a chieftain loyal to the English crown, would she really act as she had? As reluctant to accept his gracious gestures as if she were loath to trust him or anything Norman? Adele and her retainers were responsible for the deaths of her clansmen, but Duncan—as yet—had done nothing to hurt her.

Suddenly fearing that she might give herself away long before Duncan could learn the truth about her, Maire resolved then and there that she must behave differently until she had a chance again to escape the castle. And that must start with enjoying a bath—

"Here's the screen, miss. Will it do here, or should we move . . . ?"

"No, no, that will be fine," she murmured to a pleasant-faced Irishwoman. Maire was astonished that all was done so quickly, the bath prepared, thick towels and a pale blue wedge of soap laid atop a small table that had been brought forth, the screen arranged round the tub.

And such a screen, too. As the servingwomen filed quietly from the room, Maire studied with unabashed admiration the four embroidered panels, never having seen such fine needlework.

She loved to embroider, could not count the hours she'd spent with needle and thread in her hand; in truth, she had done little else until she'd regained the use of her legs and begun to spend more time out of doors. It was still some solace to her that if her life could not be like other women's, at least she had been blessed with such a skill. But Maire stared in wonder at needlework so beautifully wrought, she doubted she could equal it.

She rose just to glide her fingertips over a panel, the blanket dropping to her feet but she paid no heed, wholly fascinated by embroidered wildflowers, fluttering birds, and delicate green vines framing what appeared to be scenes of a gently led life: a young, dark-haired girl surrounded by forest creatures she fed by hand, then the same child with what appeared to be her parents giving loaves of bread and drink to the poor on a feast day.

But what truly caught Maire's eye on the third panel was the scene of two lovers sharing a kiss beneath a shaded bower, the child—now a willowy beauty—swept into the embrace of a strapping knight clad in armor. Emotion tugged at Maire's heart, her eyes growing blurred at the next scene of a solemn marriage before a priest, and later, that of a new mother lovingly holding a babe in her arms. She so wished for such a life herself. It was her fondest dream and yet it was as far from coming true, as if she wished that her legs overnight could be made healthy and whole!

Sighing raggedly, Maire traced the threads depicting the tiny newborn babe with trembling fingers, then abruptly turned her attention to the tub. She had to admit the steamy water looked inviting, and perhaps it would soothe her tired limbs if not her spirits. She drew her gown over her head, wondering if the effects of Clement's healing potion still lingered. She determined not to drink another drop of anything he might bring her.

She wanted her wits about her—no more herbal brews. She even smiled to herself, remembering Niall's complaints two years ago when he had been made to drink a healer's foul-tasting remedies after nearly losing his life to MacMurrough arrows. He had swayed Triona to fetch him ale from the kitchen instead . . .

Fresh heartache filling her at such thoughts of her family, Maire dropped her camise to the floor; she removed the heavy stool for which she had little use from the tub and sank naked into the warm water, wishing more buckets had been brought so it might fully cover her. The tub was so large it probably would have taken another dozen. Yet the water came almost to her waist and she had only to cup her hands to pour some over herself, her nipples puckering at the chill in the room despite the blazing fire.

It made her decide to bathe quickly, and she reached for the soap, a lilac-scented luxury not unknown to her, thanks to Ronan's raids. But it slipped from her wet fingers and slid across the floor, nearly to the door leading to where the servants had gone to fetch the screen, Maire saw with a small sigh, frustrated by her clumsiness.

That must be the room beyond the latrine, where Duncan had slept that first night, which made Maire wonder nervously as she gripped the sides of the tub and started to rise with some effort if he intended to forgo his bed again and sleep on a cot. Her face began to burn. Saints help her, surely so. If only he hadn't kissed her, she wouldn't be plagued with such wild imaginings at all—

"Stay there, woman. I'll get the soap."

Chapter 12

Stay there? Maire fell back into the tub so awkwardly that water splashed everywhere, logs hissing and sputtering, the lovely screen spattered with droplets while she was blinded, her heart pounding wildly as she groped for a towel to cover her breasts.

Stay there? Had Duncan truly thought she would race him for the soap, even if she could? Quickly wiping the water from her eyes, Maire could hear his footsteps and she sank even lower into the tub, paying no heed that much of the towel was sodden now and drifted around her.

Jesu, Mary, and Joseph, she had no intention of leaving, of even moving! Maire clutched the towel under her chin and stared incredulously as Duncan came around the screen. He had stripped from his armor, though surely the sweat-stained tunic that clung to his powerful body must have fitted beneath it, and he held in his hands a goblet and the soap. He kept his eyes fixed firmly upon her face, his expression impossible to read.

"Forgive me, but I imagined you would cover

yourself. I brought you something to drink from Clement—I met him on the stairs. Anise wine to calm you."

As Duncan set the goblet on the table and dropped the soap with a plunk into the tub, Maire could only nod her thanks, relief flooding her when he abruptly turned and moved beyond the screen although he didn't leave the room. She sat frozen, startled even more when she heard a vehement curse from the direction of the windows. Was he going to remain, then, while she bathed? Surely not—

"I told Clement I doubted it was any illness that made you try to flee with Adele and Fitz-Hugh, and he agreed . . . which is why I came back to ask your forgiveness, too, for how harshly I spoke to you. Damn that infernal woman! That she allowed her fool to hound you—to make sport of you so cruelly. If I hear of such foul treatment again, by the blood of God I'll—"

"Truly, Lord FitzWilliam, it wasn't so bad a thing." Maire sought to appease him, as moved by his unexpected apology as that the force of his anger on her behalf shook her. Yet she gasped when he appeared once more at the screen as if in two strides, his expression both thunderous and grim.

"Not bad, woman? You would rather face wolves than remain safely at my home?"

The burning intensity of his gaze unnerving her as much as the same affront she'd heard in his voice when he'd left the room so abruptly earlier, Maire shook her head, her face grown as warm as her bath. "No . . . I'm sorry. It wasn't wise—"

"No, it wasn't—God's teeth, but how can I blame you? Adele's retainers laughing at you, the bastards amusing themselves at your expense. You were brave enough to bear it as you did . . ."

Duncan fell silent to stare at her so strangely that Maire suddenly lost all ability to breathe. She saw no pity in his eyes as much as something very close to admiration, which struck her all the harder, as no man had ever looked at her in such a way before. Aye, she had been praised enough for her embroidery but this was different . . . reminding her of how Ronan often looked at Triona . . .

Maire dropped her eyes, her heart slamming in her throat, while she heard Duncan shift his stance.

"You're chilled. I should let you bathe."

"Chilled?" Almost stupidly, she looked at the goose bumps puckering her arms, then glanced up to find Duncan's gaze had lowered to something else altogether. Her nipples tightening all the more that his eyes were upon them, now she truly could not breathe. Stricken, she clasped the soaked towel to her breasts, her voice sunk to a whisper. "Aye, please . . . before the water grows cold."

He was gone before she could blink, another low curse following him as he disappeared into the dark passageway leading to the other room. She started at how hard he shut the door behind him, nearly slamming it, but she allowed herself no thoughts as to his mood as she grabbed for the slippery soap.

She doubted she had ever bathed so quickly, even washing her hair within a few moments' time when usually she liked to linger over such a task. But now she simply wanted to be done and dressed and in bed before Duncan might return, and she imagined it would be soon, given that he must still have much to do. He had said to his knight Gerard de Barry that he planned to join him . . .

The prisoners jumping once more to her mind, Maire felt an utter traitor as she climbed carefully from the tub and toweled herself dry, then quickly donned her linen camise. It would have to do. She had no sleeping gown. She ignored the goblet, with its questionable draught—anise wine, aye, but with some opiate added too?—and made instead straight for the bed, all the while working the tangles from her thick hair.

She had no comb, either, but her fingers were deft. She was actually grateful as she climbed into bed that no other amenities had been provided for her that her guilt at her present comfort would be so much greater.

Those poor men—no, one man and two others no more than boys . . . from clan O'Melaghlin, Duncan had said. She knew little of them other than that they had lost their rich pastureland to the conquering Normans years ago, much as the O'Byrnes, and imagined their hatred burned as hot. Hot enough to slaughter an entire herd of cattle?

So Gerard had claimed yesterday, but in truth, Maire could not imagine any rebel Irish doing such a wanton thing in such hard times. To steal them, aye, for fresh milk and meat for their clansmen, their families, their wee babes. But to kill the beasts and leave them to rot? She could not help thinking that something there did not ring true.

Sighing heavily, Maire rolled onto her side and drew the covers well over her shoulder. That she lay so snugly upon so fine and clean a bed grated upon her conscience, too. Were the three O'Melaghlins being flogged or worse at this very moment, their beds filthy straw strewn over a cold dungeon floor? Jesu give them courage, if only there was some way she could help them.

Yet what could she do? She seemed no more likely herself to escape from Longford Castle than to sprout wings, given what had happened no more than an hour past. And if she didn't keep her wits about her and behave as if Duncan FitzWilliam were no enemy to Eire at all but a kind benefactor . . .

Maire's gaze flew to the door closed so firmly against her, a sudden thought plaguing her mind.

If she wanted him to think her appreciative of his gracious treatment, she should surely have thanked him by now. So the daughter of a chieftain who'd bowed to Norman rule would do. But she hadn't said a word, mayhap only once come close yesterday just before he'd taken her to see Clement. Her decision to remedy matters made, she tried to quell her sudden nervousness as she left the bed by telling herself that going to him tonight was the wisest thing to do . . . yet he had also come very close to slamming the door.

Not wishing to fathom what might have made Duncan angry again, Maire went to the massive chest at the foot of the bed where her blue cloak had been neatly folded, and swept it around her shoulders. Her flimsy camise was hardly enough garb in which to appear before the man, offering no more covering than that sodden towel—

"Begorra, Maire O'Byrne, have you gone mad altogether?" she whispered to herself as she walked to the door, suddenly not so sure that she should disturb him.

It didn't help that everything Adele had said to her about Duncan having no vent for his lust now that Flanna had been sent away came rushing back to her, and Maire almost changed her mind. And Duncan had kissed her, too, while she slept. She told herself as her hand moved shakily to the latch that it must surely have been pity, but after what she had seen tonight in his eyes—

Jesu, Mary, and Joseph, what did any of that matter? Doing her best to gather her own courage, Maire had only to think of how Duncan would look at her if he knew her to be the sister of Black O'Byrne, and she was able to thrust all such concerns from her mind, though her nervousness remained.

It grew, too, as she made her way down the short passageway and past the latrine to the adjoining room where light shone from beneath the closed door. She could hear the creaking of a chair, her hand rising to knock at the same moment heavy footsteps came toward her and the door was flung wide. She gasped at the flood of light, backing up as Duncan almost ran into her.

"God's teeth, woman!"

Duncan had to brace his hands against the wall to catch his balance, as startled to find Rose in the passageway as she appeared to be that he had come so suddenly upon her. Her eyes wide and round, she said nothing, only staring at him, while he swept his gaze over her blue cloak, his gut clenching.

By the blood of God, was she dressed to try and flee again? Yet why, then, had she come . . . ?

"I'm sorry . . . I thought to speak to you," came her voice in almost a whisper.

Duncan was struck more than he wanted to be by its sweet timbre. He was struck, too, by her words, and found himself staring back at her almost densely. She'd made little effort to speak to him of her own will before, their exchanges provoked more by his none too gentle demands for a response, much as what had happened earlier. Yet she didn't appear upset or pressed. Was it possible she might have remembered something of her clan?

Duncan glanced past her to the bedchamber, then thought better of it and took her arm. She blinked at his touch but did not hesitate when he drew her with him.

"Come, we'll talk in here." He guided her into the refuge he seldom allowed anyone to enter and around the oak table which took up much of the space. Duncan gestured for her to take the high-backed chair he'd abandoned moments before while he sat down opposite her on the cot.

At once her face reddened, and he followed her eyes to the single woolen blanket folded at one end of a mattress that was more a pallet atop the narrow wooden frame. Then she glanced back at him, at his shoulders, at his chest, as if gauging that the cot was not nearly large enough for him, which made him guess easily her thoughts.

"It's not as bad as it looks—much better than the cold ground. That's all I knew for years . . . a soldier's lot."

He had shrugged while she only blushed further, which made Duncan wonder again how much contact she had had with men. Not much, surely, as he saw her swallow nervously, her beautiful gray eyes so luminous in the lamplight and yet anxious, too.

Had no man ever come near to court her? Had none dared to see past the unfortunate infirmity she bore with such grace that Clement had been moved to tears in telling him how Rose had walked with the composure of a queen while the great hall rocked with laughter around her?

Fresh fury surged inside Duncan that the woman he'd made clear to everyone was a guest in his home had been so sorely mistreated, and he thought again of the harsh words he intended for Adele and Rufus the Fool.

"M-mayhap, Lord FitzWilliam, we should speak at another time . . ."

Duncan realized he must be scowling. Rose

suddenly appeared uncomfortable, perched like a bird at the edge of her chair as if ready to fly, her voice grown uncertain. He saw then a measure of cream linen peeking beneath her cloak and realized, too, that she must have made herself ready for bed only to decide she wanted to talk to him. In truth, he had been on his way to talk further to her, much weighing heavily on his mind. Leaning forward, he hoped his low voice would calm her.

"My anger isn't for you, Rose. I was thinking of Adele and her blasted fool, and how I failed that you be well treated under my roof—"

"No, no, you've been very gracious to me and I—well, I wanted to thank you, truly."

She'd spoken in such a rush that she seemed almost surprised at herself. Duncan's frustration that she'd not come to speak of her clan was somewhat soothed by her words. It had undeniably cut him that she might consider him of the same brutal ilk as Adele and her knights, but how could he blame her for that either? He and Adele were blood kin, much as he might wish otherwise.

"I'm not an ogre, Rose," he said earnestly, leaning closer. "I told you from the first I would not hurt you. And if I could alter what happened to your clansmen, I would, I vow it! But nothing can be done save that you're returned safely home, and soon. Do you remember anything more at all . . . ?"

She had begun to shake her head before he finished, which made Duncan's frustration again grow sharp.

"So we've still only your name . . . while I learned little from that accursed meadow," he said more to himself, imagining again the slaughter she must have witnessed at the amount of dried blood staining the grass. "Your clansmen's bodies were gone—Adele had told me that was likely, but I wanted to see for myself, no matter she said a rider had disappeared into the trees only moments before the first arrows—"

Duncan fell silent at Rose's sudden ashen pallor, which reminded him all the more that Clement had pointedly advised again she be treated with gentleness. The friar hadn't been pleased to see him come storming down the stairs—God's teeth! He didn't need Clement's censure to know it hadn't helped matters for him to become angry that Rose had wanted to flee, yet it seemed he had been nothing but vexed since yesterday.

Damn him for a fool, he should never have kissed her! That had started the trouble. No woman since Gisele had occupied his thoughts as this one. He had told himself a hundred times that only her wretched plight had captured his mind, yet it hadn't been thoughts of her slain clansmen that had sent him for the sanctum of this room. Even now, looking at Rose's midnight hair drying in soft tendrils around her face and throat made his loins tighten.

He'd been an utter fool, too, to disrupt her bath! Had he truly thought he'd be immune to her nakedness simply because he hoped soon to be rid of her? Immune to the taut, rounded beauty of breasts he'd already touched, to dark woman's hair like a tempting shadow beneath that wet towel where his fingers had already—

"Enough, man, enough," Duncan said so gruffly to himself that once more Rose appeared uncertain as to whether she should stay or go.

She even started to rise, a pale flash of thigh making him clench his teeth, but he stood first, which at once made her sink back into the chair, her lovely eyes grown wide. Pained that she still seemed so uneasy around him no matter all he'd said to reassure her, he decided in the next instant that perhaps it was a very good thing, given the days ahead. God grant him strength if she ever looked at him other than as a nervous virgin . . .

"Ease yourself, Rose, it wasn't my intent to distress you," he said to soothe her, keeping his voice low. "We'll speak no more of your clansmen unless you wish it. And I'll not have you suffer again as you did tonight. Until I've found your family, you'll be safer at my side. I leave tomorrow morning for Dublin, and you will accompany me."

Chapter 13

Dublin? Maire was so stunned that she stared dumbly as Duncan held out his hand to her, her mind running away with itself.

Jesu, Mary, and Joseph, she must accompany him to Dublin? And for how long? Ronan would never find her there, and even if he did, that walled city was dangerously filled with Normans—

"There's a chance your clan has already sent word of its loss to the Justiciar John de Gray. If so, I could see you home all the sooner," came Duncan's voice to pierce her stricken thoughts. "If not, perhaps a courtier at Dublin Castle might recognize you, someone known to your father's clan. I decided it worth the journey, though I can spare only three days—"

"Three days?" Relief overwhelming her that it would be no longer, Maire accepted Duncan's assistance and rose to her feet as he nodded, his expression become ominously grim.

"I've prisoners, Irish rebels. You saw them?"

Her knees gone weak as she murmured a soft

"aye," Maire had a terrible sense she knew what he would say when his fingers tightened around hers.

"The bastards will hang if I've heard nothing from their chieftain by then. Gerard captured two of the O'Melaghlin's grandsons and his own harper—and if it's true these rebel chieftains love their musicians as well if not more than their blood family, the O'Melaghlin will come to Meath."

As Duncan once more guided her around the rough-hewn table spread with leather-bound books and parchment maps and then out into the passageway, Maire felt the blood pounding in her ears at his harsh words. Would the O'Melaghlin heed Duncan's threat? Yet what then . . . ? Somehow she made herself speak, grateful for the shadows which hid her burning face.

"You . . . you would release the prisoners if the chieftain—the O'Melaghlin came to Longford Castle?"

"No, they'd remain my hostages—and that, only if he swore to peace. If the O'Melaghlin refuses, the prisoners will die."

Duncan's pronouncement lay like an icy hand gripping her heart. Maire hoped she didn't appear too shaken as he drew her into the bedchamber and turned to face her, searching her eyes.

"Enough talk of rebels, Rose. It's no matter to you."

"I-I only asked as I've already caused you so much trouble," Maire blurted out, growing anxious that she might have seemed too interested in the prisoners' plight. "You've concerns enough here without having to journey to Dublin. Messengers sent across the land on my behalf, strife between you and your sister—"

"That strife existed long before Adele came upon you and your clansmen." His tone grown bitter, Duncan's gaze went to the embroidered screen arranged around the tub, his expression as hard as stone. "Long before I was born, and my mother was made to bear it. But she had my father then, to protect her . . ."

Duncan fell silent, a faraway look in his eyes that touched Maire for the somber regret it held, too. It struck her suddenly that the screen had been brought from a room as intensely masculine as the man, with its spartan furnishings and unadorned walls, a room she had sensed at once was a private refuge. For such a lovely thing to be kept there, it must surely hold some special meaning.

"It's very beautiful, the screen," she murmured, her breath catching as Duncan's grim gaze met hers. "The embroidery—"

"My mother's. The work of a madwoman, or so my three half brothers claimed. They had her locked away when my father died, and I never saw her again. And I was too young—Enough!"

He'd spoken so vehemently that Maire started, Duncan's face grown almost tortured as he threw a glance at the bed.

"You'd do well to get some rest. We'll be leaving not long after dawn."

Maire nodded, Duncan appearing so weary at that moment, too, that she couldn't help saying as he turned to go, "What of you, Lord FitzWilliam? You can't have slept much at all . . ."

He'd stopped to look at her so strangely that Maire felt a blush burn her skin.

"I—I meant that mayhap you might want the bed. I could take the cot—"

"My bed is yours, woman, for the duration of your stay," came his voice in so husky a timbre that Maire shivered as if he'd touched her. "But I'm grateful for your kind concern . . . and that you came to thank me. Sleep well."

Maire could but stare as he left the room, a strange warmth engulfing her from head to foot. The unsettling effect of his voice combined with the odd intensity in his eyes lingered even after she had doused the few oil lamps, climbed into bed, and drawn the covers to her chin.

She had only been behaving as she must! Maire told herself over and over, wishing the disconcerting feeling would go away. As a chieftain's daughter accustomed to Norman rule. She hadn't truly been concerned for Duncan—her enemy, one of the conquering horde who'd done so much to destroy what the O'Byrnes held dear.

Her thoughts repeating themselves like a litany, Maire closed her eyes, but she knew sleep would be long in coming for the truth plaguing at her heart. Jesu, Mary, and Joseph, she was not only lying to others but lying to herself now, too!

She had been concerned.

For a Norman.

A Norman who with each passing moment was becoming less a foe to her than a man . . . saints help her!

* * *

"Is the woman well?"

Duncan nodded as Gerard heavily took the chair opposite him, though he didn't look away from the fire. The great hall filled with shadows and silent but for the crackling logs, they sat for a moment until Gerard shifted restlessly.

"You may not wish to speak of this now, Duncan, but I say three days is too long! We should hang those bastards from the battlements tomorrow and to hell with the O'Melaghlin—"

"And risk further strife when we've a chance for peace? Dammit, man, hanging every rebel in Meath or all of Ireland for that matter won't bring back your brother!"

Duncan had shouted, all thoughts of Rose thrust from his mind as Gerard's face tightened angrily against him. But he would hear no more of an argument that had raged back and forth since he'd met up with his men in West Meath and learned of the capture. Lowering his voice, he sat forward in his chair.

"If the O'Melaghlins had slain Robert, I might give you a free hand, but they're not the ones to blame. Save your wrath for the O'Byrnes if they ever stray this far north again, and I'll help you myself tie the rope around Black O'Byrne's neck. But there will be no hangings tomorrow. Do you hear me, Gerard?"

His knight not answering but turning to glare into the fire, Duncan sighed heavily. He debated for a brief moment leaving Reginald Montfort in charge of the castle while he was away in Dublin, yet he knew Gerard would not cross him. Over the years they had saved each other's lives in battle countless times, and he trusted no other man as well.

He had known Robert and Gerard de Barry since he had left Northumberland as a youth to serve in King John's army. Younger sons like them with no inheritance of which to speak, there had been little other choice for them than such an occupation. In Duncan's case, his three half brothers had kindly seen to that. Bitterness welling inside him, he shoved thoughts of the men he considered no better than thieves and murderers from his mind and focused once more upon Gerard.

"Did the prisoners finally speak?"

"The younger two," came the gruff response, though at least Gerard had turned from the fire to look at him. "The harper was better able to resist the whip—stubborn old goat, but I don't believe any of what was said. The O'Melaghlins slaughtered those cattle just as surely as they've been stealing them since we came to Meath—"

"And I'll suffer no more of it, damn them." His voice as grim as Gerard's face, Duncan clenched his fists against the chair. "No more raiding cattle, no more torched fields. If the O'Melaghlin doesn't swear to peace, my hand will be forced. There will be no more prisoners, only corpses . . ."

Just as his hand had been forced two days ago with his own kind, Duncan thought darkly, imagining the Justiciar might have heard already, too, of his swift execution of justice. But he doubted a dissenting word would be spoken, any man still loyal to the traitors Walter and

Hugh de Lacy, former earls of Meath and Ulster, no better than dead.

By the blood of God, he would allow no rogue Normans or rebel Irish to harry him from his land! He'd never known a home before Ireland and he would fight as he had done for everything he'd gained in his life to establish some measure of peace over the barony King John had granted him. And he would have peace, even if it must be held by the sword.

"Do I have your word, then, that we'll wait no more than three days?"

Torn from his thoughts, Duncan met Gerard's burning eyes as his knight rushed on.

"If the O'Melaghlin refuses to come to Meath, a lesson must be taught—and at least I'll have won some vengeance whether it's the O'Byrnes who murdered my brother or not that hang from the tower. God's breath, someone must pay! You must grant me that much!"

Gerard's vehement plea ringing from the rafters, Duncan made to speak, but a flurry of amber silk caught his eye. His gut clenched as Adele came toward them, a stricken look on her face.

"Dear God, how terrible! I couldn't help but overhear . . . your brother, Gerard? I'm so sorry."

Overhear? Imagining that Adele might very well have been listening to their conversation before she'd decided to make her presence known, Duncan was not pleased to see her lay her hand with sympathy on his knight's arm as Gerard rose from his chair.

"How long ago was this tragedy?" Adele shot a look of reproach at Duncan and then glanced back at Gerard. "My dear brother failed to mention a word of your loss to me—oh, please, you mustn't stand on my account, I know how tired you must be. Let's sit and you must tell me everything. How dreadful for you, Gerard! Did you say Robert was murdered?"

That she knew Gerard's brother's name confirming she had indulged herself in their entire conversation, Duncan almost cursed aloud when Gerard retook his chair while Adele sank to her knees and settled herself in front of him, her eyes focused compassionately on his face. Disgusted, Duncan rose to leave but Gerard's still-ravaged voice stopped him.

"Three days, Duncan? Do I have your word?"

The loss of Robert de Gray, both friend and loyal comrade in arms, having cut him almost as deeply as it had Gerard, Duncan nodded. "You have it."

He said no more, angered to see that Adele's hand had crept to Gerard's thigh, her beautiful face illuminated to perfection by the firelight. She didn't spare him a glance, her eyes only for Gerard, as Duncan turned and strode from the great hall, his half sister's concentrated attention reminding him of a hawk bearing close for a kill.

Damn the woman! He had warned Gerard of her more than once, but he wasn't the man's keeper. Adele had marked his knight as fair quarry from the first she'd seen him, no doubt waiting for the right moment to pounce only to have finally found it.

A seductive listening ear, a touch, sweet soothing words—God's teeth, it was nothing more than sport to her! Hopefully Gerard would realize as much, as well as consider his bride-to-be awaiting their marriage in Sussex before doing anything rash. Callous, coldhearted sport, just as the senseless slaughter at that meadow . . .

His grim thoughts turning once more to Rose, Duncan climbed the last steps to his rooms, wondering if she slept. He had left her some time ago, thinking to meet Gerard in the dungeon, but had gotten no farther than the great hall, where he'd slumped wearily into a chair before the massive stone hearth and remained there while the castle grew quiet around him.

No one had strayed near, as if sensing he wished to be left alone—none of his knights, no servants as they cleared away the remains of the meal, not his six hunting dogs, who had done no more than nuzzle his hand before trotting off to sleep elsewhere, not even Faustis, who'd come close at one point only to change his mind and retreat at Duncan's dark glance. And Adele and her retainers must have retired to their quarters to escape whatever wrath they thought coming at their first chance.

Yet she had obviously decided to venture forth—to find him and attempt to make more excuses for herself and FitzHugh? If so, she'd been swayed easily enough from her purpose upon seeing Gerard. Or perhaps she thought her actions concerning Rose were of so little consequence to not merit further discussion . . . ?

Duncan swore under his breath as he entered the dimly lit anteroom, determined that she would hear from him before he left for Dublin. But all he wanted right now was rest. He saw the glint of armor atop the bench that he'd stripped out of so quietly as to not disturb Rose at her bath, almost deciding then to wait to speak to her when she was done. Yet when he had seen the soap skidding across the floor . . .

"Blasted fool." His words were no more than a harsh whisper as he went into the next room, but Duncan nonetheless glanced at the bed. He saw no movement; upon drawing closer, the sound of gentle breathing assured him Rose was fast asleep. He did not linger, wouldn't allow himself to after he'd been so reckless yesterday as to kiss her, but passing by the screened tub made him stop.

He was tired to the bone, but he stank, too. As ripely as any man who'd ridden south into Wicklow and then all the way to West Meath and back in less than two days. Yet the screen would have to go. His gut twisting, he couldn't bear to look further at the embroidered scenes of his mother's life, the screen usually kept folded and shrouded in the other room.

Quickly and silently he did so, and when he returned he glanced once more at the bed to ensure Rose still lay deeply sleeping. Her lithe form took so little room on the huge mattress; he found himself remembering all too well the brief yet stirring sensation of her naked body in his arms, and he turned away, scowling.

Try as he might, his thoughts would not be rid of her, especially the look of concern in her eyes when she'd asked if he might wish to use the bed. And she'd spoken so gently, reminding him of another whose voice had been as sweet . . .

Struck anew that he would compare any woman so favorably to Gisele, Duncan felt the same desolate feelings that always gripped him, yet strangely, they didn't seem as sharp. Sharper was the sudden thought that tomorrow might be the last time he saw Rose if some in her clan had gone to Dublin, which made him scowl all the deeper as he hastily stripped out of his clothes.

God's teeth, he would be well rid of her! It was true, she'd brought nothing but trouble to his house—though not on her own account. He could imagine how much she wished to be home, even if she couldn't yet remember more than her Christian name. Yet she had finally seemed more at ease around him tonight, just before he'd left her, her soft words making him speak of things long kept to himself.

His jaw growing tight, Duncan was glad that he'd put away the screen as he stepped into the tub and sank into water that had long lost its warmth. Only then did he realize he had no plain soap, only the fragrant wedge that lay at the bottom of the tub. By the devil, he would smell like lilacs. But better that than to use none at all.

He began to scrub his chest and under his arms, the scent wafting around him . . . making him think all too blatantly again of Rose.

Of how her nipples had prodded so seductively against the sodden towel, her legs long and pale and lovely, showing no hint of any infirmity. Of how her tangled hair had shown black as midnight against milk white skin he already knew to be soft and smooth as the finest silk. That she had sat in this same tub, the same water that he used now to rinse his body having streamed over hers, seemed suddenly so intimate a thing that he felt his loins grow painfully heavy and hard.

Gritting his teeth, he bathed quickly, amazed that in water so cold— By the blood of God, what was this woman doing to him?

He couldn't climb from the tub fast enough, grabbing a towel from the table and taking only a moment to dry himself in front of the fire. And still his enormous erection persisted, which made him stride naked for the adjoining room lest Rose did awake and spy a sight no virgin need face until her wedding night.

Chapter 14

"A good journey, Rose. And may you find your clansmen in Dublin! It would be a pity for you to have to come all the way back to Meath."

Adele's parting words still rang in Maire's mind as if they'd just been uttered rather than hours ago. She winced, too, as she remembered the daunting look Adele had given her as she had ridden from Longford Castle beside Duncan.

The woman hoped never to see her again; that had been more than plain. Jesu, Mary, and Joseph, what would Adele do when Maire did return? She alone knew there was no family awaiting her in Dublin, no outraged clan gone to protest to the Justiciar of a loyal chieftain and his men ruthlessly slaughtered. Her only hope lay in that Ronan might have learned her whereabouts, and even now was dogging their progress to Dublin, waiting for the right moment to attack . . .

That thought chilling her, Maire's gaze flew to Duncan astride his spirited bay stallion only two lengths ahead of her, at the lead of a phalanx of fourteen mailed knights and as many men-at-arms that bristled with weaponry. She could sense his tension. The heavily wooded valley they had ridden into moments ago was not a route he would have normally taken, she'd heard him say to Reginald Montfort. But it was shorter, and he had said, too, given that they only had three days before they must return to Meath, that the sooner they reached Dublin, the better.

Three days. Maire shivered beneath her cloak, and it wasn't because the day was cool; she hoped for the prisoners' sake that the O'Melaghlin would agree to peace. Yet even so, his grandsons and the old harper would remain Duncan's hostages. To live out their lives as slaves at Longford Castle? Maybe even in the dungeon?

Such a possibility was too bleak to contemplate. Maire's hands tightened nervously on the reins, and she scanned the thick trees, wondering again if Ronan and his men might be lying in wait to rescue her. Yet she felt as much dread, not wanting any to lose their lives on her account. Not any O'Byrnes or any of Duncan's knights or—

"You look pale, Rose. Do you want to dismount a moment and rest?"

Startled that Duncan had fallen back to ride beside her, Maire met his eyes. Her heart began to pound so fiercely that she scarce could speak. It didn't help matters when his knee pressed against her legs, Duncan's stallion bumping close to nip at her docile roan gelding. At once Duncan gave his unruly mount a sharp tug on the reins.

"God's teeth—easy, now. Easy!"

Grateful for the distraction as Duncan settled his horse, Maire swallowed hard and told herself for what seemed the hundredth time that glimpsing a man at his bath was no reason to become so unsettled whenever he spoke to her. But her face was burning, too, and she could only wonder what Duncan must think to see her not so much pale anymore as blushing to her roots.

"I-I'm fine . . . truly," she somehow managed, true enough Duncan was now studying her intently. "There's no need to stop. I . . . I was only thinking of my clansmen—that they might be in Dublin and . . . and how they must have worried for me. You're so kind to take me there, Lord FitzWilliam."

She didn't know how he might answer, but she hadn't expected the frown that came over his handsome face as if her words had displeased him. She was as startled when he suddenly kicked his stallion forward and retook his place ahead of her, leaving her to stare in confusion at his back.

A broad muscular back she hadn't been able to tear her eyes from last night when she'd awoken with a start, not daring to move or scarcely to breathe to see Duncan rise dripping and naked from the tub. Her cheeks flaring with heat, she wondered again that the screen had been gone, his body in the dying firelight so physically beautiful she had stared in heart-stopping awe as he toweled himself dry, his powerful muscles flexing . . .

Maire dropped her eyes and stared blindly at the reins curled around her trembling fingers, that she would have watched him so blatantly, so wantonly, shocking her as much today as the sight that had met her when he turned abruptly from the fire. She knew little of men, but she wasn't so raw an innocent that she hadn't recognized his arousal— Saints help her!

Maire pressed a hand to her burning face. How could she be thinking of such things when an attack by her clansmen might be only moments away? Almost dazedly she saw that the ancient oaks had become thicker, the leaves overhead so green and dense that it seemed to have grown darker, too, only a thin shaft of sunlight here and there breaking through.

And the tension among Duncan and his men had heightened—she could feel it. She noticed that Duncan's right hand had moved to the hilt of his sword, while the other held fast to the reins. As a seasoned fighter, had he sensed something she had missed . . . a movement in the distance? The warning snap of a branch? Or was it gut instinct ruling him?

Jesu, Mary, and Joseph, to think that blood might soon be spilled, that men might die, Norman and Irish. Truly it was too much for her to bear. There had to be another way, surely! If Triona were here in her place, what would she do?

Praying for even a trace of her sister-in-law's brazenness and courage to conquer any situation, Maire glanced desperately around her. The air had grown damp and heavy and she smelled it then, the undeniable muskiness of a bog borne on a westerly breeze. But how far away . . . ?

An outcropping of rocks ahead suddenly caught Maire's eye, halfway up a rise, and a plan began to form in her mind. It could work; it had to work! If Ronan and his men were watching them from some hidden point even now, they would see her ride away and spare themselves an attack, surely. Ronan was not one to risk his clansmen's lives heedlessly, always taking the cautious path. Aye, and even if they weren't anywhere near, even if they were searching for her miles away, she would finally be free if her plan succeeded to ride home to Glenmalure.

Her gaze flew to Duncan. Maire was stunned by the strange emotion that struck her, regret mixed with something she couldn't name. But with the outcropping fast approaching, she had no time to dwell on anything save for finding the bog as soon as she could get past the rocks. Her nervousness so great that she feared she might somehow give herself away, Maire pulled up on the reins and slowed the gelding to a stop.

At once Duncan twisted in his saddle, concern lining his face as he wheeled his stallion around and came to her side.

"Rose . . . ?"

"Forgive me, Lord FitzWilliam, but if we could rest . . . only for a moment. I am tired and—and if I could . . ." Her blush in earnest, Maire hoped Duncan would understand as she shifted uncomfortably upon the sidesaddle. To her dismay, he only stared at her, a frown deepening.

"Baron, I believe she must attend to herself," came Reginald Montfort's gruff voice, the older knight drawing his mount alongside Duncan's. "Her needs—"

"Dammit, man, I know what she meant!"

Maire had started at Duncan's voice, which held annoyance as well as a trace of chagrin. As he glanced around them, she quickly rushed on.

"If I may, Lord FitzWilliam, those rocks up there. I need a few moments, no more. It's not so far—"

"Go on, then. We'll wait for you here."

Unspeakable relief filling her at his words, Maire could see that he wasn't pleased by the delay at such a densely wooded spot but she didn't linger to hear him change his mind. Flicking the reins, she guided the gelding up the slope, and didn't dare to look back either. She knew Duncan was watching her as the clatter of armor and restless horses spurred her on.

Within moments she had reached the rocks, her relief again so sharp that the limestone outcropping loomed well above her head that she'd begun to tremble. But she told herself firmly that Triona wouldn't be shaking in fear if she were in Maire's place. Triona would boldly forge onward, and Maire did so too, pausing only briefly behind the moss-covered rocks to catch her breath before she let go with a piercing scream and dug her heels into the gelding's sides.

"Oh, no! Saints help me!"

She shot out from behind the rocks as if her mount had been suddenly spooked, Maire still crying out in terror while she veered the gelding up and over the rise. She was filled with remembered fright when she heard men shouting far below her and the crashing of horses through the woods, Duncan's voice rising above the rest in a vehement curse that made her kick the gelding into a reckless gallop down the slope.

Swiping the hair from her face, she rode for her life, so grateful Triona had spent long hours teaching her how to handle a horse that she could have wept. But she was too busy screaming and wending the now-terrified gelding through the trees, the musty smell of a bog growing sharper.

Her lungs burning, Maire gave no heed to thick woods that had grown so dark she might have sworn it was dusk, and headed straight for a hazy wall of sunlight not far in the distance. She could no longer hear any men's voices. The gelding's frantic hooves pounded in her ears, but she knew her pursuers were riding hard to catch up with her, and she abruptly ceased her screams.

Hopefully they wouldn't know which direction she had gone now, and even if they did . . .

Maire's plan burning in her mind, she came upon the bog so suddenly, bursting through the trees into what appeared a low-lying clearing, that she was nearly pitched from the sidesaddle when she yanked hard on the reins and the gelding reared in fright. A breathless prayer on her lips as his hooves came down only inches from the treacherous quagmire, she snatched wildly at her cloak and flung it onto the brown decaying matter that stank so foully her eyes stung.

She thought only fleetingly of Duncan's face once he came upon her cloak, deciding with an undeniable pang that it was better he think she and the gelding had drowned in the bog than that he still might find her. The sound of men roaring her name carrying through the trees, she kicked the gelding into motion and skirted along the spongy bank, deciding it was best to hide and set out again once Duncan and his men had retreated.

She saw a huge gnarled oak and rode toward it, doubting that her exhausted horse could go much farther without a brief rest even if she wanted to. And she needed nothing more than to snatch her breath—

"By the blood of God, woman, where . . . ?"

Maire had barely reached the oak's concealing shadow to dismount shakily as Duncan burst from the dense trees almost as she had, his vehement roar fading into stunned silence while his stallion snorted and reared in the air. She could tell from his stricken expression that he had spied her cloak, and she watched in disbelief as he vaulted from his heaving horse and plunged into the bog.

Jesu, Mary, and Joseph, was the man mad? Didn't he know that such quagmires could trap a hapless soul within its depths before a cry of help could even be sounded? And he wore heavy armor! Horror gripping her, she saw him grab her cloak and then he sank from sight, leaving nothing but heaving brown muck to mark where he had gone under.

"Saints help him . . . no."

In a daze Maire felt herself move, her hands

shaking so badly she feared she wouldn't be able to haul herself into the sidesaddle yet somehow she did, then kicked the lathered gelding into a hard gallop back along the bank. All the while she kept her eyes riveted to the spot where Duncan had disappeared—

She gasped as his head suddenly emerged from the bog, his arms thrashing to catch a hold, any hold. But there was none, the water-laden peat giving way beneath his fingers, while Maire rode as she had never done before.

She didn't think, didn't heed the shouts of approaching men as she nearly fell in her haste to dismount and struggled her way over too-soft ground to reach the agitated stallion. He almost shied from her but she firmly caught his bridle, so grateful that Triona had taught her to be unafraid of horses.

"Duncan! Duncan, catch the reins!"

Pitching them over the steed's head, Maire flung the reins onto the churning muck as Duncan lunged to reach them. Yet the bog seemed determined to thwart him, and his hands caught only air, the stinking stuff drawing him farther into its depths with his every movement.

"Again, woman! Throw them again!"

She did frantically, stepping so close to the edge that she felt the soggy ground threaten to give way beneath her. She'd never known such relief when Duncan's outstretched hand closed in a tight fist around the reins, his stallion tossing its head and whinnying shrilly as Maire grabbed the bridle and pushed against him to make him walk backward.

"Aye, boy, that's it," she urged him in a voice

gone hoarse from the strain, tears blinding her eyes. "Keep going . . . aye, please, please, you must keep going . . ."

Hearing a labored intake of breath, Maire glanced behind her to see Duncan's face wracked with effort as he fought to haul himself up and over the crumbling bank. She pulled all the more desperately on the bridle until the stallion had dragged Duncan to solid ground. Overcome by emotion as much as exhaustion, she sank to her knees and crawled to him even as he rolled onto his back, his chest heaving, every inch of him soaking wet and covered in muck.

"Duncan—"

"God's teeth, woman!"

Maire gasped as Duncan pulled her into his arms so fiercely that she fell atop him, staring into his stricken eyes.

Chapter 15

"I thought you had drowned . . . like Gisele. Your cloak—"

Duncan didn't finish, his voice as ravaged, Maire never having known such a lump in her throat as he drew his thumb across her cheek, coming away wet with her tears. She couldn't speak, yet she didn't know what she would have said to him first. She was just so grateful that he was safe. She would never have forgiven herself—

"Lord FitzWilliam!"

She stiffened, more in stunned embarrassment to be sprawled so intimately atop Duncan as Reginald Montfort and two other knights sharply reined in their horses and dismounted at a near run. Yet Duncan didn't release her even as more riders came thundering through the woods while shouts went up that they had been found, his arms tightening around her.

"You are well? Not hurt?"

"No . . . no, not hurt." Knowing she must summon a wealth of lies to explain what had happened, Maire was relieved to be spared if only for a few moments as Reginald noisily cleared his throat.

"Forgive me, Baron . . . it looked as if you needed help but, uh . . . God's breath, shall we wait for you elsewhere—"

"Assemble the men, Montfort."

It was near painful to speak, Duncan's lungs still burning from exertion, yet that wasn't the full reason his throat was so tight. He paid little heed as his knights hastily retreated through the trees, and fixed his eyes once more upon Rose.

Her face had grown bright pink at Reginald Montfort's words, and she'd stiffened further in his arms, but Duncan wasn't ready to release her. He didn't want to release her. By the blood of God, just to know she was alive and unharmed when he had feared her . . .

His throat clenching all the tighter, Duncan saw suddenly in his mind's eye another cloak, not blue but yellow gold, floating on the murky surface of a pond. A pond where Gisele had stolen early one morning from her parents' manor to meet him, except she had slipped—

"L-Lord FitzWilliam . . . ?"

Duncan met soft gray eyes, not the stunning green that had haunted him for so long, and was struck that he could have felt so intensely for this woman what he had known for Gisele that terrible day. Yet he had, he couldn't deny it, struck as much that Rose had returned to using his title which all too keenly made him want to hear his Christian name upon her lips again.

"Lord FitzWilliam, we should go. Your men—"

"Call me Duncan, woman," he bade her gently, while her eyes flared wide in surprise. "It's only fitting since you saved my life—"

"Oh, no, it was your steed, truly. I could have done nothing without him."

"Maybe so, but you handled him with skill I've seen in few women . . ." Falling still, Duncan felt her nervous intake of breath even as he stared at her, a strange niggling of doubt suddenly gnawing at his gut. It seemed now, too, that she was reluctant to meet his eyes, which made him roll over with her and pin her lightly to the mossy ground while he kept his voice as even as he could in spite of his unwelcome suspicion. "Those rocks, Rose. What happened?"

"Th-the rocks?"

"When you lost control of your horse—"

"Aye, that was it exactly! He was fine, the poor creature, then something startled him . . . and so suddenly, too. He reared and I almost fell and—and I lost the reins. If I hadn't held on to his mane . . ."

She fell awkwardly silent while Duncan studied her face . . . the heightened color of her cheeks, her lovely eyes holding more than a trace of apprehension as if she feared he might not believe her. And he wanted to believe her, yet his suspicion that she might have for some reason contrived the entire incident only grew as he thought of her cloak.

She had worn it about her so snugly. Could a headlong ride have wrenched it loose? And that she hadn't plunged straight into the bog if her mount had been so terrified and she'd lost all control of him—God's teeth! Only his competence with horses had made him rein in his stallion just in time when they'd come crashing through the trees, while he had dived into the muck like an utter fool, thinking . . .

Duncan knew he was scowling, by sheer force of will telling himself not to press any farther as her face had gone pale. And she shivered, too, almost as wet as he that he'd held her in his arms for so long, the front of her blue silk gown smeared with brownish muck. Imagining the stir their disheveled appearance would make at Dublin Castle, he almost wished he still smelled like lilacs. The stench alone that clung to him was enough to raise eyebrows and tear the eyes.

Cursing to himself, Duncan shifted from her and rose to his feet, then held out his hand.

"Come."

She accepted his assistance without a word, and he drew her up to stand shakily beside him, her eyes grown as wide and anxious as the first days she'd spent at Longford Castle. It stung him, while her continued silence as he led her to her mount made him wonder if perhaps he had wrongly suspected her, and her explanation had been true.

By the devil, what had come over him? Was it so easy for him to forget that Clement had warned him to treat her gently? How could he think she would have wanted it to appear she had drowned? It was more likely her cloak had come undone before she managed to regain control of her horse and then ridden back to help him—and what of her screams? What of her tears? She must have been terrified; even the most accomplished rider was prey to mishaps now and again.

"May . . . may I ride with you, Duncan?"

His hands already at her waist to lift her to the saddle, he felt all suspicion fade as she glanced nervously at the gelding.

"After what happened, I don't think I . . . at least not right now . . ."

She didn't say more while Duncan felt his anger at himself deepen. He nodded for one of his waiting men to look after her horse, and then led her to his stallion.

Moments later, Rose tucked safely in front of him as they rode back through the woods, a borrowed cloak warming them both, he wondered again that he could have suspected her, especially when he felt her relax within his embrace and lay her head against his shoulder. Her midnight hair smelling of lilacs, it made him want to curse aloud that they were bound for Dublin where her clansmen might soon bear her away with them. But he kept silent, even as his arms tightened possessively around her.

"By God, has no one seen her?"

Ronan's roar shattering the tense silence, he slammed his fist upon the table in impotent fury and eyed the dozen exhausted clansmen who stood before him.

"You asked at every village? You split up and each man took a different route?"

"Aye, Lord, just as you commanded and when we heard any news, it was always the same," came Flann O'Faelin's weary voice, the huge carrot-haired Irishman's expression grave. "A large force of Normans had been seen riding north three days past but none recognized them to fathom a guess where they might be bound. And they might not have been the devil's spawn we seek. Women were among them, aye, one a blonde of surpassing beauty it was said, riding a fine gray steed, but no one could remember seeing Maire—"

"The bastards dragged women about on their slaughter?" Ronan glanced at Niall, who so far had said nothing, his younger brother's face as wretchedly grim as he felt, which was answer enough.

Niall, in fact, had said little these past days while they'd waited impatiently for Flann and the others to return, his anger intense that he'd been made to stay behind instead of joining the search for Maire. Yet Ronan had feared Niall might be recognized by those who'd slain their clansmen. Who could say if any had glimpsed his face before he'd ridden into the woods? When the O'Byrnes of Glenmalure found the Normans who'd taken Maire, and by God, they would, Ronan wanted it to be as terrible a surprise as that which had come upon poor Fiach and the others.

"Maire had to be among those women," he said fiercely, more to himself than anyone, wondering if she might have been borne in such a manner that none could see her face. That would mean she had been injured—God help them, if so, those spawn would pay doubly! His wrath mounting, he met Flann's gaze. "Did you hear word of any other host of Normans traveling north?"

"No, Lord, none."

"Then it had to be them. Yet no one could name the bastards?"

"No, Lord, and no word of their progress beyond daylight could be found. The last they were seen was ten leagues south of the Hill of Tara in Meath. It's as if they were swallowed by the night—"

"More likely a castle than the night," came Niall's low voice. "They must have been pressing hard to their destination to ride on after dark, aye, and that would mean they knew a hot meal was close at hand, beds aplenty, a stable large enough to accommodate them—dammit, Flann, did you say ten leagues?"

The giant Irishman's nod made Ronan's gut knot, even as Niall rose from the bench and caught his arm.

"She has to be there, Ronan, in Meath, and I would swear near Tara! We've only to learn which castle—"

"And whether or not the spawn moved on from there the next day."

Ronan's grim words falling like a pall over everyone present, he was struck by the sudden despair in Niall's eyes. His anger directed at no one more fiercely than himself, his voice was tight as he turned to Flann.

"I'll need ten men to ride with me, no more. It might be days before we return, weeks mayhap—as long as it takes until Maire is found and safely back among us. See that all are well armed and ready to leave by dark."

"Aye, lord, it will be done."

Ronan said no more as his clansmen silently

filed from the feasting-hall, but turned to the blazing fire while Niall sank onto the bench. All he could see in the flames was Maire surrounded by Normans, Maire possibly hurt, mayhap worse—

"By God, those bastards will die!"

His fury echoing around them, his momentary feeling of helplessness was nearly as acute. He, too, had burned to ride with his clansmen, but he'd made enough raids north of Wicklow that someone could well have recognized him asking questions and put Maire's life at further risk. At least now they had a reasoned place to start, while he prayed that she had somehow kept her relationship to the O'Byrnes to herself. Since he had learned of her abduction, it had never once left his mind how truly dangerous was her plight.

"I should never have allowed her to learn to ride, to leave Glenmalure, none of it!" His jaw clenched, Ronan stared blindly into the fire. "She was safe here, yet Triona—"

"Good God, brother, so now you blame your wife again that Maire was granted a chance at knowing more than half a life?"

Niall's harsh words striking him like blows, Ronan wheeled to face him, not surprised that Niall stood now as if ready to do battle.

"Dammit, man, I blame no one but myself! To have her walk again, aye, that I would never take from her, but the rest was pure folly and has brought nothing but harm to her! A half life, Niall? I'll never forgive myself that I hadn't insisted upon it! By God, she might be dead for as much as we know!"

At Niall's stricken look Ronan almost wished he could take back his last words. The two of them faced each other across a chasm that each day seemed to be widening no matter Triona's efforts to keep peace between them. She would have done so now if she hadn't been at their dwelling-house caring for Deirdre, who'd suffered a scratch to her hand after pulling her kitten's tail. Just thinking of his wife and daughter served to ease some of his anger, and he sighed heavily.

"Niall, this isn't helping Maire—"

"No, it's not, and I'm glad to hear you recognizing it after all these months. I wish you'd thought as much when you told Maire you'd bring no more suitors to Glenmalure to meet her—dammit, Ronan! Didn't you see the light dying in her eyes? She never wanted for more than a husband and children and to have a chance to lead her life like other women. Aye, she might have been hurt by Colin O'Nolan, and I know you'd have done anything to take it from her, but that didn't give you the right—"

"By God, enough!"

"No, Ronan, it's not enough, not yet! Did I tell you that right before I left Maire in that meadow she was crying? Aye, with joy for me and Caitlin but sorrow, too, that she might never know the same for herself. So I'm telling you now that Maire isn't dead, and when we do find her, you'd do well to grant her a chance to find even half the love you share with Triona if you truly care for your sister's happiness at all!"

Niall stormed past him before Ronan could summon an answer, and when he did, it was to utter a vehement oath that fell to no one's ears but his own.

Niall was already gone.

Chapter 16

"There, child, that's so much be[illegible] couldn't have you looking a[illegible] did—or smelling as you did, at supper ton[illegible] oh, my, no."

Clucking her tongue, the apple-cheeked servingwoman made a last adjustment to the gold girdle wrapped around Maire's waist, then stood back to survey her handiwork with a knowing eye. In the next instant, clearly satisfied, her kindly face broke into a broad smile.

"Ah, child, how fair you are! Like an angel—it's no wonder you moved Lady de Gray's heart. And how generous my mistress was to see that you lacked for nothing, do you not think so?"

Maire could only nod, still stunned at the graciousness extended to her from nearly the moment she and Duncan had arrived at Dublin Castle and been ushered into the Justiciar John de Gray's private meeting room. A tall, robust man with a stentorian voice to match, he had barely begun to listen to Duncan's recounting of why they'd come from Meath when the Justiciar summoned his wife, Lady Enid, as if knowing she would take Maire under her wing so he and Duncan might talk alone.

And the lovely older woman had, gauging at once that one of her maids-in-waiting was Maire's size and could spare a gown or two to replace the soiled blue silk that, though dry, still stank like the bog. Maire's brief explanation of what had happened had horrified her, and Lady Enid had insisted that Maire lie down and rest while a hot bath was prepared and fresh clothing brought to a well-appointed bedchamber. One of Lady Enid's personal servants was sent to see to her every need.

Even now the servingwoman continued to fuss over Maire, plump fingers arranging a transparent white veil edged with embroidery of gold and lavender thread around her shoulders. Maire felt as if she scarcely recognized herself in the Norman garb. She had never donned so much clothing, or so it seemed. Silken white hose to just above her knees held with delicate ties and soft matching slippers, a thin linen shift much like her camise, then a lavender gown with long fitted sleeves and shimmering folds that fell to the floor and hugged her form like nothing she'd ever worn.

The strange girdle only made things worse, accentuating the slenderness of her waist, while gold plaits were tied just above the juncture of her thighs, making Maire blush that the eye might be drawn there. And she'd never worn anything on her head, the gilt circlet holding the veil in place not so much uncomfortable as unfamiliar.

At least her long hair hung loosely, which had

disappointed the serving woman who had wanted to braid and arrange the thick, freshly washed mass in coils above Maire's ears. At that point a sigh and soft words that she was Irish, not Norman, had been enough to dissuade the woman, but she had insisted upon combing Maire's hair until it shone.

"Well, now, child, it seems I've nothing more to do—except show you the way to the banquet hall." A worried frown touched the serving-woman's brow. "I fear it's no short way—"

"I'll see her there."

Maire gasped to find Duncan standing just inside the door, hours spent wondering what he might be doing answered in part by his handsome attire. He wore a calf-length tunic of black edged with gold, black hose, and black boots. The dampness of his dark hair suggested a recent bath, which only brought to mind the night before, causing Maire's heart to thunder. It seemed his eyes swept her as thoroughly as hers had swept him, but more slowly, and with an admiring warmth that suddenly made it difficult for her to breathe.

Jesu, Mary, and Joseph, at least it was that rather than the suspicion she had glimpsed in his eyes at the bog, though she had done her best to assure herself that asking to ride with him had convinced him further that her hastily conceived story was true. She had truly never thought she would need a story, nor considered that anything she said might ring false given she'd shown such skill with horses. And she had never, ever imagined that Duncan might dive into the treacherous muck when he saw her cloak. Saints help her, what that might mean had kept her mind spinning and her heart often racing—

"You look beautiful, Rose."

His voice was so husky that she shivered, her breath falling still altogether as he came forward and took her arm. Maire had never known any man to say such a thing to her. And he was looking at her so strangely, differently than he ever had before. Duncan's handsome face grown sober, he stared into her eyes for so long and heart-stopping a moment that the servingwoman coughed lightly and excused herself, though she threw a knowing smile at Maire just before she left the room.

That only made Maire's knees feel weaker as Duncan drew her with him, and she knew as surely that something was happening to her, something incredible and dangerous and impossible that she would be a fool not to fight and shove forever from her mind. Yet it seemed her thoughts and feelings had forged a will of their own, mayhap even from the first moment she had seen Duncan FitzWilliam.

"Shall we walk or might I carry you?" came his low query as they, too, left the bedchamber. "It would be less taxing—"

"No, please . . . I'd like to walk." Her face burning, she accepted his proffered arm. "Truly, Lord Fitz—Duncan, I'm not a child that must be assisted here and there."

"I never imagined you a child. Come."

She'd seen no affront in his eyes, but Maire sensed a slight stiffness in his shoulders that she immediately decided was best, no matter her sudden regret that she'd been unkind. Mayhap now he would not ask such a thing again, the intimacy of him carrying her too much to bear after hours spent sharing the same saddle. She did not want to think of how much she had liked the sensation of his arms around her, his hard thighs hugging her hips . . .

"Have you always blushed so easily?"

She met his eyes with a start, as disconcerted by her wild imaginings as that he would so unexpectedly ask her something of her past. Warning herself that she must be all the more careful not to arouse further suspicion, she answered as calmly as she could. "I . . . I don't know. Mayhap if I could remember . . ."

His heavy sigh as she fell silent wasn't what she had expected either, nor his frown as they left the guests' hall that formed only a small part of Dublin Castle. Wondering what might have displeased him, she tried to ignore the curious glances thrown their way by well-dressed courtiers bound, too, she imagined, for the banquet hall.

"You'll see many staring tonight, but don't let it trouble you," came Duncan's voice as if reading her mind. "Most all by now have heard of your plight—Lord de Grey chose to make no secret of it. He hopes someone may recognize you, especially since no word has yet come to Dublin from your clan."

"No word?" Maire prayed at this news that she looked convincingly dismayed as Duncan shook his head. He said no more, and she didn't either, only too grateful to focus instead on the growing crush of courtiers.

It was true, people were openly staring, Maire realized, as the din of the banquet hall grew louder. Not so much at her awkward gait but at her face, while Duncan's frown only seemed to grow deeper. Yet he drew her more closely against him, too, which confused her as much as made her flush to her toes. His hold upon her seemed almost possessive, as if he wanted everyone to see . . .

Begorra, would her imaginings not cease? Dismissing the impossible thought, Maire blinked as they reached the soaring entrance to the banquet hall, the massive room illuminated by scores of blazing torches. And it was already teeming with humanity, the roar of conversation making her head spin. Yet as she and Duncan moved into the throng, she heard a strange drop in the clamor as heads turned and people stood back so they could pass.

"That must be her—God's blood, she's comely but I've never seen the wench before," came an aside from a stout Norman near to Maire's right. "Have you, FitzGilbert?"

She didn't hear the answer but didn't need to, knowing none would recognize her. As Duncan led her toward the high table, where she saw Lady Enid lean over to say something to her husband, Maire was suddenly distracted by a trio of lovely young women who glided out of their path but kept three pairs of eyes fixed enviously upon her.

"Can you believe Lord FitzWilliam has agreed to wed that Irish chit?" hissed one.

"Only if he must, Clare, that's what I heard."

"Of course that's the only reason!" whispered

the third. "Why else would he want to be burdened with a cripple?"

Maire stared after them in shock while Duncan continued to draw her through the throng that had suddenly become no more than a dizzying blur of voices and faces. She doubted he had heard those women, doubted she had heard their words herself. *Duncan was thinking to marry her?* It couldn't be true.

"Take care on the steps, Rose."

Dazedly she nodded, as grateful for Duncan's assistance at that moment to climb to the dais as she was certain she would have stumbled without it. Only Lady Enid's kind smile seemed strangely to steady her; the older woman, resplendent in green brocade that heightened the rich auburn of her hair, arose to offer the cushioned chair next to her own.

"Ah, child, how charming you look. Sit here by me."

"She is lovely, FitzWilliam," seconded John de Gray in his great booming voice as Maire sank into the chair. "A man could do worse in a bride—if her clan demands you wed her to satisfy them. Perhaps we'll learn of her family tonight. God's breath, listen to the stir!"

Maire heard no stir, the crescendo of conversation filling the hall nothing to the blood pounding so fiercely in her ears. Out of the corner of her eye she saw Duncan take the seat beyond the Justiciar, but she couldn't look at him, she was so stunned.

"Child, are you ill? You've grown pale."

"I—I didn't know," she murmured more to herself than Lady Enid, though she met the woman's concerned gaze. "Duncan never said anything to me about . . . about a marriage . . ."

"Ah, dear, isn't that the nature of men not to mention something so close to a woman's heart?" Lady Enid twisted in her chair, her voice filled with mild reproach. "For shame, Lord FitzWilliam, that you haven't shared your honorable intent with this poor girl."

"In truth, my lady, I thought there not enough time before supper . . . and the matter a delicate one not to be rushed. Yet I see now that I was wrong to delay . . ."

Duncan said no more, as angry with himself as he was deeply stung that Rose appeared so ashen. And she hadn't once looked his way, her eyes even now downcast, while Lady Enid sighed and threw an exasperated look at the Justiciar.

"Thanks in no small part to my lord husband—ah, dear, but there's nothing to be done about it now."

With a wave of her hand, Lady Enid signaled for the meal to begin, but Duncan suddenly had no appetite for meat or drink. His frustration only grew as Rose seemed as disinclined to taste the array of savory dishes served to her plate or to take even a sip of wine, and still she refused to look at him.

"Dammit, FitzWilliam, am I speaking to myself?"

Reluctantly, Duncan shifted his gaze to John de Gray. The Justiciar studied him with annoyance.

"I said, do you think there's any chance it wasn't the O'Melaghlins who slaughtered those cattle but some of Walter de Lacy's men still loose about the countryside?"

"It doesn't matter. Those rebels have plagued Meath long before I came to Ireland, and I'll suffer no more. If the O'Melaghlin chooses not to heed my summons, his harper and two grandsons will hang."

John de Gray didn't readily respond, but took a long draft of wine, which gave Duncan another chance to focus upon Rose. Still she hadn't touched her plate, and he could tell she wasn't listening as Lady Enid went on and on about the excellence of her cooks, no doubt in an attempt to coax her to eat. Did the thought of marrying him displease her so much that she would starve herself?

"You want her, don't you?"

Duncan met John de Gray's shrewd dark eyes. "I agreed to marry her."

"But only if her clan wishes it? I daresay, Baron, you'll take her as your bride whether they demand such retribution or not—unless I've judged wrongly."

Duncan said nothing, but he clearly didn't have to speak as a speculative half smile stole over the Justiciar's face. Yet it faded as quickly as it had come, John de Gray leaning toward him, his voice grown stern.

"I want peace in Leinster, FitzWilliam. When her clansmen come forward, and I trust they will soon, given that you believe their chieftain has been slain, you will wed the wench if they so wish it—or offer yourself first to wed her, I care not which. But if they oppose such a match . . ."

Duncan's gut clenched as John de Gray

paused to glance over his shoulder at Rose, and he saw then that she sat as still and pale as a statue, perhaps listening to every word—

"You will give her up, Baron. Are we understood? I'll have no clan warfare begun over a wench, however fair. You will give her up."

As if the matter was firmly settled, John de Gray sat back in his chair and stuck his knife into a glistening slice of roast venison while Duncan had never felt farther from being hungry. He stared out over the crowded banquet hall. That no one had yet come forward to say he recognized Rose was an ominous sign that none would this night. And by the blood of God, now that his mind was made, he wanted the matter done!

At first he had hoped that her clansmen hadn't come to Dublin, his relief intense when John de Gray had said no word of any slaughter had yet reached him. So intense that Duncan had readily agreed to take Rose as his bride if her clansmen so demanded it, startling himself at how much he realized he wanted her. But with none of her family here, and no one coming forth with any knowledge of them, how long now before he would know their wishes? Dammit, before they might know his? And she still remembered nothing, not even if she had always blushed so easily, so no help lay there—

"My lords, the poor child isn't well. If you'll excuse us, I'll accompany her back to her room."

Duncan lunged from his chair as Lady Enid helped Rose to stand, but John de Gray caught his arm.

"Seat yourself, FitzWilliam. My lady wife can

see to the wench. We've many matters yet to discuss."

Duncan looked from John de Gray to Rose as she was assisted down the steps, then he sat with a low curse; the Justiciar was King John's highest official in Ireland and not a man with whom to quarrel. But as John de Gray began to relay news of the royal court in London, Duncan listened with half an ear, his eyes never leaving Rose until she had disappeared with Lady Enid from the banquet hall.

And even then he couldn't focus his attention, his gut churning. By the devil, had the thought of wedding him made her so ill she must take to her bed?

"God's blood, man, you're smitten."

Duncan met John de Gray's gaze, the Justiciar holding out to him a brimming goblet of wine.

"To the marrow, from the looks of it, so you'd best drink—for now. But later, pray, FitzWilliam . . . that her clansmen when they come forth want you wed to the wench rather than to put your head on a pike."

Chapter 17

"Ease yourself, child, and rest, it's no wonder you're not feeling well. How much could any young woman bear in so few days? Yet I'm certain Lord FitzWilliam meant you no injury by neglecting to tell you his intentions—ah, dear, men."

Maire said nothing while Lady Enid shook her head and tucked the counterpane around her shoulders; in truth, she'd said little from the moment she'd left the high table, no matter she was touched by the woman's kindness. She wanted to sleep, to sleep and wake somehow in Glenmalure in her own bed and pretend all this strange madness had been no more than a dream . . .

"Ah, no, child, no tears." Sighing, Lady Enid sat on the edge of the bed and brushed her hand across Maire's forehead. "Duncan FitzWilliam is a good man, and honorable, my lord husband has never spoken anything but highly of him. That he has agreed to right a terrible wrong committed by others should show you his integrity. If your clansmen want you to wed him, I know he'd not mistreat you. And it's time Lord FitzWilliam marry, past time with so rich a barony, we've often remarked upon it. You'll want for nothing, child—ah, me, enough. I should let you sleep."

As Lady Enid rose, Maire swept wetness from her eyes that, now begun, would not seem to stop. She heard Lady Enid sigh again, and saw her glance at the apple-cheeked servingwoman who hovered nearby. Maire had been helped to undress and assisted so capably into bed that her head still spun from that alone.

"Leave us," came Lady Enid's soft voice. The servingwoman with a last concerned look at Maire, hastened to oblige. Only when the bedchamber door was quietly closed did the Justiciar's wife once more settle herself onto the mattress, and she took one of Maire's hands in her own.

"Do you wonder of love, child? Is that why you weep?"

Unable to answer for the sudden lump in her throat, Maire glanced away while Lady Enid continued gently.

"I knew my husband for only a short time before we wed, a few weeks, no more, but I haven't regretted it. He often tries me—like tonight, yet I love him dearly. Our affection for each other only grew with the years. And I saw how Lord FitzWilliam looked at you tonight, child. That promise has already taken root. Love will grow strong and deep between you, I know it."

Love? Between a rebel O'Byrne and a Norman? Her eyes filling with fresh tears, Maire felt the torment inside her only mounting as Lady Enid squeezed her hand.

"Would it help for you to know how quickly Lord FitzWilliam agreed to take you for his bride? My husband told me the words were no sooner from his mouth than it was done, and even he was surprised. We know little of the baron's private affairs, except that he was to have married years ago but the poor girl drowned . . . Gisele de Clare was her name—"

"Gisele?" Maire had no more than whispered while Lady Enid nodded and went on.

"He lost her only days before their secret wedding, or so the parish priest revealed to her family, and they brought their grief and anger all the way to King John, creating quite a stir. Her parents blamed Lord FitzWilliam much for her death, for they hadn't approved the match. He was only a mere soldier then. I don't recall anything said of punishment meted out to him—ah, dear, his own suffering must have been enough. That he's a baron and still no wife? But perhaps, child, in you he's finally found—"

"Please, no more." Her mind truly spinning now, Maire felt her eyes stinging even worse, Lady Enid's face become a blur. "If I could sleep . . ."

A soft sigh greeting her words, the Justiciar's wife gave Maire's hand a last squeeze and then rose from the bed.

"Forgive me, child. Of course rest is what you need. But when you awake in the morning, I hope all will look brighter to you. I will pray that your fears are eased."

Maire wanted so badly to offer some thanks, but she kept silent as Lady Enid left the room; she wished as much to be alone and sensed that any word might encourage the kindly woman to linger. Tomorrow she would thank her, but not now. As the door closed, she rolled onto her side and clutched the pillow to her mouth, finally allowing her sobs to overtake her.

She hadn't cried, really cried, since that night last autumn when Colin O'Nolan had spurned her, but even that memory paled to the utter wretchedness she felt now.

It was all so cruel.

Fiach O'Byrne and her other clansmen ruthlessly slaughtered.

Her family with no knowledge as to whether she lived or where she might be . . . at Dublin Castle, no less, where Ronan and Triona had nearly lost their lives only two years past.

And now Duncan FitzWilliam agreeing to marry her—and Lady Enid speaking of love. *Of love!*

Balling her hand into a fist, Maire punched wildly at the pillow as her sobs shook her, shook her so fiercely that she soon doubled over from the pain.

But it was nothing to the pain tearing at her heart, the dream she'd cherished for so long as close as it had ever been or ever would be again, she knew it! And it was all so terribly cruel. Duncan was a Norman. To think of marriage to such a man, even loving such a man, was no more than trying to catch air. So why did it make her want such madness to be possible all the more desperately?

Maire had no sense of how long she cried, but, finally spent, she lay silent and exhausted and trembling on the bed, the pillow sodden from her tears. Only then did she hear it, a low intake of breath and she froze, her heart thundering.

"Is it that horrible to you, woman? The thought that we might wed?"

Her senses dazed and her eyelids swollen from weeping, Maire couldn't tell from where Duncan's voice had come, but she knew he was very close. And the room was so dark, the low fire in the hearth casting more shadow than light that proved of little help.

She struggled within the linen tangle of her sleeping gown to sit up, gasping when she felt two strong hands grab her and haul her backwards from the bed. Within an instant she was enveloped in an embrace so powerful that her legs gave way beneath her, but Duncan held her too close, her back pressed against his chest, for there to have been any chance she might fall.

"Have you been crying so fiercely because of me, Rose?"

She heard pain in his voice even as his embrace grew tighter, and she wanted to scream then and there that her name wasn't Rose but Maire . . . Maire O'Byrne, and finally have the wretched madness come to an end. But what then of Ronan and Niall and Triona and Deirdre and any of her clansmen that such a confession might put at terrible risk? Tears once more stung her eyes as she wondered wildly what to say, nothing burning brighter in her mind than at least, in this instance, the truth.

"I cannot . . . I cannot marry you, Duncan."

She had no strength to even gasp as he turned her around in his arms, a log crackling into fresh flames casting light upon his grim face.

"Woman, have you remembered your clan? You know they would oppose—"

He'd fallen abruptly silent as she shook her head, Maire's throat tightening at the relief she saw in his eyes which tore all the more deeply at her heart. Once again, she grabbed desperately for some measure of the truth.

"It's Adele. You heard her that first night . . . I-I'm no fit bride for you. She'll never allow it—"

"Allow it?" Duncan's voice incredulous, Maire watched as a host of emotions played across his striking features from relief again to a sudden hardening that came close to chilling her. He drew her closer, staring into her eyes as if he dared her not to believe him. "Adele has no say in my life, woman, and she never will. Was that at the heart of your tears?"

He searched her face so intently that Maire lost all voice to answer, and it seemed her silence made Duncan become even more grim.

"God's teeth, I'll throttle her if she utters another word against you—does another thing to distress you. Forget all that she said—"

"I can't, Duncan, and I cannot become your wife!" Maire felt him stiffen at her sudden outburst but she rushed on recklessly, determined all the more to find some way to dissuade him. "Why would you want such a thing? To bring discord into your house . . . aye, a-and it wouldn't be fair to you, cruel even, to have you bear such a burden! I saw scores of young women in the banquet hall tonight, all of them lovely and healthy and whole. Any would make you a better bride, not a woman like me—"

"Like you, Rose?"

He'd cut her off so huskily that Maire sucked in her breath, the look in his eyes not at all what she would have expected.

"Tell me what's not beautiful in a woman who holds her head high like a queen when others laugh and point and stare. And as for healthy and whole . . ."

Maire's heart leapt to her throat as he drew her against him, his voice grown huskier still.

"Can you see me, Rose?"

"A-aye."

"Can you hear me? Speak to answer me?"

Maire tried to but in vain, nodding when she found her voice gone altogether as he bent his head close to hers.

"Can you feel my arms around you?"

She could, aye, she could, hard and muscled and strong. Shivers plummeted to her toes when he drew her even closer, his lips hovering only a whisper away from hers.

"Ah, woman, and you can taste?"

His breath warm and scented with wine, she opened her mouth to catch her own breath that had all but fled, even as his lips found hers, pressing down so gently at first that Maire sighed in wonder and went limp in his arms. But she didn't fall, though she felt as if she were tumbling headlong into some dizzying abyss when his kiss swiftly became one of plunder, his embrace grown as fierce.

She thought only to hold on for dear life, her

arms stealing around his neck to hold him close, her fingers ensnaring in his hair, her sigh becoming a broken moan when Duncan swept his tongue deeply into her mouth. Engulfed as if by flames, distantly she sensed a coolness, too. Then, as Duncan's hands heavy and warm beneath her sleeping gown cupped her bare bottom and pulled her against him, Maire suddenly trembled from head to foot.

And still he kissed her, wildly, possessively, his groan coming to her ears even as she suddenly felt him draw away from her, Duncan lifting his head to stare into her eyes.

"Woman, never think again that you're not healthy and whole . . . ah, God."

His voice hoarse, he was shaking, she could feel it, and almost with determination he held her away from him, the back of her legs bumping against the bed. It made her start, and she saw him glance from the mattress and then to her face, his low curse shattering the charged silence. She had no more than blinked when she was swept from her feet and laid on the bed, Duncan's voice as raw as he covered her with the counterpane to her chin.

"My decision is made, Rose. We will wed. By the blood of God, whether your clan wishes it or not."

He said no more, leaving Maire to stare after him, her heart thundering as he strode from the room.

Wishes it? If Duncan only knew. Tears biting her eyes again, she forced them back, not allowing herself to cry further. It would do no good.

Just as she knew it was no use any longer to

fight what burned so deeply inside her; she had already lost. From the moment Duncan's lips had touched hers . . .

"Begorra, Maire O'Byrne, you're a fool. Saints help you, you're a fool!"

Curling into a ball, she hugged her sodden pillow and stared blindly at the dying fire.

Chapter 18

"Perhaps, Lord FitzWilliam, all she needs is to know you a little better to ease her fears. What has it been—five days? You're really no more than strangers to each other, and that must change."

Lady Enid's fresh advice ringing in his mind, Duncan strode toward the bedchamber he couldn't have left faster last night . . . or he wouldn't have left at all.

It still astounded him that John de Gray had suggested he go to Rose's room when Lady Enid had returned to the banquet hall saying she'd heard Rose begin to weep as soon as she'd shut the door. Or perhaps it had been the pointed look Lady Enid had thrown her husband when he'd at first only advised Duncan to have another goblet of wine. God's teeth, women did have a meaningful way with their eyes. In the next instant, John de Gray had groused that Duncan might want to check on her, and he hadn't hesitated.

He had already been on his way there this morning when Lady Enid had waved him down and informed him that she'd just been to see Rose herself, and that she seemed in lighter spirits. It had been all Duncan could do not to make some ill-advised comment when Lady Enid had suggested he continue whatever he'd done to cheer Rose, along with a gentle plea for him to heed her well-intentioned advice. He fully intended to—at least the latter, while the other . . .

Duncan swore under his breath, the undeniable tightening in his lower body only a hint of what he'd suffered last night. His first mistake had been in kissing Rose, the softness of her lips, the sweet taste of her, enough alone to haunt him deep into the morning. But when he'd dragged her sleeping gown above her hips and—

"Enough, man, you'll have a babe made before she's a bride," he said gruffly to himself, not surprised that the idea didn't displease him. His impatience only growing that the entire matter of the marriage be done and settled, it only tore at him further that it might be days yet before he could claim Rose as his own—if and when her clan came forward. That they hadn't made him wonder if plans for battle were already being drawn.

Scowling, Duncan forced the grim possibility from his mind, telling himself for the hundredth time that if so, it altered nothing. Not to him.

He had never thought another woman would come close to sharing a place in his heart with Gisele, but now that he had found her, he was not about to let her go—John de Gray and his warning be damned. If need be, he would go to

London to the king to ask that such a demand be overruled. If Rose's clan proved reluctant, he'd already decided as much. There were more ways to preserve peace than to risk losing what he'd thought never to find again. Dammit, that bog had been close enough . . .

Duncan's throat growing tight, he was tempted not to knock and instead throw open the door, he wanted so to see her. But startling Rose was not how he wished to begin their day together, and as ever, Clement's advice, too, to treat her gently, remained forefront in his mind. Yet his kiss last night hadn't been so gentle—

"By the devil, man, knock on the blasted door," he muttered, feeling more like a callow boy than a man who commanded more knights and men-at-arms than many a baron in Ireland. Wondering what Gerard de Barry would think that he'd finally decided to wed, his friend having long encouraged him to seek a bride to preserve the barony he'd gained, Duncan rapped twice.

"Rose?"

He heard a flurry of sound, then footsteps, disappointment filling him when a serving-woman answered the door, the same one who'd been attending to Rose last night. Smiling cheerily, she brushed past him as if eager to leave them alone, which suited Duncan. His gaze flew to where Rose turned in her chair to look at him, two bright spots of color warming her cheeks.

She didn't appear unhappy to see him, if but a little nervous, which made Lady Enid's advice flood back to him. He felt suddenly awkward standing there, halfway in the door, half out; it had been a long time since he'd made any special effort to woo a woman.

"You . . . you may come in, if you'd like."

Her voice as sweet and soft as her lips had been last night, it was enough to spur him into motion. Duncan was struck by renewed purpose at her tentative smile. He'd not seen such a thing from her before.

Or to hear her laugh. What a wonder that would be. An intense longing filling him for the day when she would be well enough to reveal more about herself, he knew what was important right now was for her to learn more of him. And she did seem of lighter spirits, just as Lady Enid had said, which only made him further take heart. Perhaps given what he'd said to assure her last night, her fears had already begun to ease.

He sank to his haunches beside her chair, a swift glance taking in the pale pink gown she wore, which so suited her delicate coloring, and he noted as well the square of embroidery in her lap.

"Lady Enid kindly brought me something to do."

Duncan met her eyes, a softness there that he hadn't seen before either, though she seemed to grow uncomfortable at his scrutiny and glanced down at her needlework.

He did, too, seeing that the stitches were as finely wrought as those of his mother, and he remembered suddenly how Rose had commented upon the beauty of the screen. He realized she must have a deep fondness for such a womanly skill to wield a needle so well. Duncan felt as if he'd been given a precious gift to have discovered something more about her.

"When we return to Meath, I'll see that you have all you need to embroider to your heart's desire. And gowns. As many as you wish, I'll have made for you. Lady Enid was gracious to give you this one"—he touched her sleeve, grateful when Rose didn't pull away from him though she had blushed as pink as her gown—"and the one you wore last night, but you must have your own. As my wife, you deserve nothing less. Now come."

He stood and she looked up at him in confusion, the same slight uncertainty tingeing her gaze, too. It made him all the more determined that by the end of the day, he would not seem such a stranger to her.

"Set aside your needlework, Rose, we've something else to do."

He could barely contain his sudden impatience to be gone from Dublin Castle as she did as she was bidden, then accepted the hand he held out to her. As he drew her up in front of him, it was all he could do not to pull her into his arms, too. Then he impulsively decided, why the devil not? He swept her from her feet so suddenly that she gasped, and strode with her to the door.

"I know, woman, you're not a child to be carried. But it pleases me, and it's faster, fair enough?"

He was smiling, and if his teasing words alone didn't sway her, that seemed to. She offered no resistance, staring at him as if in wonder, while Duncan felt his own mood lighter than he could even remember.

Maire shifted in the saddle, trying not to think of how much it pleased her to feel Duncan's arms so tightly around her just as he had said it would please him that they ride together.

Jesu, Mary, and Joseph, everything seemed to be pleasing him this morning!

That the spring day was balmy and the sun shone bright as they'd rode from the huge stable, had moved him to smile again and so handsomely that Maire had felt her heart begin once more to thunder. Just seeing him standing at the door to her bedchamber had aroused that overwhelming sensation, and it hadn't seemed to stop, Maire made more acutely aware with each passing moment of what she'd resigned herself to last night. She loved the man. God help her, she loved him.

But that would have happened to any daughter of a chieftain loyal to King John, she had told herself over and over as sleep had evaded her long into the night. Just as Lady Enid had said, Duncan FitzWilliam was honorable and good. What such young woman wouldn't be delighted to become his bride? Her protestations had swayed him not a wee bit last evening, and there were none left to her save the truth. A truth she risked revealing if she didn't appear to be warming to Duncan's attentions—saints help her, she had no pretending to do there!

"That's the place I wanted to show you. Do you see it?"

Maire glanced at his face to find him not smiling now but grown sober as he reined in his dark bay stallion. She followed his gaze to a barren jutting of land lying south of where the River Liffey spilled into the sea.

"We landed our ships there. A quarter of King John's army while he and the rest marched north from Waterford . . . nearly two years ago. I would have never known then that Ireland would become my home."

Duncan's arms tightening around her, Maire was reminded all too vividly by his words of how Ronan and her clansmen had hoped the Normans would all butcher each other when King John had come to Eire to crush the rebellion among his own vassals. Yet Duncan had survived, and prospered—

"I was a knight then," he continued close to her ear, his warm breath eliciting shivers inside her. "But I was made a baron for saving the king's life. A recompense. I came close to dying that day—"

"Dying?" Maire's outburst ringing around them, she flushed with chagrin as he nodded.

"The king's army was bound southward for Dublin, the earls Hugh and Walter de Lacy defeated and fled to France. The bastards had wanted to make Ireland their own kingdom—and still some of their men remain who long for nothing more than their return. It was such as those who broke through the king's guard and attacked, but thankfully there were enough to stop them. I heard later that King John swore if I hadn't caught a sword blow intended for him, he would have lost his head."

Maire shuddered, and Duncan must have sensed it for he drew her close.

"I tell you this not to distress you, Rose, but that you might know my mind, my heart. I don't want to seem a stranger to you, now that we will wed."

He spoke with such certainty, such finality, but how could he know the impossible barrier that lay between them? As he kicked their mount into a gallop toward a copse of trees, Maire said nothing, the pain she'd felt so terribly last night coming once more to gnaw at her heart.

It was not to be, she repeated unhappily to herself. *It was not to be!* Nothing would alter that, no understanding between them, no fervent wishing, no prayers, no tears. Yet would it be so selfish for her to forget, if only for a little while, that she came from a rebel clan who would sooner see Duncan dead than making his home in Eire?

"Let's rest here. Does this spot please you?"

She had been so lost in her thoughts, that he'd slowed his horse to a stop before Maire realized they had reached the trees. Somehow she mustered a small smile.

"Aye, it's fine, truly."

It was a beautiful place, hauntingly so; as Duncan lifted Maire to the mossy ground she saw that ruins lay scattered under the birch and oak. The remains of an ancient church? She crossed herself as Duncan turned to lift a cloth bag from his saddle, the meal he had purchased for them before they left Dublin's towering walls, which she could still see in the distance.

The fortified city was as imposing and bustling a place as Triona had described it to be. Maire had been glad to leave behind them the noise and so many Normans everywhere she looked. Duncan had said only that they were going for a ride, and now she wished they were still astride the stallion, who contentedly began to graze upon a tuft of lush grass, instead of stopped at this all too quiet, all too eerily intimate spot that seemed to echo with long-ago truths and secrets. Her mind running away with itself, she started when Duncan took her hand.

"Come."

His strong fingers laced with hers, she was compelled to move with him, Duncan taking care to lead her around foundation stones that shown ghostly pale and weathered in the dappled shade. Yet she paused, in spite of her unease to be taking their meal in what had once been a sacred place, when she spied wild roses as red as blood trailing up and over a tall cornerstone, the first such roses she'd seen since leaving Glenmalure. Her heart aching, she had never felt so utterly torn as Duncan drew close to her.

"You're fond of roses?"

"Aye, I've always loved—" Catching herself, Maire met his eyes to see they had darkened while her face suddenly felt as if it were afire. She said nothing further, she couldn't, as he studied her for what seemed an unbearably long moment, then he squeezed her hand, a hint of a smile crossing his handsome face.

"We will sit here, then."

She could only nod, grateful at how weak her knees had grown to sink onto the cloak he spread out for them in front of the rose-covered cornerstone. But he didn't join her until he had plucked several blooms, their perfume heady as he held them out to her.

"I've seen them as red only on the Hill of Tara, amid the ruins there. When you told me your name, I thought of those roses . . ."

His gaze falling to her lips, Maire wondered wildly if he meant to kiss her again. She hoped he might after how she'd just forgotten herself—saints help her, anything to distract him! Her fingers trembled as she took the roses, brushing his, and she sucked in her breath when still he stared at her as if trying to fathom her thoughts.

Jesu, Mary, and Joseph, might she have given herself away? She had never known relief so intense when he finally turned from her and drew his heavy sword from his belt, then placed it on the ground within arm's reach at one end of the cloak and sat down beside her.

Gazing at the weapon, Maire was reminded too painfully of the chasm that separated them, years of unbridled hatred and fear and a river of blood as red as the fragrant roses she lowered to her lap. As red as the wine Duncan offered to her after he had laid out the simple meal of bread and ewe's cheese and a dried berry tart. She took a sip from the leather flask, knowing her hands were still shaking, but there was no help for it.

And she could see he noticed, his fingers once more grazing hers when he took the flask and helped himself to a long draught. Yet his eyes never left her face, and desperately Maire tried to think of some way to shift the focus from her discomfort.

"That wound, Duncan . . . when you almost died. Is it the scar upon your chest?"

He didn't readily answer, looking at her even more intently, then he gave half a laugh.

"Forgive me. I was trying to think when you might have seen me unclothed . . . then I remembered that first night."

He gave another laugh, his expression almost as chagrined as a boy's, which touched Maire even as she thought of the other time she'd seen him naked. Lowering her eyes to hide her burning face, she heard him sigh, his voice grown sober.

"Yes, you've judged rightly. I lay abed for nearly a month while Gerard managed things for me, no easy task for so large a barony. And it wasn't made any easier for him when his brother was murdered."

The sudden harshness of his tone making Maire meet his eyes, she was struck that Duncan's face had become so hard.

"His brother?"

"Right in front of his eyes. He'd gone to West Meath where he'd left Robert and a dozen knights to guard a castle there—little more than a ruin then, since Walter de Lacy's men had laid torch to it when they'd fled before King John's army. Yet it wasn't so completely damaged that Irish rebels weren't drawn there as well, the bastards forever looking for plunder. They came upon Gerard and the others so suddenly . . ."

Duncan fell grimly silent as if the topic were

too bitter for him, and Maire didn't know if he would continue.

"O'Melaghlins?" she asked softly, wondering if that might be why Duncan had chosen to deal with his prisoners so harshly. He shook his head, his eyes grown ice-cold.

"O'Byrnes. Come north from Wicklow."

Chapter 19

Maire stared at Duncan in disbelief, his voice as fierce as his gaze.

"Gerard lives for the day Black O'Byrne crosses his path again—and I'll join him to watch that murderer hang. Robert no more made a move for his sword and he was struck down, the others made to lie upon the floor while he bled to death before them. It was my Irish tenants who put a name to the rebels, saying the O'Byrnes and their chieftain were feared throughout Leinster. By the blood of God, they'll know fear if any dares set foot again in Meath."

Duncan no longer looking at her but off into the distance, Maire sensed as surely as her blood had run cold that he meant every word. She had heard that tone before . . . from Ronan whenever he spoke of Normans. Jesu, Mary, and Joseph, could there be more hatred held by two men? Her situation suddenly grown all the more precarious, she swept hair from her face with trembling fingers as icy.

"God's teeth, enough talk of rebels."

Duncan had spoken more to himself than

Maire, though his gaze caught and held hers as he continued.

"That's only one scourge with which a baron must contend. Others face as much on their land, and what's left of Walter de Lacy's men bedevil Meath to this day."

"Were those the ones . . . ?" She faltered, still stricken about what she'd heard of Ronan. Yet she told herself desperately that she must act as if what Duncan had revealed held no consequence for her—aye, none!—and somehow found her voice. "Clement told me you hanged three men—"

"Rogue Normans. Traitors. It was easily done."

"But for an Irish girl?"

Duncan didn't readily answer, staring at her again, his eyes darkening to almost black. Maire shivered, glimpsing pain there too.

"I protect all that is mine—though I came too late to help the girl. Just as I would protect you with my life."

Maire didn't doubt he meant it, his voice grown so low and vehement that fresh shivers coursed through her, his gaze as intense. She felt marked, claimed, even as he reached out a hand to draw her toward him.

"No rebel Irish or treasonous Normans will drive me from my land. It is my home—our home, Rose, once you become my bride. Adele and any others who oppose our marriage be damned."

Duncan so close now that Maire knew he would kiss her, she couldn't breathe, her heart pounding as much at the fierce determination in his eyes as that she knew even at that moment Ronan was as determined to find her. That these two men might meet and come to blows . . . saints help her, each intent upon killing the other—

"No, please!"

Her hoarse cry echoing in the trees and sending a flock of birds fluttering into the air, Maire twisted away from Duncan and stared blindly at the roses scattered in her lap. She knew she had startled him almost as much as herself, sensing his tension while she'd never felt her face so warm. She didn't know what to say, yet she had to say something, anything to explain why . . .

"F-forgive me, Duncan, but it isn't right, aye, it isn't right—"

"What isn't right, woman?"

"That . . . that we should kiss here—in this place." Wildly, Maire looked around her. "It was a church once, aye, and look over there!" She pointed, chills striking her indeed, that a cluster of worn gravestones, half-buried by trailing vines and underbrush, could have missed her attention until now. "It isn't right, truly—"

"It couldn't be more right."

He'd taken her arm again, drawing her toward him as Maire met his eyes in astonishment to find him smiling at her—smiling!

"If a church, wouldn't weddings have taken place at this spot?" came his teasing query while he pulled her closer. "We will soon be husband and wife. What could be more sacred than to honor those who came before us . . ."

He didn't finish, his lips covering hers and so gently, Maire felt as if all thought fled even as all sensation centered upon his mouth warm and yet so achingly light against hers. Unconsciously she parted her lips and leaned toward him, a sigh escaping her, a soft plea giving voice to the yearning that suddenly flared inside her as his arms tightened fiercely around her.

For one blinding instant his mouth grew hard, passionate, and she was lost, utterly lost, her fingers clutching at his tunic while his hand found her breast, his thumb circling a taut nipple through the pale silk of her gown. But when she started and moaned, he drew away from her almost abruptly, his breathing ragged, no hint of teasing left in his eyes. Her breath was gone and she waited, her senses reeling, her heart racing, his mouth still so close to hers, so close . . .

"Woman, we'll be no strangers to each other in more than mind and heart if I kiss you so again . . . unless you wish it. You must tell me . . ."

She stared into his eyes, realizing as a blush crept over her face at the raw huskiness of his voice, conscious thought swiftly returning, that he was asking if she wanted him to . . . if they might—

"No, Rose, say nothing. Forgive me. This is not the time or place—God's teeth, you deserve better than the ground . . ."

Frowning as if angry with himself, he released her, while Maire felt utterly shaken from the last moments, her heart still thundering.

Jesu, Mary, and Joseph, what might she have said? Flushing because she knew all too well the answer, she tried to avoid Duncan's eyes, which only made him curse under his breath while he tore off a hunk of crusty bread.

"We should eat. It's well past midday."

The sound of the wind rustling through the trees and birds chirping overhead seemed deafening to Maire in the face of Duncan's silence, his expression grim as he handed her the bread topped with a generous wedge of ewe's cheese. His darkened mood pained her, and she found herself wishing to see him smile once more, a memory to store for that day when . . .

Fresh heartache stabbing her, Maire made herself eat, but she had no more appetite than Duncan appeared to. When he handed her the leather flask after taking a draught of wine himself, she knew the weighty silence couldn't continue between them. Mayhap even now he was thinking again of what she'd said of the roses, mayhap wondering, too, why she didn't seem more pleased at the way events had turned, and that alone spurred her to speak.

"Duncan?"

He met her eyes, and she felt such a rush of emotion for this man she'd not known lived and breathed only days ago that she found it difficult to continue.

"I . . . I want to thank you. It was a kind thing—you agreeing to marry me—"

"Kindness had little to do with it, nor pity. I told you that last night."

Aye, so he had, Maire blushing deeply as she remembered his stirring words, his impassioned kiss, his hands upon her. Duncan's gaze grown intense, she sensed he shared her thoughts, too.

"I want you for my wife, Rose. I've said those words only once before, and thought never to say them again to any woman. But when I believed I'd lost you at the bog . . ."

His voice died away, and Maire followed his eyes to the weathered gravestones, wondering with a pang if he was thinking of her at that moment or another woman from long ago. Yet was that so terrible a thing? He must have suffered so wretchedly, just as Lady Enid had said. Maire's throat grew so tight that she could only whisper.

"She was very beautiful, wasn't she? Gisele?"

Maire saw the flicker of pain cross Duncan's face even as he once more met her gaze.

"Yes. Like the sun."

She could tell just in how he'd answered, his voice heavy with memory, that he must have loved Gisele very much. Yet might he feel for her even a little of what he'd known before to want her to be his bride? A fervent wish filled her that she could so move his heart. Maire dropped her gaze to the fragrant roses forgotten in her lap as tears suddenly stung her eyes.

Fool. Aye, so she had called herself last night and so she was again today! Would such a love even be enough to overcome the impossible barrier that birth and circumstance had thrust upon them? It was not to be! How many times must she—

"Rose."

Maire started, as much at the warm timbre of Duncan's voice as that his fingers gently lifted her chin to face him. His eyes searched hers.

"Who told you of Gisele?"

Maire didn't readily answer, fearful that the emotion in her voice might betray her even as a tear slid down her cheek. She drew in her breath when he wiped it away with his thumb, somehow saying brokenly, "L-Lady Enid. And Flanna and Adele made mention of a . . . a ghost, though I didn't know until last night of whom they spoke."

"A ghost." Duncan sighed heavily though his eyes never left hers. "So Gisele's been for six years now, haunting me, and it wouldn't be fair that you not know what came before. I found her cloak floating in a pond . . ."

His voice grew hoarse and Maire's heart went out to him, that he should still feel such anguish. But she wasn't prepared for the vehemence with which he spoke again.

"Her family opposed me from the start—I was penniless, thanks to my three half brothers. After our father's death they disavowed my mother, saying she had never truly wed my father and no record could be found to prove it, the priest who performed the ceremony long dead. They shut her away in a tower and claimed her mad, while I became no more than the bastard my father had spawned—half-Scots as well, which made me no better than the dirt beneath their feet. A barbarian child to be spit upon and cuffed at every turn, only my name marking me as a FitzWilliam."

Duncan's tone become so bitter, Maire was struck even more that his hands had clenched into fists as if he struggled to contain his anger.

"They took everything from me, my inheritance, my birthright, but I left Northumberland at sixteen and made my way on my own. And Gisele waited for me—we'd known each other since we were children. After years in King John's army, I made my suit to her family, but a soldier's pay and the promise of knighthood wasn't enough. I was believed a bastard . . . and for that I've my own blood family to blame. Their treachery cost me Gisele's life—we were to wed secretly, there was no other way, our every meeting concealed from her family. Even the last one that morning when she drowned—God's teeth, and Adele comes to Ireland now that I'm two years a baron and demands she choose for me a bride!"

Maire could only stare while Duncan's fury echoed around them, her heart pounding at all he had revealed. Yet the roar of blood in her ears grew louder that his gaze hadn't once strayed from hers, his voice as vehement.

"*I* have chosen my bride—as Irish as the land that's become my home. It's only fitting that our children will bear the blood of their place of birth in their veins. They'll fight all the harder to protect it, just as I do now."

Duncan fell silent, still staring into her eyes, though he reached up a hand to touch her face. Maire slowly drew in her breath as once more he traced a thumb over her cheek, something burning in his eyes which made her heart seem to stop as he spoke almost to himself more than her.

"Only God can say . . . but perhaps it was meant to be this way all along . . ."

His thumb moving to gently caress her lips,

Maire couldn't move, couldn't even breathe, Lady Enid's words suddenly burning as intensely in her mind.

I saw how Lord FitzWilliam looked at you tonight, child, that promise has already taken root.

Jesu, Mary, and Joseph, could it really be that Duncan might love—

"My lord!"

Maire gasped even as Duncan grabbed his sword and lunged to his feet and she struggled with his help to rise, too, while Reginald Montfort came galloping astride a lathered steed toward them. The grim-faced knight had barely reined in his mount before Duncan exploded.

"Dammit, man, what the devil—"

"Baron, forgive me, but you said where you could be found if there was need. Word has come from Meath! The O'Melaghlin refuses to answer your summons. And he has sworn that if his grandsons and the harper aren't freed to return home, he'll slay five of your tenants for every day that you hold his clansmen imprisoned beyond week's end."

Duncan's oath was blistering to hear, and it seemed in no more than an instant Maire had been lifted onto his stallion and Duncan vaulted into the saddle behind her. Gone was his fervent expression of moments before, his thunderous scowl truly ominous to behold.

She could only imagine what he intended to do about the O'Melaghlin's threat and his prisoners, and she thought again of the hatred he bore for Ronan, icy chills overwhelming her. As Duncan kicked his steed into a hard gallop, she braced herself against him while his arms tightened protectively around her, the rose she'd swept up from the ground without thinking crushed in her hand.

Chapter 20

Maire still held the wilted petals hours later, the bright glare of guttering torches held aloft hurting her eyes as much as mere shifting in the saddle made her ache with weariness.

Only the formidable walls and towers of Longford Castle looming ahead gave her some comfort that the long ride was nearly done. They had stopped only twice since leaving Dublin, Duncan pushing his men as hard as himself that they might reach the castle not long after dark.

Lady Enid had protested that Maire be made to keep such a fierce pace, but Duncan wouldn't hear of allowing others to escort her to Meath the next day, which had warmed Maire as well as filled her with despair. At least then she would have had no fear of Duncan and Ronan coming face-to-face if her brother had managed to discover her whereabouts and been waiting somewhere outside the city to rescue her. She was exhausted—much in part because the entire journey she'd dreaded a surprise attack; Ronan would not do otherwise.

But no attack had come and the well-lit battlements of Longford Castle soared now above them, the fortress ablaze with torches. She could hear men shouting from inside the walls and a great creaking of chains as the drawbridge was lowered, while Duncan drew her closer against him. He'd not allowed her to ride by herself either, concerned she would not be able to keep up.

"We're home, Rose. Forgive me for the haste but there was nothing to be done."

Home? Fresh pain cut Maire, the memory of the emotion she'd seen burning in Duncan's eyes haunting her still. Yet even if it was what she so wished for, what she'd long dreamed of, Longford Castle could never be her home. She only nodded, her gaze lifted to the towering gatehouse as they rode across the drawbridge, the pounding of hooves deafening.

When might she leave again? Would she be with Duncan? He had said that he wanted to keep her safe at his side, though she knew he was the one who would not be safe from Ronan as long as she remained with him.

Yet what was she to do? She'd spent the journey, too, wondering futilely how she might leave the castle without notice and wishing Flanna had given her some word as to how she had planned to help her. But Duncan's former mistress probably hated her now. Maire could hope for no aid there—

"God's blood, Duncan, I thought you'd never arrive!"

Maire had started at the shout that filled the courtyard, Gerard de Barry running to meet them as commotion seemed to erupt from every corner, more men rushing from the castle, stable hands scrambling forth to help with exhausted mounts. She was astonished, too, when women and children began to stream into the courtyard. The clamor of babes crying and horses snorting and people suddenly all trying to speak at once made her head spin as Duncan reined in his steed.

"They've come from the village and surrounding manors," Gerard shouted above the growing din while Maire heard Duncan swear fiercely. "The news is spreading about the O'Melaghlin—dammit, Duncan, we should hang the prisoners this very night and show that bastard we don't bow to threats!"

Maire was surprised that Duncan said nothing more, instead grimly dismounting and pulling her into his arms. He didn't set her down but carried her across the teeming courtyard and into the castle while a surge of humanity coursed behind them. Gerard de Barry came hard on Duncan's heels.

Inside the bedlam was as intense; pockets of alarmed Irish tenants, men, women, wide-eyed children, and somber-faced knights shepherding their own families joined the throng and followed Duncan into the great hall. Maire stiffened when she saw Adele standing by the massive hearth and looking as regal as a queen, Rufus the Fool and Henry FitzHugh flanking her while her other knights milled nearby. The woman's eyes grew ice-cold upon spying Maire. Yet Maire was thankfully distracted when a short, balding fellow came running and wringing his hands toward Duncan.

"My lord, my lord, what are we to do? Where will they all sleep? We've provisions enough, the storerooms are full, but if more come and I know they will—"

"God's teeth, Faustis, enough!"

Duncan's roar served not only to silence his frantic steward, but the entire great hall. No sounds were left but for restless babes and the urgent shushing of their mothers. With all eyes turned toward him, including Rose's, her lovely face pale—as much, he sensed, from exhaustion as the frantic commotion he had hoped not to encounter—he kept his voice stern.

"All may remain here tonight, but in the morning you will return to your homes."

"But, lord, we cannot!" cried a ruddy-haired Irishman who Duncan recognized as one of his more prosperous tenants. "Aye, we would be mad to—unless you release your prisoners. The O'Melaghlin has vowed to kill—"

"And I say the O'Melaghlin would be mad to make good his threat and he knows it well for the battle that would come. By the blood of God, I will have peace! Word will be carried this very night to West Meath—an offer of three days more within which the O'Melaghlin may meet me here to speak terms or my hand will be forced."

"Another three days, Duncan?"

Gerard's voice incredulous, Duncan had known such a protest would come as he met his knight's eyes.

"It must be. Much has changed since we spoke—"

"But you swore to me . . . you gave your word that we'd wait no longer than three days to hang those bastards—"

"So you did, brother, I was there to hear it!" Adele rushed to Gerard's side in a flurry of emerald samite. "The prisoners were to hang tomorrow."

His gut clenching as much at the cloying smell of her perfume as the glance exchanged between the two, Duncan did not miss either, how intimately Adele placed her hand upon Gerard's arm. It was all Duncan could do to keep his voice calm.

"I gave my word, Gerard, that is true, but much has changed as I've said." Duncan's concern was great as he paused to set Rose upon her feet, her unsteadiness making him keep an arm firmly around her waist. Then he met Adele's eyes, his words at that moment meant especially for her. "Rose will be my bride—it has been agreed between me and the Justiciar John de Gray. I trust *all* will treat her with the honor and respect her place as my future wife commands."

To Adele's credit, she made no rash reply though her face had grown pink, while Rufus the Fool ducked behind Henry FitzHugh when Duncan shot him a dark glance. Yet Gerard's low curse drew his attention, his knight's stance gone stiff with fury.

"What of Robert, Duncan? Will I have no justice? God's breath, you swore! Does that mean nothing?"

Gerard's anger echoing around them, Duncan didn't readily answer. Only their long years of friendship made him bear what he would have considered a personal attack from any other man. Swallowing his own anger, he kept his voice low.

"You've long encouraged me to take a wife, and now I've chosen one—all the more reason that I wish for peace. What are three days more if they prevent needless bloodshed? Look around you, Gerard! Will you tell these people that your own thirst for vengeance is worth more than their lives, their children's lives? If we hang the prisoners on the morrow, you know it would bring war—"

"Or it would bring the O'Melaghlin to his knees, but do what you will, Duncan. You're the baron of Longford, not I."

Gerard turned and shoved his way through the crowd before Duncan could utter another word, his worst fears confirmed when Adele spun around and rushed after his knight. Imagining well what must have transpired during his absence, he swore vehemently under his breath and glanced at Rose.

She wasn't looking at him but at some distant point in the great hall, her face grown more ashen as he followed her gaze to where Flanna stood with the strapping Irish tenant she'd agreed not too unhappily to wed. Duncan stiffened. God's teeth, what next? His castle overrun, Gerard bewitched by Adele, and now a former mistress to plague him?

"Flanna will be gone in the morning, Rose, I vow it," he said to reassure her, drawing her more closely against him. "You've nothing to—"

"Please, Duncan, I'm so tired. If I could retire . . ." Heartache filled Maire at the concern suddenly lining his face, her knees already weak at the unexpected circumstance that had presented itself to her. Still incredulous that Flanna was among the panicked tenants who'd rushed for safety to Longford Castle, she somehow made herself continue. "I'll be fine, truly, and I know the way—"

"That may be, woman, but all those steps?"

He moved to lift her but Maire shook her head and laid a hand upon his chest to stop him, her face firing that so many people were watching them. Yet one particular man standing nearby had spurred her resistance, and she hastened to explain herself while Duncan stared as if surprised at her fingers splayed over his heart.

"You've so much to do, aye, a messenger to send, your people to attend to—far too much to see to me now. But . . . but Clement could help me."

As Duncan glanced beyond her at the friar, Maire held her breath as much over what he might say as the desperate plan taking shape in her mind. Her gaze once more flew to Flanna, the young woman lifting her chin and staring right back at her. Jesu, Mary, and Joseph, would Duncan's former mistress even want to speak—

"Clement, I've need of you."

Maire hoped she didn't appear too relieved at Duncan's command, though she was trembling as the stout friar hastened forward and gently took her arm.

"Ah, child, you look so weary. Of course you long to retire."

She couldn't reply, a great lump forming in her throat when Duncan released her and stepped back to let them pass, his eyes still full of concern.

"Take good care with her, Clement."

As the friar nodded, Maire leaned on him heavily, turning away from Duncan so he wouldn't see the tears suddenly stinging her eyes. The sea of faces around her no more than a blur as they left the great hall, she was grateful for the rising din of anxious voices that carried after them to mask anything she might say.

"Ah, dear, such troubles, such troubles."

Maire could only unhappily agree as Clement sighed and shook his head, that she intended to ask him to bring Flanna to Duncan's rooms to see her provoking as much unflagging resolve as pain. So, too, did the rose petals she still held, but she clutched them all the tighter and climbed the tower steps.

"Lord, I swear it was her!"

Ronan stared into his young clansman Shea O'Byrne's flushed face, tempted almost to shake him to ensure that he remembered well what he'd seen. As it was, Ronan already held him hard against a tree trunk while the rest of his men were gathered close around, Flann O'Faelin looming at his side in the bright moonlight.

"Tell me everything again from the start, by God, man, everything!"

"It was as I said, lord!" Shea blurted out, his breathing still ragged from a breakneck ride to camp. "I'd been to the village to seek any word of the spawn who killed Fiach and was heading back here when they rode out of the east—I ducked into the trees to wait for them to pass. A host of Normans, thirty or better, and more than half as many torches among them so it was easy enough to see. Your sister Maire was at the front, lord, held by a man I can only guess was the baron of Longford—Duncan FitzWilliam's his name."

"Duncan FitzWilliam." Ronan's expression must have grown so fierce that Shea looked shaken now as he nodded his head.

"Aye, lord, but I learned little else of him. The village was in an uproar, and many had already fled to Longford Castle. I heard the baron holds three prisoners from clan O'Melaghlin in West Meath as well as your sister—"

"By God, he will die."

His vehement words echoing around them, Ronan released Shea and met Flann O'Faelin's eyes, the huge Irishman as grim-faced as the rest of his men. His relief that Maire was alive as intense as his fury at what she must have suffered while in Norman hands, Ronan didn't attempt to speak further—he couldn't. Instead he strode into the clearing, agonized that he stood no more than a league from her—a damned league!—and still could do nothing.

He didn't have to see the castle to know that its walls were impregnable, a stinking moat no doubt surrounding battlements lined with sentries ever alert for intruders, a drawbridge as well guarded the only entrance. And subterfuge was too risky, detection of any possible ruse too likely. He could barely stomach now that Maire had finally been found that he must wait even an hour more to help her, but he had little choice.

All he and his clansmen could do now was watch for when she might emerge again with this Duncan FitzWilliam, baron of Longford, and then wait for the right moment, and Ronan would be ready. Just as he had already determined, the attack would be swift and sure and as fatally unexpected as that which had struck Fiach O'Byrne and the others in Wicklow—

"Do we ride, Lord?"

Ronan wheeled around, Flann O'Faelin a hulking shape in the moonlight. Ever conscious of his men's welfare no matter he burned for swift action, he knew that only patience and stealth would win the day.

"Aye. As close to Longford Castle as we can and still have cover. Shea said there were woods enough that would serve."

"Woods mayhap filled with Normans."

Ronan gave a grim laugh; Flann knew as well as he that such a likelihood wasn't anything they hadn't ably encountered before. But there was only one Norman he wanted now, Duncan FitzWilliam, baron of Longford. The thought of Maire held captive by the murdering bastard was enough to send Ronan striding with a string of furious oaths to his horse.

Chapter 21

"The moat?" Maire stared incredulously at Flanna as the pretty young Irishwoman nodded, still not straying farther into the bedchamber though Maire had invited her to come and sit by the fire. "Truly?"

"Aye, no other way around it. I did as much myself once, when I was fifteen and one of Walter de Lacy's vassals ruled this place. Better to jump into the moat than be raped by a mob of drunken knights . . ."

As Flanna fell silent, Maire felt a sick lump in her throat, not only for what Duncan's former mistress must have suffered at the hands of those who'd come before, but that her plan to escape Longford Castle was quickly fading.

She swam poorly, no matter Triona had tried to teach her as a way to strengthen her legs, and would more probably sink like a stone than make it to the other side even if she could evade the guards on the outer battlements. Jesu, Mary, and Joseph, and now to have Flanna studying her suspiciously . . .

"It was kind of you to agree to come and

speak to me," Maire offered for the second time, imagining what Flanna must be thinking. "And to wish me well with Duncan—truly, so much has changed since last we spoke. I was only curious as to how you'd intended to help me a few days past . . . it seemed such an impossible thing. I was so fearful then that Adele wanted me for a maid—"

"And now you will become a wife."

Flanna's words held no rancor, and Maire was relieved that her gaze held little suspicion now either, though Flanna sounded somewhat amazed as she went on.

"Aye, I wouldn't have believed it if I hadn't seen with my own eyes how Lord FitzWilliam looks at you . . . and how he never looked at me."

Maire flushed uncomfortably, the lump in her throat only growing. "I-I'm sorry, Flanna—"

"Sorry? Why should you be? I never loved him—I couldn't. Too many Normans had come before . . . but I see that's far different with you. It's plain you care as well for Duncan, though how you could look at him so and still seem so sad . . ."

Maire felt her face afire—Flanna had judged her so well—and she quickly sought an excuse to divert her. "I grieve yet . . . my clansmen."

"Aye, it's no matter, and with such a harpy as Lady Adele beneath your roof I'd be unhappy too. You've only to ask, you know, and I'd swear Lord FitzWilliam would toss that blond witch into the moat just to please you. Wouldn't that be a fine sight?"

For the first time in what seemed like ages,

Maire actually smiled, and she thought wistfully that in Flanna she might have found a friend. Aye, if things were different, and she wasn't so desperate to leave this place, so desperate to do anything to protect Duncan. Heartache nearly overwhelming her, she lowered her eyes for the damnable tears that never seemed far away.

"Well, I'd best go downstairs," came Flanna's soft voice, not at all bearing the wary stiffness with which she'd first spoken to Maire. "Lord FitzWilliam wouldn't be pleased to know you're not resting, and Clement made me swear I wouldn't stay very long—as did Hagan."

"Hagan?" Maire met Flanna's lovely green eyes to find her blushing, a tenderness touching the young Irishwoman's face.

"The man I agreed to wed. Lord FitzWilliam said I had a choice—I told you that first day I'd not known a Norman more fair-minded—and he assured me Hagan was a good man, a widower for two years now and eager for a bride. I had no words then to thank him, but it seems I've much to thank him for now. Nor would I have thought I'd be glad you came to Longford Castle, but I am, my lady—"

"No, no, please, call me Mai—" Maire stopped herself just in time, stricken, then quickly amended, "Rose will do, truly."

"Aye, very well, Rose."

Grateful that Flanna hadn't seemed to think anything amiss, Maire could only imagine she was eager to return to Hagan as Flanna threw a warm smile and then disappeared out the door. That left Maire alone, and she gazed almost numbly around the vast bedchamber, unwilling to believe that there was no route left to her to spare Duncan from coming face-to-face with her brother.

What would Triona do? Her brazen sister-in-law would think nothing of evading countless guards and jumping feetfirst into a moat, or even cleverly disguising herself as a villager or servant and secreting herself among those leaving the castle in the morning, but Maire had no way to conceal a cumbersome gait that would give her away at a glance. She would obviously have to wait and hope for some chance that Duncan might take her with him again on a journey, and that she might somehow elude him—saints help her, but what of Ronan?

Her plight becoming all the more impossible in her mind, Maire rubbed temples that had begun to pound. She imagined Duncan might soon be joining her, and her gaze flew to the crushed rose petals she had laid on a table by the hearth.

It tore at her to do so, but she went and scooped them up and threw them into the fire, not wanting Duncan to see them. He might only be reminded of what she'd said at the church ruins, a blunder she still couldn't believe she'd committed. And now what she'd nearly said to Flanna . . .

"Begorra, Maire O'Byrne, you'll find yourself in a dungeon yet if you don't take care," she whispered to herself, watching as the blood red petals curled and blackened and crumbled into ash. Yet would Duncan truly do that to her? Given what she'd seen burning so fervently in his eyes, might he be able to see beyond his hatred for her clan? For Ronan Black O'Byrne?

Maire turned from the hearth with a sigh, not even wanting to hope. She even pushed away thoughts of Duncan's unexpected leniency with his prisoners, and the offer of three days more within which to talk peace with the O'Melaghlin—a change of heart that had truly astonished her.

He was a man like none she'd ever known, Norman and yet born of a Scotswoman who must have done much to foster within him a sense of fairness and honor that had missed the rest of his family altogether. Maire still could not believe what he'd suffered at the hands of his half brothers, the treachery, the cruelty . . . and his mother shut away in a tower after her husband had died. Maire no more believed the poor woman had been mad than that she hadn't been truly wed to Duncan's father—the embroidered screen attested to that.

Maire suddenly questioned how Duncan could have come by the thing. Wouldn't his half brothers have wanted to destroy such an exquisite testimony of love and gentleness? Determined to ask him, she felt almost a relief to have something else to think about if only for a little while.

She was struck by a desire to see the screen again, and wondered if Duncan would mind that she visited the adjoining room she'd sensed at once was a private refuge. She knew that she couldn't rest, her exhaustion all but fled in her anxiousness to talk to Flanna.

Maire took up a guttering lamp and was already halfway down the passageway before her decision was fully made, a warmth enveloping her as she drew closer to the opposite door. Reminded of the first time she'd gone to this room—could it be only two days past?—and how nervous she'd felt, she wasn't surprised at her reaction.

Before she'd fully opened the door, she could sense Duncan's formidable presence just as surely as if he'd been there, and she felt too, her heart begin to thunder. Begorra, the man didn't even have to be near and she was lost!

She ventured a step inside, drawing in her breath at the screen propped and shrouded against the wall. Clearly he couldn't bear to look at the beautiful needlework for the brutal injury done his mother—

"God's blood, what do we have here?"

Maire gasped as the door was slammed shut behind her, and she spun around so awkwardly that she nearly toppled into the oaken table, the lamp crashing to the floor. In the next instant it was righted by a rough-looking man, wearing a dull shirt of mail beneath his cloak, who straightened and swept her with a glance that froze her blood.

"Lord FitzWilliam's latest mistress, perhaps? I've heard no news that he's taken a wife."

Maire couldn't speak, her gaze falling to the hunting knife the Norman held, the blade flashing in the lamplight. He followed her eyes, a low chuckling that held no humor breaking the ominous silence as he lifted the weapon to her breast.

"Lay yourself back on the table, wench, and make not a sound, do you hear? I've been a bit bored waiting for the good baron to retire for the night, and it's a fortunate thing you've come along to amuse me."

"Y-you're waiting to see Duncan?" Maire heard herself say almost stupidly through the terror gripping her. A slow smile spread across the man's shadowed face.

"See him? Kill him, you mean. Ah, but don't let that distress you—we've other things to think of, you and I."

The knife tip slipping beneath the curve of her breast, Maire heard a faint snagging of pink silk and she sucked in her breath, which only seemed to amuse him. He laughed softly, his own breathing coming faster, but he sobered when she took a step backward, her movement clearly angering him.

"Lie down, damn you, now!"

She started, trembling from head to foot as she glanced behind her at the table still spread with maps. "I . . . I can't. It's covered—"

A roar of impatience burst from the man and he lunged to sweep rolls of parchment and books to the floor, the knife gone from her breast. With a cry, Maire shoved against him with all her strength and knocked him off-balance. The man crashed into the table while she groped wildly to throw open the door. She'd never known such a surge of fear when she heard him curse behind her, Maire no more having stumbled into the dark passageway when she felt a hand clamp onto her shoulder.

"No! Saints help me, no!"

She heard a pained outcry, dazedly realizing she'd dug her fingernails into his flesh even as she lurched away from him, suddenly free from his hold. Tears bit her eyes. Desperately she willed her legs to move, knowing he was just behind her, his breathing harsh, his curses filling the air.

"Rose—God's teeth, woman, what . . . ?"

She saw Duncan appear at the opposite doorway the same moment the man caught her, his arm going around her neck to half strangle her, Maire's knees finally giving out. She went down, but her attacker jerked her to her feet in front of him, the cold knife blade pressed against her throat.

"Stand back, FitzWilliam, damn you, stand back!"

Through eyes glazed with tears Maire heard Duncan swear and saw him pull the sword from his belt, but she knew as surely that he could not help her. Her captor's breath warm and sour at her neck, she was virtually carried into the bedchamber, her legs refusing to support her. She'd never seen Duncan so pale, no, not even at the bog.

"I said back away, man, or I'll cut her throat, don't try me!"

"He said—he said he was waiting to kill you, Duncan!" she blurted out hoarsely to warn him, the man's arm growing all the tighter around her neck.

"Yes, so I was, but that will have to wait for another time, won't it, FitzWilliam?"

The Norman moving her with him to the

door, Maire felt as if she were choking, while Duncan risked a step toward them.

"Let her go, man, and I swear you'll have safe passage from the castle—"

"Do you think me a fool, FitzWilliam? If you hang your own kind as easily as you did my comrades the other day, what makes you think I would ever trust your word? Stand away!"

With that, Maire was hauled through the bedchamber door, grown so dizzy from the vise grip around her throat she scarcely realized they were halfway down the tower steps until she heard Duncan's roar.

"Give her over, man, and I'll fight you now if it's revenge you seek. The woman played no part—"

"She does now—out of my way, all of you!"

Her captor's vehement demand sending people who'd gathered wide-eyed at the bottom of the steps scattering to give them room, several knights drawing their weapons, Maire fought for breath as once more Duncan's voice thundered behind them.

"Do as he says, stand away, damn you!"

Maire had no strength left to struggle even if she'd dared to; she felt herself more fully dragged along by her captor than before as they moved through a doorway and out into the courtyard still ablaze with torches. The noise and commotion only grew, shouts filling the night. A demand at her ear for a horse to be brought sounded as if it had come from a far distance, she felt so starved for air.

She couldn't see Duncan, all hope failing her a

moment later when she was half-thrown onto a nervous mount, her captor vaulting into the saddle behind her and once more pulling her up in front of him like a shield.

"We will face each other again, FitzWilliam, that I swear!" came the man's fierce shout as the horse was spurred forward. Maire feared that the drawbridge would not be lowered in time before they crashed into it. The knife still pressed to her throat, she knew if she left the castle with her captor she was lost.

They passed through the outer gatehouse, Duncan's voice commanding his startled guards to fall back, while Maire waited until she heard the horse's hooves striking wood, the drawbridge beneath them. Only then did she grab desperately at the reins. Their mount was already so spooked by the furor that it took little to make him rear and spin.

She gasped, the Norman cursing violently as he tried to regain control, the animal coming so close to the edge of the drawbridge as to plunge them all into the moat.

"Damn you, woman, damn you!"

Maire saw the flash of the knife, his arm unlifted and she closed her eyes, her cry of terror cut short when she felt the Norman suddenly jerk against her. A low gurgling came at her neck, while Duncan lunged toward the horse and caught the bridle even as her captor tipped to one side and fell facedown onto the drawbridge.

"By the blood of God . . ."

She stared just as was Duncan at the owl-fletched arrow sticking from the Norman's back.

In the next instant she lifted her gaze to the nearest trees a hundred yards away. She knew of only one man who could shoot an arrow from such a distance and so fiercely find its mark. A man who even now might be aiming right for Duncan . . .

"No. Ronan, no."

Her voice no more than a ragged whisper, she nearly fell from the saddle in her haste to dismount, Duncan sheathing his sword and catching her before her feet had touched the ground. Even as her arms flew around his neck, he ran with her into the gatehouse, his command splitting the night.

"Raise the drawbridge, now!"

Chapter 22

If Maire had thought the commotion intense moments before, now it seemed that the castle had come alive with the sounds of preparation for battle. She buried her face against Duncan's shoulder as he shouted more orders to his men, her heart thundering that Ronan and her clansmen—and Niall too, was he out there?—were the cause of the uproar.

How had they found her? Jesu, Mary, and Joseph, if Ronan's aim hadn't been so true and so timely, would she now even live or breathe?

"Montfort, take her inside!"

Maire felt Duncan's arms tighten fiercely around her for only the briefest moment, and then she was given over to the older knight, whose face was grim in the torchlight.

"O'Melaghlins?"

Duncan didn't answer, his gaze so intent upon Maire's face that she wondered then if he might have guessed the truth. Somehow she made herself speak in hopes to divert him, her voice still barely above a whisper.

"My clansmen, Duncan. Do you think they heard from someone in Dublin—"

"I care not. No one will take you from me. *No one.*"

Duncan waved Reginald Montfort away before Maire could utter another word, yet she doubted she could have spoken for how tight her throat had grown. It seemed all else had faded around her as she was carried across the courtyard, her eyes straining solely for Duncan though he had disappeared into a tower leading to the battlements.

Long hours later, Maire dozed fitfully, the fire in the hearth burned to no more than glowing embers as, once more, she opened her eyes with a start and looked around the bedchamber.

She knew Duncan hadn't returned. She would have sensed him, even if asleep in the next room. So where might he be? Saints help her, had any more well-aimed arrows come flying out of the night from Ronan's bow?

Fresh anxiety seizing her, she nonetheless tried to quiet her fears by telling herself that if anything was amiss, someone would surely have come to tell her. That thought had sustained her, too, through the first harrowing hour when she'd been unable to tear herself from the window, the commotion in the courtyard gradually settling into a watchful state of tension.

She'd stood there until her legs had fallen numb, still straining for any sight of Duncan, and she imagined she had glimpsed him a few times along the battlements though she couldn't be sure. It had seemed her eyes were forever clouded by tears, and finally she'd retreated from the window and prepared herself for bed, grateful for any task to occupy her.

It had amazed her that no matter the uproar in the castle, the servants had still come with a basin of hot water for her to bathe and a tray of food that had gone untouched. The young freckled serving maid whose name Maire learned was Ona had been one of them. Maire was deeply touched that the girl said she'd been so frightened for her. Ona had seen the Norman drag her down the tower steps.

Maire closed her eyes and rolled onto her side, a sick feeling welling inside her as she remembered the knifepoint pressed to her breast.

She wouldn't have been able to step foot in these rooms if Reginald Montfort and several guards he'd called to accompany him hadn't searched them thoroughly; the knight had grimly said as much would be done throughout the entire castle for any other intruders who might have secreted themselves among the tenants who'd fled there that day. One of Walter de Lacy's men, Reginald had cursed him. And to think the Norman had been lying in wait for Duncan . . .

A shudder shook Maire, and she tried to force the terrible memories away. It brought her some comfort that a guard had been stationed at the top of the tower steps, but she so wished Duncan was here. She so wished to know that he was safe—

"Enough, man, take yourself away and get some rest."

Duncan's voice carrying to her from outside his apartment, Maire felt her heart jump just to hear its husky timbre. Yet she lay still, too, and pretended sleep, suddenly nervous that they would once more be sharing such close quarters . . . especially now that so much had changed between them.

Or had anything really changed? The warmth spreading out from her stomach as she heard him quietly enter the bedchamber was much as she had experienced whenever they were together from almost the first moment she'd seen him.

She was glad her hands were tucked beneath the pillow, for how he might see them trembling; she wasn't surprised he had come close to stand beside the bed even as she was sure he might hear the furious beating of her heart. Somehow she made herself breathe evenly no matter she felt as if she couldn't draw breath at all. Yet when he reached out to touch her cheek, his fingers barely grazing her, she was certain she'd given herself away for the tiny sigh that escaped her.

He sighed too, but heavily, and she discerned his sudden tension even though he hadn't moved. She sensed so clearly he was thinking about the Norman, and she remembered with a pang how ashen his face had been, his deep brown eyes as stricken at that moment as filled with helpless fury. If Ronan's arrow hadn't struck her enraged captor, would Duncan's sword have been wielded in time to save her?

As if sharing her thoughts, Duncan swore fiercely under his breath and strode from the bed. Maire dared to open her eyes to see him disappear down the passageway to the other room. To his cot? Longing and keen disappointment filled her, and she found herself wishing she hadn't feigned sleep if only to ask him if all was well.

She doubted he would have returned to the tower to rest if he still expected an imminent attack, and she wondered what the morning would bring. Would he and his knights ride out at daybreak to search the distant woods? She knew Ronan and her clansmen would not be found, their stealth in hiding giving her some comfort that he and Duncan would not come face-to-face. And she must see somehow that they never did, aye, truly!

Maire sighed heavily, too, such anguish overwhelming her at the thoughts roiling in her mind that moments later she scarcely heard footsteps once more enter the room. Not until she heard a low splashing of water did she glance in surprise over her shoulder, and she froze to see that Duncan had stripped to the waist and stood before the basin set upon a table near the dying fire.

She lost breath altogether. His back was so broad and powerful that she could not look away or even think to as he bathed quietly and quickly, no doubt because the water was cold. It seemed so intimate a thing to watch him, and she flushed to her toes when he ran his hands under his muscled arms and down his chest. Her fingers twisted in her linen sleeping gown an instant later when he bent to splash his face and then straightened to thrust his fingers through his dark hair.

She saw him look down at himself, and she followed his gaze to his calf-length breeches, thoroughly dampened now and stuck to his lower body like a second skin. She did not have to wonder long at his thoughts. Her heart truly began to pound when he suddenly peeled off the soaked garment to stand naked at the basin and still she could not, would not, tear her eyes from him.

She'd never known her face to be so warm when he cupped his hands to draw water that streamed down the front of his body to pool at his feet, cupped more water to stream down his back and muscled flanks. The fire was not so low that she couldn't see his skin wet and glistening, and she sucked in her breath when he grabbed up the towel she'd used to dry herself.

It made him turn suddenly to look at her, and Maire was caught, staring.

She didn't move, didn't blink as he dropped the towel to the floor and came toward her, Maire feeling his eyes upon her as blatantly as hers were yet upon him. Even now she could not look away, though she began to tremble at the aroused state of his powerful body; she knew then that this night would be different from any others.

And she knew desperately she wanted it to be so even before he reached her. Maire gave herself to him with her eyes even as he climbed into bed beside her and pulled her fiercely into his arms. In an instant her sleeping gown was as soaked as his skin, the pounding of his heart against her breast the most stirring sensation she had ever known.

"Woman . . ."

His voice hoarse and almost breaking, Maire didn't need to hear more, all the terrible emotion they'd known that night captured in one word. He kept silent for a long breathless moment, merely holding her, his arms hard and strong and warm, and Maire knew she would have been content just with that. But she knew, too, shivering suddenly at the vehement whisper at her ear, that Duncan had no intention to stop there.

"No one will take you from me, woman, do you hear?"

She nodded, while Duncan pulled her all the closer.

"After this night, you will be my wife in all ways save the blessing of the Church . . . and that will come soon enough, I swear it. I swear it!"

He said no more. Maire buried her face against his chest even as she felt his hand tug her sleeping gown above her thigh, her hip, only to cup her bottom and pull her against him. She so wanted to believe they could have a chance for happiness, even for a night, dear God, even for one night. As his lips found hers and he rolled her onto her back, his naked body blanketing her, she pushed any lingering thoughts of Ronan, of her clan, of the fearful chasm that separated her from the man she knew she so desperately loved, and gave herself over to his kiss.

Already Duncan was shaking, his desire as wild and unleashed as her own as his lips ravaged hers, his tongue sweeping hot and deep into her mouth. If he had meant to be slow and gentle, Maire knew innately at the heat exploding inside her that they were far beyond such leisure now, and she wound her arms around his neck to welcome the incredible onslaught of his passion.

She could never have imagined the wonder of desiring to be one with a man, to belong to him, and she shook, too, with the force of her own need. Distantly she heard a ripping sound, her sleeping gown torn impatiently from her body so she lay naked now and trembling beneath him while he poised himself above her, her legs thrust apart by his knee, his lower body pressing heavily against her. Yet suddenly he tore his mouth from hers and stared into her eyes, his breathing deep and ragged.

"Woman, you must tell me if you wish . . . this. You must tell me—"

"Aye, Duncan, aye," Maire said in a voice she scarcely recognized as her own, full of pleading and so hoarse it was more a whisper. Yet she thought no more as he groaned and spread her legs wider, his aroused flesh hard and insistent at the heart of her thighs for the briefest, most agonizing instant before he drove himself into her, claiming her, possessing her as his own even as Maire cried out beneath him.

She knew piercing pain, but his kiss, the weight of him, the driving force of his hips made her soon forget even that and she gave herself over to the wildness of it, the pure wonder of it, an incredible pressure building where their bodies were wet and burning and joined as one. It was both madness and ecstasy, this heretofore unknown thing that made her hold onto him as fiercely as he held her, her fingers clutching at his back.

She scarcely knew at what point her trembling ceased and a wrenching cry burst from her throat, her body arching to the pleasure spilling over her, through her, while Duncan drove himself into her one final time and stiffened, a deep, full throbbing felt at the very heart of her. His mouth against hers, he drew her all the harder against him, his impassioned whisper almost lost to the clamor of their breathing.

"Ah, God, Rose . . . sweet Rose. Now they cannot take you from me. They cannot!"

Maire felt tears suddenly burn her eyes, but even her false name upon his lips this night, this one precious night, she would not allow to distress her. Saints help her, she would not!

As his mouth possessed hers, she kissed him back with all the depth and truth of her love, abandoning herself to him even as she felt his body grow hard and urgent inside her once more.

Chapter 23

Maire knew without opening her eyes that Duncan would not be there. The disheveled bed was empty beside her.

She distantly remembered his whisper in her ear that he would return by midday, his last caresses, his tender kisses more a dream than conscious memory, she'd been sleeping so soundly. Still with her eyes closed, she brought her fingers to her lips, by touching them able to conjure his presence as if his mouth were warm and insistent upon hers. It made her draw in her breath, the wonder of the night they'd spent together rushing back to fill her completely.

She belonged to him. Utterly. She felt her face begin to burn at the fierceness of their lovemaking, only the last time so gentle as he'd rolled her, dazed and near satiated, onto her side, his fingers bringing her to aching fulfillment while he took her slowly, oh, so slowly. Even now she shuddered just as they both had shuddered together and then finally fallen asleep, their bodies still joined.

Maire drifted open her eyes, the hazy sunlight streaming through the narrow windows doing little to dispel the sense of possession that clung to her. And she didn't want it to leave her. Not yet.

She wanted to steep in the memories and impress them indelibly on her heart. It warmed her that she still smelled of him, the masculine scent of his body on her skin, in her tangled hair, her woman's flesh still wet from him. Did he carry with him the scent of her, too?

That thought brought a stab of pain as jarring as if she'd been struck. Maire moaned to herself, helpless to stop the memories from fading as cold reality suddenly came crashing upon her.

She knew as surely as Duncan was gone that he'd ridden out with a phalanx of knights to search high and low around Longford Castle for whoever had fired the arrow. When he found no vengeful clan arrayed to fight against him or marching forth from the trees to demand her immediate release, would he guess then the truth and return to confront her? Her only hope lay now in that he believed mayhap the O'Melaghlins—

"Ah, still abed, I see."

Maire rose in surprise on one elbow, clutching the blanket to her breasts as Adele glided imperiously into the room. Garbed in a silken gown as icy blue as her eyes, the woman didn't stop until she stood at the foot of the bed, where she glared down her patrician nose at Maire.

"And how the air reeks of sex. I can imagine Duncan has used you well—"

"Duncan would not be pleased to know you're here," Maire heard herself say stiffly, almost as much to her astonishment as Adele's.

"Ah, delightful. A few tumbles in the baron's bed and now you think you may speak to me as an equal—which is why I thought it best we reach an understanding, you and I."

"Truly, I see that we have little of which to speak," Maire began only to be cut off by an angry wave of Adele's hand.

"You insolent Irish whore! If you believe for an instant I or my brothers will ever tolerate you as Duncan's wife, you are wretchedly mistaken—"

"And if you think you have so much to say in the matter, I suggest you'd best share your mind with Duncan and not me! Aye, considering what you and your fine brothers did to him and his poor mother so long ago, I can well imagine what sort of answer you'll be hearing!"

Adele snapped her mouth shut, and Maire was even more surprised at herself, thinking she might have absorbed a wee bit of Triona's legendary brazenness after all. But she was angry, too, as much as she'd ever felt at anyone to think of the misery borne by Duncan because of his family. She even went so far as to yank the blanket around her and rise as gracefully as she could from the bed; she lifted her chin as she faced Adele, so indignant now that her cheeks were hot as flame.

"Get out of these rooms and don't ever again think yourself welcome here. Do you hear me? And mayhap you might consider gathering your people and taking yourself away from Meath this very day if Duncan's choice seems so intolerable to you—"

"Enough! I'll not listen to you speaking to me like this!" Spinning on her heel, Adele walked stiffly to the door while Maire, feeling all the more flushed-faced and emboldened, followed a few steps after her.

"Aye, you deserve to be tossed into the moat for all the terrible things you've done, you . . . you heartless witch!"

Imagining the look on Triona's face if her outspoken sister-in-law had heard her, Maire wouldn't allow herself to think she'd gone too far, no matter Adele turned at the door to face her. The woman's eyes glittered, her voice ice-cold.

"Me in the moat? Take care, Rose, that you don't find yourself drowned—"

Adele didn't finish, the young serving maid Ona suddenly appearing behind her—much to Maire's relief. Adele turned and pushed past the poor girl so callously that Ona nearly dropped the pitcher she carried, water sloshing down the front of her apron. At her cry of dismay, Maire at once went to her, fearing the serving maid had been scalded.

"Ona . . . ?"

"No, no, miss, I was startled, is all."

Smiling almost sheepishly, Ona bobbed her head in a deferential manner Maire wasn't accustomed to at all; the serving girl had done so last night, too, as had the other woman who'd accompanied her with the food tray. It seemed Duncan's announcement that she was to be the

Lady of Longford had affected most everyone . . . including Adele.

Disbelief suddenly struck Maire that she could have spouted so angrily. She went back to sink onto the edge of the bed as Ona filled the washbasin with steaming water.

Jesu, Mary, and Joseph, what madness had overcome her? The woman had caused the slaughter of her clansmen! And had Adele's last words mayhap held some veiled threat?

"I'm sorry, miss, but there wasn't enough hot water yet to fill a tub. The kitchen's still in an uproar—so many people to be fed—"

"It's fine, truly," Maire said softly, grateful once again that Ona had arrived at such a timely moment. As the serving girl laid the fresh towels she'd carried under her arm onto the table, Maire felt her face grow warm as Ona then bent to mop up the puddle on the floor with the towel discarded there.

"Have . . . have any begun to leave for their homes?" she asked, not surprised she suddenly felt so flushed again at the memories that puddle evoked.

"No, miss, not yet. Lord FitzWilliam ordered that all remain until he returned to Longford Castle. It was a large force that went with him—aye, almost all of his knights."

Maire swallowed hard at this news, imagining they must have bristled with weaponry. Her only comfort that she felt little fear for Ronan and her clansmen, evading Normans for rebel Irish as instinctive as breathing, she wondered suddenly how the three O'Melaghlins had come to be captured. Duncan had never said.

It made her wonder, too, how the prisoners fared and if they'd even been told they had won a three-day reprieve from the noose. If Gerard de Barry was tending to them, his hatred for rebels was so great that she imagined he would sooner taunt them with torture and death than tell the truth. Overcome with a desire to see the O'Melaghlins, if only to offer some hope, and more than eager to find some distraction from worrying about what Duncan might soon ask of her, Maire called out to Ona just before the serving girl disappeared out the door.

"Wait! Do you know the way to the dungeon?"

Ona spun around to stare oddly at Maire. "Th-the dungeon, miss?"

"Aye. Would you take me there? After I dress, of course. It won't take me long to bathe. You could sit on the bench and wait for me."

The serving girl nodded, though she still looked surprised as she retreated and shut the door. Maire dropped the blanket at once and went to the basin, her heart already pounding. Yet she doubted any would stop or even question her, surely not given all seemed to know she was Duncan's intended bride.

"Sweet Jesu, Mary, and Joseph."

"My lady?"

Maire started as the somber-faced guard twisted round on the narrow steps to face her. "I . . . I meant only—it's so cold down here," she said quickly, shuddering more for the slimy moss covering the walls than that she was chilled. The man merely nodded and then began once more to descend into the dark bowels of the dungeon, a guttering torch held out in front of him.

Already having reconsidered her decision to visit the O'Melaghlins several times since Ona had brought her to the far tower, her strongest urge to turn back had come when a half dozen guards had looked at her as if she were mad when she'd made her request to them. Surprisingly and much to her relief, the only reservation expressed to her was that the steps were many and steep, and she'd assured the thickset commander of the guards who led the way now that she would be more than up to the task, if a little slow.

Already he'd moved ahead of her, his shadow eerily elongated upon the dank, curved walls as they descended farther, Maire imagining he would grow impatient indeed with her on the way back up. She'd counted forty steps, forty-one, forty-two . . . saints help her, were they descending to the very gates of hell?

Relief filled her again when she saw that the commander had finally stopped and waited for her in front of a bolted wooden door. It didn't take much for her to conceive what she might see after Ronan had described that other dungeon to her, yet she prayed she wouldn't be confronted with any rotting corpses. Nearly overcome at once by the musty air reeking of sweat and urine, she feared to breathe as they stepped inside a vast chamber lit by oil lamps set into the walls.

"This way, my lady."

She wanted to lean just a moment and rest,

but couldn't bring herself to touch the thick support timbers they passed or the walls glistening with moisture. Nor did she want to study overmuch the filthy straw they walked upon for the rats she feared she might see, or the iron implements of torture she glimpsed about the chamber. It was all so horrible.

If Duncan ever learned the truth about her clan, would she be dragged to this place? She couldn't imagine he would do such a thing now, but she had only to remember the hatred in his voice when speaking of the O'Byrnes to still wonder, her heart aching at the thought.

"Up on your feet, the lot of you! You've a visitor—soon to be the Lady of Longford, so mind your tongues!"

As the guard thrust the torch toward what at first appeared an empty corner, Maire felt her throat tighten at the three prisoners who struggled weakly to rise, the heavy scraping of chains at their ankles accompanying their movement. "No, no, please, they can stay where they are, truly."

In spite of her words, the commander of the guards didn't amend his order but stared with disgust at the O'Melaghlins who squinted uncomfortably at the torchlight. Maire stared too, stricken by their haggard appearance, all three stripped to the waist and clearly having suffered a severe lashing from their bloodied shoulders. And the O'Melaghlin's grandsons, brothers she could see now from their shared features and dark curly hair, were no more than boys!

The long-haired harper looked as if he'd fared the worse though, no matter his advancing years, one eye swollen shut, his bearded face bruised though he still lifted his head proudly. Saints help them, had Duncan recently seen these wretched souls?

"I doubt Lord FitzWilliam would be pleased you linger here, my lady," came the commander of the guard's voice to distract her. "You can see the prisoners fare well enough—"

"I see one old man and two boys sorely mistreated," she cut him off, amazed at herself again for the hard glint of reproach in her tone. "If I may speak to them for a few moments . . . alone."

The guard looked at her with some affront, then shrugged and moved away, but not before depositing the torch into a wall sconce. Maire's gaze flew back to the O'Melaghlins, and at once she gestured that they must sit. Yet they continued to stand, staring at her not as much warily as in confusion, and she quickly sought to explain her presence.

"I'm sorry, I—Jesu, Mary, and Joseph, this is terrible what's been done to you! Have you been given food and drink?"

The three seemed so surprised at her outburst that they glanced at each other first before answering, the old harper finally nodding his head.

"Aye, miss, a wee bit of food, some water. 'Tis kind of you to ask—"

"A wee bit? Enough to fill your bellies?"

Again they looked at each other, their silence telling Maire much. Determined that she would ask Duncan that the O'Melaghlins be better fed, the situation reminded her so much of when

Caitlin MacMurrough was abducted from her home and held by Ronan in Glenmalure, Triona boldly standing up to him to secure her gentler treatment. Would Duncan hear her out? Reminded, too, by what Flanna had said of him wanting to do anything to please her, Maire resolved at least to try and do some good while she still remained at Longford Castle.

That thought once more making her throat grow tight, she heard the commander of the guards cough with impatience some distance away and she rushed on.

"Do you know that three days more have been granted to the O'Melaghlin to come to Meath to talk peace?"

Maire got no ready answer, her words seeming to have fallen on deaf ears as the three rebels simply stared at her. It was the harper whose spindly legs suddenly gave way beneath him, and he sank to the straw while one youth, the sturdiest-looking of the three, caught his arm to help him while the other boy still stared in disbelief at Maire.

"W-we're not going to hang today?"

Chapter 24

Maire's heart going out to the O'Melaghlins that they hadn't been told the news just as she suspected, she shook her head and drew closer. At once all three seemed to notice her awkward gait, but their eyes quickly jumped back to her face as if she were an angel who'd appeared to deliver them.

"There may be little I can do to ease your way here, but at least you know all is not lost—"

"Why do you care to help us, miss? Why?" came the harper's incredulous voice, while Maire tried to swallow the sudden lump in her throat.

She couldn't answer, not with anything close to the truth. Instead she glanced over her shoulder to see the commander of the guards had begun to pace near the steps, and she knew she didn't have long.

"Tell me, please. How did you come to be captured?"

Again the three looked at each other, and it was the boy who'd asked if they weren't to hang who finally spoke. "We'd gone to the place where the cattle were slaughtered—my grandfather Rory O'Melaghlin and our clansmen. It was not of our doing—"

"Aye, but we've borne the blame!" interrupted the harper, his red-rimmed eyes ravaged. "'Twas Normans that killed the beasts, their own accursed kind burning the baron's fields, too, and so we've been blamed no matter we seek only to live in peace on what land's left to us."

"Aye, so it's true, but ease yourself, Finian," urged the youth who'd sunk to his knees beside the harper while he glanced with apology at Maire. "Go on, Tynan, tell her."

The boy nodded, a name now to him that made Maire all the more deeply feel their plight.

"We hoped to salvage the meat before it began to rot—to see such waste after so harsh a winter. We were nearly done when we saw the Normans coming upon us. My grandfather cried for everyone to ride into the hills, there weren't enough of us to fight them. But Finian fell from his horse—"

"I told the young fools to ride on," interjected the harper. "To leave me—"

"Aye, and who then would play the harp and sing the ancient legends in Grandfather's hall?" the other boy demanded gruffly, clearly fond of the old man.

"Innis and I"—Tynan glanced at his brother—"went back to help him but by then it was too late to escape. The Norman called de Barry taunted us to run, to take up a sword, but I knew he wanted nothing more than to cut us down."

"Aye, he's no love for Irish rebels," Maire heard herself say softly while Finian, Tynan, and Innis stared at her now in silence. "Nor does Lord FitzWilliam . . ." She fell silent, too, her heartache suddenly so fierce that she looked down at her hands, tears stinging her eyes. Only a low grunt of impatience from the commander of the guards made her start, and she glanced up to see him striding toward her.

"I must go," she murmured to the O'Melaghlins, who stared at her still, especially the harper whose eyes held a curious light as if mayhap he had read her mind, her very soul. Unsettled, she had wanted to assure them that she would do whatever she could to help, but the commander of the guards was already upon her.

"Enough, my lady, I know the baron would not be pleased—"

"Aye, so you've said." Unable to speak to the man anything but stiffly as she wondered how many stripes he'd laid upon the O'Melaghlins' backs, Maire brushed past him without another word. She heard him pull the torch from the wall sconce, not having to glance behind her as increasingly angry tears burned her eyes to know that Finian, Innis, and Tynan had once more been swallowed by darkness.

"Rose?"

The sunny bedchamber disconcertedly empty and quiet, Duncan felt unease grip him. His gaze flew to the open doorway leading to the opposite room, doubts filling him no matter he knew the castle had been searched exhaustively for any more intruders.

As if he were reliving those horrible moments of the night before, he strode into the passageway with his hand upon the hilt of his sword, but he sensed at once that he wouldn't find Rose in his private room either. And she wasn't, a quick scan of the shadowy interior, the floor still strewn with books and maps, making him curse vehemently under his breath for the terror she must have suffered.

He had been a hairbreadth from striking the Norman from the panicked horse when that arrow had flown out of the dark, yet to this moment Duncan didn't know if he would have been in time to save Rose. He, too, had seen the knife descending, his heart beginning to pound and his hands to sweat at the vivid memory.

The long hours spent waiting for an attack last night had been torture, as much for the thought of how close he'd come to losing her as that her clansmen might appear en masse at his gates in the morning to demand her release. But they hadn't appeared, and a thorough search of the countryside within a half league of Longford Castle had shown no evidence of a large force . . . only a small one, perhaps eight to ten horses, at the point from where he guessed the arrow had been shot.

Duncan swore again as he strode back through the passageway, more convinced than ever that some O'Melaghlins had been lurking in the trees, and no clansmen of Rose's. His strong suspicion that the arrow hadn't been aimed at the Norman as much as himself did not bode well for his hopes for peace. Yet if he believed that to be so, why, then, did it plague his mind still that Rose's captor had been skewered so squarely in the back?

Forcing down instincts that told him it was no mere accident of chance, Duncan looked to the rumpled bed and told himself he would have done nothing differently no matter he no longer believed Rose's clansmen had come—yet—to try and wrest her from him. And now they wouldn't have her; she was his wife just as he'd said in all ways save the Church's blessing.

God's teeth, he would wed her now, this very day if Clement hadn't advised him to wait to speak to her clansmen. That Duncan had taken the matter fully out of their hands was likely to endear them even less to the present circumstances. Yet Clement had said also, clearly chagrined to speak of such a delicate matter, that if Rose be gotten with child, what more could her clansmen wish for her sake than to see her properly wed?

Duncan scanned the room, at the crumpled towel dropped across the washbasin, at the blanket pooled on the floor, and sensed Rose had been been in some haste to leave the tower.

He had hoped to find her still abed, where he had planned to join her, needing no red-faced encouragement from Clement. He'd burned to take her in his arms again even as he kissed her good-bye early that morning and whispered he'd return by midday, stunned by the force of his feelings for this one woman. To have babes with her . . . by the blood of God, a family? Only days before he had thought never to take a wife, and now he couldn't imagine his life without her!

Overcome by the vision of a future he'd never dreamed he would possess, Duncan lingered no more but left his apartment, wondering anew where she might have gone. He fairly ran down the steps, feeling more a callow boy than ever before, so eager to see her, so eager to once more hold her in his arms.

The castle was alive with commotion, tenants and villagers clearing the great hall in droves to return to their homes; he'd deemed it safe to do so given no large force of vengeful Irish lay in wait to wage battle beyond the fortress walls. And if a small contingent of O'Melaghlins was nearby and intent upon fomenting trouble, Duncan imagined they would hear soon enough from their chieftain to desist if the O'Melaghlin was wise and had taken his latest offer to heart. For the sake of peace, he hoped so—

"Duncan!"

He grimaced, trying to avoid Adele in the bustling throng even as her voice shrilly rose once more to accost him.

"Duncan, wait!"

He stopped reluctantly, bracing himself for the onslaught as soon as he saw the white, pinched look around his half sister's lovely mouth. For the first time, he wished she were amusing herself with Gerard if only to spare him having to listen to her.

"Duncan, I insist you speak to Rose as to her manners toward her guests."

He stared at Adele almost stupidly, her words to him making little sense. "Manners? Guests?"

"Myself, of course, and my retainers. A short

while ago she had the gall to ask me to leave Longford Castle . . . and she called me a witch!"

Again Duncan could but stare, wondering if he and Adele were speaking of the same sweet Rose. He couldn't imagine her calling anyone a witch or demanding anything of anyone.

"Well, brother, have you nothing to say? She also threatened to have me thrown into the moat! Clearly she has no idea of hospitality, of civility, which is all the more distressing to me considering you plan to take her for your wife. No proper Norman girl would speak so to guests."

"And what did you say to encourage this . . . this tirade?" he demanded, more to appease Adele so he could be done with their conversation than that he believed a word of what she'd claimed. "I can well imagine—"

"I went to give her my good wishes."

"Went?"

"To your rooms, of course. She was still abed—"

"Dammit, did you say something to upset her?" As Adele clamped her mouth shut, two bright spots of color appearing at her cheeks, Duncan suspected then that Rose might have fled his apartment because of his half sister, which made him scowl deeply. "Have out with it, woman—"

"Very well, I will, since I had no chance to say my piece last night when you made your grand announcement. This wretched idea of yours to take her as your bride cannot stand! She's not fit to be your wife—an Irish chit of what family we haven't a hint! And a cripple as well, why, she looks as if she's sure to topple just to take a step—"

"Enough, Adele, you go too far."

"And I say you go too far! You have a duty to the name of FitzWilliam to marry well and in a manner the family can be proud—"

"Proud? By the blood of God, woman, have you forgotten thanks to my family I'm known throughout the realm as a bastard? What matters then whom I wed?"

She'd fallen silent at his fierce roar to gape at him as had anyone in earshot, servants, knights, and tenants alike, most stopping in their tracks until Duncan gave a look that sent them hurrying on their way. As for Adele, she wasn't daunted for long. Her voice sank to a hiss.

"I've influence at Court, Duncan, King John and I have long been more than . . . acquaintances. One letter to him and I can stop this marriage. He'll agree a Norman bride is what you need to preserve the barony—"

"Send your letter, woman, and seek your answer, but don't forget it was my saving the king's life that won me Longford Castle and all else I hold in Meath. I'll send a letter of my own, and the Justiciar John de Gray. Then we'll see if spreading your legs to a king bears more weight than the service of those willing to give their lives for him."

He didn't wait for her reply and doubted she possessed one. At least for the moment, her face was as indignantly red as he'd ever seen it. Instead he strode away, shrugging off their encounter as best he could and doing his best as well to force down his fury. God's teeth, the woman could rile him!

And what she'd said of Rose, he almost wished it were true. He would have enjoyed seeing Adele's face then, too, to have been called a witch.

Yet it was impossible. The only times he'd heard Rose come close to raising her voice was in anguish over things he'd asked her, and then at Dublin Castle when she had insisted she could not marry him. Thinking of her impassioned response to him last night, it was clear she was relinquishing any fears she might have held. He wondered anew if she might be that much closer to remembering more of her clan. He wanted to face them and have the matter of their marriage agreed to and done, and well before any letters need be sent to King John.

"Duncan!"

He looked down the length of the smaller assembly hall, astonished to see Rose coming toward him in as much a rush as she was able. And behind her was the commander of the guards for the dungeon, the burly fellow appearing none too pleased to be following in her wake.

Duncan's gaze flew back to Rose, concern filling him that she looked so pale and clearly winded. Her breathing labored as if she'd just exerted herself, he gestured for her to wait for him to reach her but she ignored him, her expression doggedly determined.

"Duncan, this cannot go on! You must do something!"

Longing to embrace her, he was as astonished, too, by her outburst as that she stopped several feet from him and wheeled to wave her arm at the commander of the guards.

"I insisted he accompany me when we heard from his men that you'd returned. I'm so glad we found you. We must speak—"

"And I've been looking for you, no idea where you could have gone."

"The dungeon, Duncan, to see the O'Melaghlins! I told the serving girl Ona to watch for you so you might know, but she must have gone back to the kitchen—"

"The dungeon, woman?"

Chapter 25

Maire gulped at how quiet Duncan's voice had grown, his stance no longer relaxed but stiff with tension. Yet she rushed on and gave him a vigorous nod, her heart thundering with indignation that had only mounted during the long and laborious climb up the dungeon's steps.

"Have you been to see them, Duncan? They've scarcely been given any food or water, they told me as much, and even the two boys Innis and Tynan have been beaten mercilessly—oh!"

He had taken her arm so abruptly and pulled her aside that Maire half stumbled, the commander of the guards clearing his throat and uncomfortably looking the other way. Yet Duncan's grip was so firm she'd had no fear she might fall though she felt concern enough at how hard his expression had grown, his voice still ominously low.

"The dungeon, Rose? In God's name, that's no fit place for you!"

Maire had expected as much, though mayhap

not his vehemence, and she decided to stay as close to the truth as she dared in her haste to explain. "Aye, Duncan, I knew you would think so, but it struck me—I don't know why . . . mayhap because of all the commotion since we came back from Dublin. I feared the prisoners hadn't been told they had three days more—that they wouldn't be executed today! And I was right. Gerard de Barry had told them nothing—"

"Nothing?"

Duncan looked stunned, and she felt his grip tighten upon her arm while he seemed to speak more to himself than her.

"I ordered it last night, after you'd retired. I went to find Gerard and told him to inform the prisoners . . . and he said this morning that it had been done."

Maire didn't know what to say, astonished that Gerard would have purposely deceived Duncan even as he suddenly shook his head.

"No, it was done and the O'Melaghlins lied to you—"

"But I know they didn't lie, Duncan, aye, think of it! It makes sense Gerard wouldn't tell them the truth, he hates them so much. He wanted them to suffer—"

"Enough, woman, we'll speak of this no more!"

He hadn't shouted at her, but his voice had been so fierce that Maire gaped at him, tears smarting her eyes. At once she saw regret cross his face, and he swept her into his arms and hugged her tightly. In that instant Maire understood that his anger hadn't been so much at her or anything she'd said as that he couldn't accept Gerard had lied to him. But such a matter was between the two of them, not her. Risking that she might press him further, she nonetheless could not hold her tongue.

"Please, Duncan, the prisoners need more food and drink. And an oil lamp at least so they're not left in the dark. If the O'Melaghlin comes to Meath, will he not look with more favor upon peace if his grandsons and Finian have been fairly treated?"

"Finian?" Duncan pulled away from her to stare into her eyes. Taking heart that he no longer sounded so angry, she blushed at his scrutiny.

"Aye, the harper. For me, Duncan, would you allow these few things for me?"

He didn't answer, but she could feel in the palpable easing of tension from his body that he had acquiesced even without a word. Just as she realized with a start as he bent his head to kiss her burning cheek that they would not be talking of such things at all if he'd guessed the truth of her clan—saints help her, that fear had skipped altogether from her mind in her desire to assist the O'Melaghlins!

"For you, woman, I'll order it done . . . but only for you."

Maire shivered at the warmth of his breath tickling her ear, and she imagined from the sudden hungriness in his eyes that he yearned to kiss her more thoroughly if not for the commander of the guards standing so near. She blushed all the more deeply as she heard the man clear his throat again, Duncan finally speaking to release him from his discomfort.

"Did you pay heed to my bride-to-be's requests? More food and drink for the prisoners, a lamp?"

"Yes, my lord, though it wasn't my intention to overhear—"

"It's no matter, man, just see that these things are done within the hour. Allow them warm water to bathe as well, and find them tunics to wear. I'd wager their clothing was ripped from their backs . . ."

As he fell silent, Maire wondered if once more Duncan was thinking of Gerard, her suspicion confirmed when the commander of the guards turned to move away. Duncan's voice was grim with one last order.

"If anyone questions you, Sir Gerard, *anyone,* tell them to speak to me. And no one is to lift a hand to the prisoners without my explicit command, or to harry them in any way. Do you understand?"

"Yes, my lord, no doubt of it."

"Good. Leave us."

The commander of the guards appeared only too eager to oblige, while Duncan seemed to have forgotten the man entirely as he pulled Maire closer.

"There, woman. Does that please you?"

She nodded, unable to speak for her heart hammering in her throat at how husky his voice had grown.

"Good enough, then. Do you know what would please me?"

She stared at him, heat creeping once more over her face as he gave a slow teasing smile.

"That I wore no armor. It's in the way."

"I-in the way?"

Now he nodded, and lifted her into his arms.

Maire's head still spun at how quickly Duncan had carried her back to his rooms, only stopping once to tell a servant passing by the steps to the tower that he wanted wine and food brought to them—but that it must be left outside the door. He did not want to be disturbed.

Those weighty words alone had set her heart pounding, but now as she sat at the edge of the bed and watched him divest himself of his mail shirt—a hauberk, he'd just called it—she felt as if he might as well be undressing her from the ravenous way his eyes swept her.

"Gambeson."

She shivered at the low huskiness of his voice, feeling as awkward as an untried maiden as he stripped off a padded garment and dropped it to the floor with his hauberk and mailed stockings, followed shortly by his undertunic damp with sweat that he peeled from his powerful body. Yet she wasn't untried, her flesh already burning as she recalled all they'd done the night before . . . though Duncan had hinted as he'd deposited her on the bed that there were things between a man and woman she still did not know.

Just as she would not have imagined that a man whose body she'd found so physically beautiful in firelight could be three times so in the bright sunshine streaming through the narrow arched windows. Unable not to, she drank in the wonder of him as he stood, taut of torso and limb, heavily muscled, before her in calf-length breeches. She found herself brazenly eager for him to be rid of them as well.

"Braies."

Maire's gaze flew to his face, that handsome teasing smile making her flesh burn even hotter as he beckoned for her to come to him. Yet she held back, staring at him in confusion even as spoke.

"Rose . . . I need your help."

Maire could not imagine how, but she obliged him, her heart so full that her clumsy gait never seemed to attract his attention. It never had.

He stared into her eyes, that alone drawing her, and she told herself as fervently as last night not to think of Ronan and mayhap Niall hiding so close by outside Longford Castle or that her determination remained as painfully fierce that somehow, she must find a way to leave Duncan. For now, she only wanted to pretend again that things were different, that happiness awaited them and not the cold comfort of memories that someday soon must sustain her.

Maire drew in her breath as Duncan caught her hands and guided them to the cord at his waist that secured his breeches. The masculine scent of him filling her senses, she untied the cord with trembling fingers while still he held her gaze, nor did he allow her to stop there. Without speaking, he covered her hands with his and guided them to the sides of his waist, where she instinctively understood and began to draw his braies slowly from his hips.

Now Duncan sucked in his breath, his massive chest rising and falling as deeply as she felt warmth building inside her, and she lowered her eyes to the thick line of hair descending from his navel to a dark thatch she'd not fully seen before. Yet just as his swollen flesh sprang free, he stayed her hands and swept his braies himself from his body; the garment had no sooner dropped to the floor when he pulled her into his arms and kissed her.

His mouth was hard, his breathing harder, Maire suddenly so dizzy she felt her knees giving way. She clung to him, lost to the power of his embrace, the wonder that never ceased to engulf her even as she knew he wouldn't let her fall. Yet his kiss had no sooner begun to deepen when he abruptly drew away, leaving her to stare up at him flushed and trembling and breathless.

"My armor is gone, woman . . . but what of this?"

His hands filled with the pink silk of her gown, already he was drawing it up and over her hips; Maire leaned into him to steady herself as he quickly pulled the garment over her head. Still light-headed, she must have lost her balance, for the next she knew, she was being carried to the bed, where Duncan divested her of her camise with as much haste.

Only when she was lying naked beside him did he finally pause to sweep his gaze over her, and she saw in his eyes stark admiration that made her know she pleased him as well. His hand trembled as he reached out to splay his fingers over her breast, long, strong fingers, and she gasped softly at the warmth of his palm that matched the stirring timbre of his voice.

"Last night I could not fully see your beauty—only touch to know it. But now I can watch you, woman . . . watch you."

As if to mark his words, he drew his fingertips across her nipple, staring into her eyes even as she sharply drew in her breath and shivered. Her response seemed only to encourage him, and he bent his head to first kiss her breast, the warmth of his breath against her skin thrilling her, before drawing her aching nipple into his mouth.

A low moan slipped from Maire's throat; she couldn't have imagined such pleasure—had he done so to her last night? He began to suckle hungrily and she thought no more, his hand gliding down her belly to cup and gently squeeze her woman's mound. That made her moan again but she fell breathlessly silent, trembling when his fingers slipped inside her while his tongue played and teased at her breast.

It was so sweet a thing, yet like torture, and she felt as if she were splitting apart to know such pleasure where his fingers circled and taunted her and that where his mouth drew so ravenously upon her. She could not have been more startled when Duncan suddenly ceased both and raised himself above her, his dark eyes burning into hers.

He said nothing, as if daring her to read his mind, and she sensed then as her heart quickened that he intended to do something of which he'd only hinted. He bent to kiss her, his mouth impassioned against hers, his tongue plundering deep, but just as quickly he was gone from her. Maire stared at him wide-eyed when he shifted his body to settle himself between her legs and then slipped his hands beneath her bottom to raise her to his mouth.

She threw back her head even as his tongue speared into her, and she tried, wholly shocked, to slide away from him but he held her fast. Her flesh burning, her body trembling uncontrollably, she could only surrender to the onslaught of his mouth, his tongue, his utter possession of her suddenly become all the more complete.

Unbidden, she opened herself to him, her fingers clutching wildly at linen sheets twisted and rumpled from the night before. As if from some distant place she could see he watched her, his eyes still burning as she burned and began to writhe upon the bed though he held her to him, claiming her with a kiss more deeply intimate than any she'd known.

From that same distant place she heard herself cry out his name, begging him for release and he gave it to her, Duncan lifting his mouth from her and rising between her thighs to thrust himself into her, filling her, Maire knowing nothing else.

Only sensation rocked her, and the purest of emotion; she did not realize until long, long moments later after Duncan had collapsed upon her, rolling to one side with her held fiercely in his arms, that tears streaked her cheeks. Not wanting him to see them, she kept her face buried against his chest for as many precious moments, simply listening to him breathe, his heartbeat slowing again to a deep rhythmic cadence.

It was so sweet, and yet as much torture as anything that had gone before, that Maire was not surprised when fresh tears came to torment her. Still she kept her face buried but she felt, too, Duncan tense, and he drew away to look at her, a finger gently grazing her cheek.

"I wanted to give you pleasure, woman, but that it has made you weep? God's teeth, have I hurt you?"

Chapter 26

Duncan's voice filled with concern, Maire hastily shook her head to reassure him though she couldn't seem to stay her tears. Jesu, Mary, and Joseph, if she didn't stop she would surely give herself away! He would sense that there was something terribly wrong, which there was—

"It's Adele, isn't it?"

His voice was angry now, and when Maire didn't readily answer, he swore under his breath and lifted himself onto his elbow.

"I know she came here—she stopped me to say as much when I was looking for you. By the blood of God, has she made you some threat?"

Maire thought at once of what Adele had said about her drowning in the moat, but she wasn't sure it had been a true threat or just a ploy to frighten her. Again her silence seemed to anger Duncan all the more, no matter her tears had finally stopped, his expression as hard as stone.

"Damn that woman! Not only does she torment you, but lies about you as well. She claims you told her that she should take her retainers and leave Meath—"

"I did."

Maire felt her face grow warm at Duncan's incredulous look, and she wondered if he might be displeased with her now. Quickly she sought to explain. "I was angry, Duncan, aye, just thinking of what your family had done to you and your poor mother. So when Adele came here to say she had no intention of abiding me as your bride—"

"You told her you'd have her thrown into the moat."

At Duncan's slow smile, Maire gaped at him, not knowing why she should be so surprised Adele would have revealed that to him.

"And she claimed that you called her a witch. Is that true? Did you call my beloved half sister a witch?"

His eyes as full of admiration as gentle teasing, Maire found she couldn't help teasing him herself. "Beloved, is she? Mayhap I'd best not answer then—oh!"

Duncan had rolled her onto her back so suddenly and gently pinned her shoulders to the bed that Maire lost her breath, but she knew she'd have lost it anyway at how handsome he was, staring down at her.

"Promise me something, will you?"

His voice husky and warm, she could only nod, the boyish gleam in his eyes doing as much to render her speechless.

"Promise me when next you call Adele a witch, that I be present to see her face?"

Maire answered his smile with her own, feeling as giddy to see this playful side of him as he seemed to be enjoying her. Yet he sobered so suddenly that she did, too, confusion filling her.

"Duncan . . . ?"

"I've never seen you smile so before, woman, never once until this day."

He spoke in wonderment and yet with regret, staring at her lips as if waiting for her to smile again. And she so wanted to, just for him, mustering another even as tears once more clouded her eyes. Saints help her, what must he think? First weeping, then smiles, then both at the same time . . .

"Ah, Rose, you're so beautiful. So beautiful . . ."

He found her lips, kissing her so tenderly that Maire felt her heart ready to burst, no more intimate a thing than she could imagine that his mouth tasted of her sex. She'd never felt closer to him and yet so far apart, nor more tempted in that moment to blurt out the truth, that she wasn't named Rose but Maire O'Byrne, than she'd ever been before.

To dare to trust him, to dare to believe that the barrier between them could be conquered . . . not by sword but with love. Was that so vain a hope?

She'd never known her heart to beat so fiercely as when he lifted his head to look into her eyes, and she opened her mouth to speak—saints give her strength! But she no sooner whispered his name than a fierce pounding came at the outer door, punctuated by Gerard de Barry's angry voice.

"Duncan, a word!"

The moment fled, Maire had never felt such emptiness either as Duncan cursed under his breath and left her, the bed vast and lonely and cold without him. Imagining what Gerard had come to say, she watched silently as Duncan swept up his braies from the floor and stepped into them, his sideways glance telling her to cover herself.

With trembling hands she obliged him, pulling a sheet to her chin while he disappeared into the antechamber. She could tell he was angry when she heard him open the door so fiercely that it slammed against the wall. But Gerard, clearly undaunted, vented his outrage before Duncan could utter a word.

"God's blood, man, are we now coddling our prisoners? Food and drink fit for our own table, a lamp, fresh clothes?"

"No large matters, Gerard, ease yourself—"

"Ease myself? First a sworn vow to me is broken, and now my authority over the prisoners is stripped away—*full authority* you gave me, Duncan?"

At Gerard's raised voice, Maire sank deeper under the sheet, imagining the look upon Duncan's face at how tightly controlled his reply sounded.

"Nothing has been stripped from you. I wish our arrangement amended, is all."

"At whose request? I heard that the O'Melaghlins had an unexpected visitor—"

"Rose won't be going to the dungeon again. We already spoke of it—she knows well I wasn't pleased. But her words to me made sense that the prisoners need fairer treatment. It's a small price to pay to further peace—"

"Peace! I see no messenger from the O'Melaghlin asking to speak to you, Duncan."

"Give them time."

"Time? And if they don't appear in three days, what will it be then? Three days more? A week? A month? I'd best have down mattresses and fresh linen sheets sent to the dungeon to make the O'Melaghlins all the more comfortable—"

"By the blood of God, Gerard, enough!"

Maire jumped at Duncan's roar, and she wondered that two men who'd clearly long been brothers in arms would square off so fiercely with each other. But even so, Duncan sounded calmer when he spoke again, which evidenced the consideration he held for Gerard.

"Dammit, man, you take this as some personal affront against you, but it is not! I vow it. The three days stand, whether the O'Melaghlin chooses to come to Meath or not. If no peace is agreed to, the prisoners will hang. Those rebels have plagued Meath long enough—burning fields, stealing cattle. I told you I would suffer their raiding no more. Now, does that satisfy you?"

Maire heard no response, but her blood was pounding in her ears so loudly that she doubted she would have discerned one.

Burning fields? Finian had claimed it wasn't them, but Normans, no doubt from all she'd heard of their ruthlessness the remnants of Walter de Lacy's men. And the cattle? Mayhap the O'Melaghlins had stolen a few now and again, but no Irish rebels, no matter how desperate, would wantonly slaughter an entire herd. Such waste in harsh times was unthinkable.

"Save your hatred for the O'Byrnes, Gerard. I've told you that before. If we've ever any in the dungeon, you'll have free rein to do with them as you will."

"Dungeon? If I come across that bastard Black O'Byrne, he'd never make it so far," came Gerard's embittered reply. "He'll die where we find him."

"Then look to that day, as will I. Do you not think I want to avenge Robert's death as well?"

Maire didn't hear Gerard's low answer, nor did she have any desire to listen further, the blood utterly drained from her face.

Jesu, Mary, and Joseph, could she have been such a fool? Had she truly believed love might overcome such hatred? And to think how close she had come to revealing all . . . The yawning chasm between her and Duncan suddenly grown all the wider and more impossible, she returned with desperation to wondering how she might leave Longford Castle.

Saints help her, might she have to jump into the moat? If it was the only answer, aye, she would attempt it, for it was horribly clear that her remaining here would bring nothing but disaster. Each moment she pretended things could be otherwise only prolonged what she knew must come. If only she could think of some other way . . .

Maire's gaze flew to the door as Duncan reappeared, her heart filled with such anguish she couldn't have summoned a smile now if he'd begged her. He looked so grim, too, as he carried a tray bearing food and a pitcher of wine to the bed, his exchange with Gerard clearly having tempered his mood. She imagined their discord must pain him, evidenced when he breathed a low curse as if still thinking of what he and his knight had discussed.

"Duncan . . . if you wish to speak further to Gerard, don't trouble yourself over me—"

"You're no trouble, woman, it's all else that plagues me." Duncan set the tray upon the bed, speaking almost more to himself than her. "Two days more after this one and my hand will be forced. Damn the O'Melaghlin for his stubbornness!"

"Mayhap it's not that as much as desperation, aye, and why else wouldn't it be so?" Maire blurted out, as surprised at herself as Duncan appeared to be. Yet she rushed on, a sudden desperate idea ruling her as well. "His grandsons and harper are to be hanged, and yet it wasn't the O'Melaghlins who slaughtered those cattle or burned your fields but more of de Lacy's men, Finian told me as much—"

"The harper, again."

Maire nodded as she drew a quick breath, astonished that Duncan had made no move to silence her, though his eyes had darkened to near black. Encouraged that he seemed to be listening to her, she didn't waste a moment.

"I believe him, too, else I wouldn't speak of it. That's how they came to be captured—they'd gone to salvage the meat for their families when Gerard and your men rode down upon them. Finian told me the O'Melaghlins have wrongly borne the blame for everything while they want only to live in peace! They desire the same as you, Duncan, yet mayhap the O'Melaghlin has given up hope and from that comes his rash threat, while you still speak of executing those dear to him in three days—"

"So what would you have me do, woman, release them?"

Maire stared at Duncan incredulously, having to gulp this time for air. His expression was so inscrutable she couldn't tell if he was serious or grimly jesting.

"R-release them?"

"Exactly. If you were in my place, given what you claim about the O'Melaghlins being falsely accused, what would you do?"

She must have turned pale, because Duncan poured a goblet of wine and handed it to her. He said not a word and waited for an answer while somehow she managed to take a sip, no matter her hands were trembling, her mind racing.

What would she do? The situation suddenly reminding her of how Donal MacMurrough had shown his gratitude to have his abducted daughter Caitlin safely returned to him, it came to her that Duncan could very well win the peace he wanted and she might have found a way to leave Longford Castle, too. Pain piercing her at the thought, she found it difficult to speak for how tight her throat had grown.

"Aye, Duncan, I would release them. Take them back to West Meath and their families, to their home as soon as you can. Gerard may not be pleased—"

"It isn't for Gerard to say."

Duncan's voice grim, Maire had no desire to touch further that subject, instead staring into his eyes even as her heart quickened that he stared so intently back at her. "It would be an honorable thing . . . from an honorable man. Mayhap to have his grandsons and harper safely home, the O'Melaghlin might even agree to help you fight against these Normans who've done harm to you both—and for that, mayhap you could spare a few cattle now and again so his people might have food?"

Maire had ventured much in that last request, she knew it well, especially when no ready answer came from Duncan, only silence. Still he stared at her and her face grew hot, and when he took the goblet from her and moved the tray to the floor, she felt warmth flood her from head to toe. Finally when he spoke, his voice low and husky, she knew she was lost.

"You've never said a word before as to what you think of me. Did you know that, Rose?"

She could but nod, her blood thrumming wildly as he climbed onto the bed and pushed her gently back against the pillows, blanketing her with his body while he took care to keep his weight upon his elbows. And still he stared at her, searching her eyes while his fingers entwined in a midnight strand of hair.

"I would release the O'Melaghlins this very hour just to hear you say again you thought me honorable . . . but tomorrow morning will be soon enough for all preparations to be made. Does that please you?"

Maire again, could only nod. She felt her heart full to breaking that he would trust so completely her word about the O'Melaghlins. To please her, she had no doubt either that he would agree to allow her to accompany him to West Meath. It would only take her concern about being left behind with Adele, and he would easily relent. Saints help her, all she must watch for then, was the right moment to elude him . . .

Maire drew in her breath as Duncan caressed her cheek, his eyes burning into hers as once more, he spoke.

"Two days past you said you could not be my wife, but now you defend me against Adele and call me honorable . . . adding to all else that has changed between us. Tell me, woman, I must hear it from your lips. If your clansmen come to demand you be returned to them, will you say that you stand beside me and wish to become my bride?"

His heart and all he hoped lay bare in his eyes. Maire somehow found the courage to answer, even though she knew such a wondrous thing would never happen.

"Aye, Duncan, ay—"

His kiss silenced her before she could finish, and well enough that he wouldn't see the tears threatening to fall. Yet she willed them away and kissed him back, passionately, wildly, only this day left to her now and one more precious night.

After that, there would be time enough to mourn when she was home in Glenmalure and far, far away from Longford Castle and Duncan FitzWilliam.

Chapter 27

Ronan angrily wiped fatigue from his eyes, willing in vain that the drawbridge be lowered and Maire appear again as she had the night before.

It had all happened so fast, he and his men no sooner arrived at the spot where he'd chosen to keep watch over Longford Castle when commotion had struck, a Norman bearing Maire in front of him attempting to ride forth from the fortress. Ronan had known instantly at the hair prickling the back of his neck that she was in danger, and he had been ready to vault back onto his horse to chase the Norman down when he saw Maire grab desperately at the reins.

That had made him seize his bow, an owl-fletched arrow set to the string before the Norman even raised his knife. By God, to think how close, how close—

"Lord, let me take the watch. You need some rest, even an hour—"

"I need nothing but my sister safely home," he cut off Flann O'Faelin, the huge Irishman not appearing surprised at Ronan's vehement reply.

Vivid moonlight illuminating both of their faces, Ronan wasn't surprised either when Flann gave a grunt and stoically persisted.

"We rode much of the day, lord, aye, evading those accursed spawn, and now more than half the night is gone, dawn soon to come—"

"Let it come and I'll be here to face it. Something is astir, Flann, listen."

As his clansman grew still beside him, Ronan strained his ears, too, to hear again the clamor of men's voices carrying to them across the barren land surrounding the castle. From where they hid at the perimeter of the trees he had a full view of the fortress, though nothing there seemed different, guards aplenty on the battlements, blazing torches lending an orange glow to the night sky. Yet he sensed deep in his gut that men might be preparing to ride out, mayhap not now but at first light, aye, just as they'd done the previous morning.

Did the devil's spawn think another day's search might bring them nearer to finding him and his clansmen? At one point the Normans had ridden so close to them that Ronan had been sorely tried to keep an arrow from his bow, the same dark-haired bastard who'd carried Maire back into the castle—Duncan FitzWilliam, he had no doubt—well within his sights.

Just as the baron had been the night before until Maire had slid from the frightened horse and thrown her arms around the man's neck . . .

A low curse escaped Ronan, his gut clenching even as he told himself for the hundredth time that she must have been terrified to do such a thing—though he could not guess what discord had led one Norman to try and ride out with Maire in his arms while the baron of Longford had come running after with sword in hand. Yet so two years ago the Normans had fought fiercely against each other, their king even coming across the water to Eire. A pity they had not all been slain then.

"Aye, lord, you're right, I hear it," came Flann's gruff whisper to distract him while Ronan shifted his legs where he stood so they wouldn't fall numb. "Fools. Do you think they make ready again to try and find us?"

Not certain, Ronan sighed heavily in answer, hoping another day wouldn't be spent in playing cat and mouse with Normans. Yet who knew how many days of watching and waiting lay ahead of him before Maire might leave that accursed place again?

He'd already sent young Shea O'Byrne straightaway back to Glenmalure to let Triona and Niall know that Maire's whereabouts at least, had been discovered, and with it went a firm order for Niall to remain there, that he might be recognized from the meadow where their clansmen had been struck down. He expected Shea's return at any time with ten extra men to better their odds, for that was the next step, doubtless more relentless waiting for the right moment to strike.

It would do no good to kill the baron outright, though that was exactly what Ronan burned to do. But what of Maire? Until she left the castle, he could not help her, and even then, he would be forced to watch helplessly if she were surrounded by too many guards. Yet if the number was right, a smaller force equal to or even somewhat larger than his twenty clansmen, more than half of the Normans would be dead before they realized from where the arrows flew . . .

"Very well, Flann, an hour's rest but no more." Sliding down against a gnarled tree trunk, Ronan set his bowcase upon the ground beside him. "By then it won't be long until we know if the bastards will amuse us another day or if we prepare to fight."

"Fight I hope, Lord, for Maire's sake."

Ronan didn't answer, made so angry by the memory of his sister in the baron's arms that he didn't trust himself to.

"If . . . if *she's* going to West Meath, then I should be able to come too! In fact, I demand it!"

Duncan groaned to himself, Adele clearly undaunted to be railing at him dressed in her sleeping gown and robe while the courtyard bustled with activity around her. God's teeth, could the morning be progressing any less smoothly?

Already it was past the sunrise hour when he had wished to leave; Faustis had gone to extremes to provide provisions for several days' stay at his westernmost castle, especially when the steward had learned that Rose would be accompanying him. And now a sky that had dawned clear was threatened by angry-looking storm clouds—Faustis frantic to see that supplies tied atop packhorses were covered well with canvas—though the promise of a spring squall was nothing to the raging tempest in

Adele's eyes as she glanced at Gerard already mounted and waiting grimly near the drawbridge.

Duncan glanced at his knight, too. Gerard's reaction upon learning of his decision to return the O'Melaghlins to their clan had been the thorniest part thus far of the morning. To say he hadn't been pleased—damn the man! Gerard's outrage had no doubt awakened anyone at Longford Castle who hadn't already been up early attending to preparations for the journey.

"Duncan, will you answer me or no? You barred me from leaving once before, and I'll not suffer it again!"

"Do you ride in your sleeping clothes then, or will you dress first while we wait for you?"

Adele sputtered in surprise, made speechless for perhaps the first time in her life, which was worth it alone to Duncan . . . almost.

"I'll give you a few moments, woman, no more before we leave you behind—"

"I'll be ready, don't you fear," came Adele's response as she spun on her heel, her loose blond hair flying around her. She threw a brilliant smile at Gerard before hurrying into the castle, which only made Duncan's jaw grow tight.

Yet perhaps such a distraction was exactly what his knight needed on the journey, he reasoned, much to his disgust upon the whole matter. The growing rift between himself and Gerard troubled him, but there was nothing to be done for it now. In a few days, though, as soon as he returned to Meath, he planned to demand Adele and her retainers leave for England, not only so Gerard might focus once more upon his upcoming marriage, but that the distress Duncan had seen in Rose's eyes when she'd asked not to be left alone with Adele be banished.

By the blood of God, he would not have the woman he intended to wed so sorely troubled within her own household! More convinced than ever that Adele had made some threat against Rose, Duncan nonetheless hadn't been able to elicit any such charge from her, which had both warmed him that she must want to spare him further discord and yet puzzled him, too.

She had obviously stood up against Adele already, but that was knowing Duncan wasn't too far away. He didn't blame her for not wishing to remain behind, touched more than he could say when she'd said simply she wanted to be with him. He swept the courtyard with a glance, at his thirty knights and as many men-at-arms mounted and surrounding the prisoners, who still appeared dazed at their good fortune, and deemed it was time enough to fetch Rose from the great hall.

Duncan felt a familiar eagerness overwhelm him as he strode toward the doorway where Adele had disappeared a moment before; he wanted to be with Rose, too, that driving need become as essential to him as breathing. He'd left her not so long ago by the fire, wanting her to be comfortable until they were ready to leave, yet it felt like hours had passed since he'd carried her from the tower.

Another thing he'd decided was that upon

their return new quarters would be prepared for them elsewhere in the castle, so she wouldn't be constantly faced with so many steps. He would see to it that she had everything she needed for her embroidery, too, just as he'd promised in Dublin. As to when she'd have time to wield needle and thread was another matter; he'd kept her busy enough with more pressing concerns these past two days, and he fully intended to continue.

Duncan groaned to himself at how reluctant he'd been to leave their bed in the dark hours of the morning, tempted to delay the tasks in front of him just so he might again feel Rose opening her arms and her sweet, willing body to him. But when she'd sleepily thanked him for deciding to release the O'Melaghlins, that alone had spurred him to rise, Gerard jumping forefront to his mind.

Fresh anger flooded Duncan at the thought of their violent exchange, but he forced it away when he spied Rose. She turned from the hearth at his approach, her blue cloak whirling around her, her eyes troubled.

"Duncan, I just saw Adele rushing to her room. She called out to me that she was accompanying you to West Meath."

"A rash move—I did so to appease Gerard more than anything."

"B-but does that mean I will be staying here?"

She suddenly looked so pale that concern swept Duncan, though he was moved, too, that she seemed so distressed at the thought they might be apart. "Leave you here with Rufus the Fool? Reginald will have his hands full enough with that one and the rest of Adele's retainers not to worry over you. Now come."

Rose appeared so relieved that Duncan couldn't resist drawing her into his arms, and he was struck that she trembled.

"Woman, are you not well?"

"No, no, Duncan, I'm fine, truly. I feared that you would leave me, is all."

"Never, woman. Never." He hugged her fiercely, inhaling the scent of her hair while she clung to him as if she might not do so again, Duncan found himself thinking. He drew away from her to stare into her eyes.

"Rose, there's little to dread. If any O'Melaghlins still hide in the woods, they'll not dare attack once they see their clansmen among us. I wager they'll be as surprised as their chieftain soon will be . . . no small thanks to you."

She didn't reply, and he chose not to press her; that she appeared less pale was soothing enough. Instead he took her hand and drew her with him, hoping his low teasing might coax her into a smile.

"Just think. If we hurry, we might be mounted and gone before Adele returns to the courtyard. Would that please you?"

Duncan received a small nod for his efforts but no more, though in the next instant Rose did squeeze his hand, which served to make amends for some of the morning's troubles. If only now it didn't rain . . .

"Ronan, look!"

He did, turning from the men who'd just arrived, his anger intense that Niall was among them. So intense that for an instant he found it difficult to focus upon the Normans surging forth from Longford Castle, though Flann O'Faelin shifted anxiously beside him.

"The spawn! Do you think they come after us . . . ?"

The Irishman's voice had faded at the same moment Ronan saw her, a strikingly lovely blond woman astride a dappled gray who met the description given to him a few days ago by his clansmen. Aye, she'd been among those at the meadow. As she rode across the drawbridge accompanied by a grim-faced knight, Ronan knew then that this was no force come again to search the woods. But where the devil might they be bound?

"Ronan, it's Maire!"

Niall suddenly beside him, Ronan had to grab his younger brother's arm to prevent him from rushing out of the cover of the trees, no matter he burned to act as well. His furious whisper cut the air.

"Damn you, Niall, will you give us away? We can do nothing to help her right now—look at their number!"

His gut clenched in dismay, Ronan sensed the same tension in his brother, their eyes riveted upon Maire as she cleared the drawbridge in close company with the dark-haired Norman who Ronan longed for nothing more now than to destroy. Swallowing hard, he saw her glance toward the trees, and his instincts told him then that she knew they were near.

But she just as quickly looked away, spurring her mount into a canter to match the pace of the large force that moved beyond the castle, sixty men at least, packhorses, and a small host of what appeared to be servants bringing up the rear. And what of the two youths and an old man surrounded by guards? Suddenly he remembered what Shea O'Byrne had told him of three prisoners held from clan O'Melaghlin—by God, Shea had said something, too, of West Meath.

"To your horses! Now!"

His low command as vehement as urgent, Ronan grabbed up his bowcase and moved to his own pitch-black steed, not waiting for Niall. That his brother, Tanist or no, had chosen to ignore his order to remain in Glenmalure so rankled him that he did not trust himself at that moment to speak further upon it. Yet deep in his heart, he knew he would have done the same. That thought helped him temper his tongue when Niall caught his arm.

"Ronan, where do we ride?"

His brother's eyes tormented, his voice hoarse from concern for Maire, Ronan nonetheless made himself answer sternly.

"To the west. We'll keep them in sight and wait for the right moment, Niall, do you hear me? There's a woman among them who might recognize you—dammit, swear to me you'll do nothing unless I tell you! Maire's life may depend upon it!"

"Aye, I swear, Ronan. I swear!"

The rest of his clansmen already mounted and waiting, Ronan said no more but nodded for Niall to move to his own horse.

God help them, twenty-two O'Byrnes against

three times as many Normans. A deafening clap of thunder breaking the stillness that had settled over the woods made him wonder if his prayer had been heard.

Chapter 28

"Delightful, how wretchedly delightful."

Maire glanced at Adele, the blond beauty not appearing so imperious now with her sodden cloak wrapped tightly around her, water dripping from the tip of her nose. Maire squinted against the lashing rain herself, and gripped her cloak beneath her lowered chin with one trembling hand while she held the reins with the other. She was soaked to the skin, and so chilled now that she couldn't stop herself shaking or her teeth from chattering.

The rain which had been more a steady drizzle much of the day had become a violent downpour what seemed like hours ago, though Maire knew it hadn't been that long. Almost at once Duncan had left her, Gerard, and a dozen men accompanying him as well as the packhorses and servants, to ride ahead to a farming settlement to prepare for them a night's lodging. He'd deemed the storm too fierce for them to continue on to his castle near Lough Ennell, no matter it was only another few hours' ride.

Watching him disappear into the blinding rain, Maire had never felt such anguish, as much because she feared for his safety as that she could do nothing yet to protect him. Still surrounded by more than twoscore knights and men-at-arms, she'd surrendered any notion that she had the slightest chance of eluding them and resigned herself that she must wait further for the right moment.

"We'll be sleeping in huts, lying upon filthy rushes and earthen floors, I know it!"

Maire made no reply, ignoring Adele and her complaints as best she could as she peered ahead into the distance. Already it had grown darker, not so much that it was late but that the storm was intensifying, the wind howling around them, the muddy ground making it difficult for the horses to keep at their pace.

Were Ronan and her clansmen faring any better? She knew they were out there somewhere, which made her fear deepen all the more for Duncan.

If Ronan weren't so cautious, ever mindful of his men's welfare, she was certain he would have attacked by now and risked the odds. But no doubt he believed her life in danger as well, that she'd been a captive brutally treated this past week—Jesu, Mary, and Joseph! Only a week to have found love and now be faced with abandoning it forever? Aye, but what else was there for her to do?

"I plan to insist we journey on to the castle—no, I'll demand it— Oh!"

Adele shrank in her sidesaddle as jagged veins of lightning burst across the sky. Maire was astonished that anything could daunt so cold-hearted a woman. She was relieved when a shout went up from a knight near the front of their entourage that the farming settlement had been sighted, and Adele actually looked relieved, too.

As they spurred the horses forward, their pace quickened, as did Maire's heart. The short time spent without Duncan had seemed an eternity, saints help her. What would she do when was alone in Glenmalure?

Forcing the distressing thought from her mind, she wiped rain from her eyes as thatched roofs appeared over the rise, the familiar smell of peat fires lending her some comfort. She saw a half dozen riders approaching, and knew as surely as her breath caught that Duncan was among them.

It seemed within an instant he had brought his great snorting steed alongside hers; Duncan looked as sodden as she but so handsome, aye, so wondrously handsome. He pulled her from her saddle before she sensed his intent and settled her in front of him, his arms hard and strong around her, his beloved voice low and husky against her ear.

"Woman, you look chilled to the marrow. But I've a warm, dry nest waiting for us—one of my tenants has kindly offered up his home and bed."

"What of me, Duncan?" came Adele's indignant voice before Maire could utter a word. "Where am I to stay?"

"There are several barns from which to choose—"

"A barn!"

"Though I'm sure Gerard has plans to accommodate you," Duncan finished, his tone grown harsh. Yet it held a hint of grim amusement, too, as if Adele's outrage had been the reaction he sought. He said no more, but tightened his arms around Maire and kicked his horse into a gallop.

"There, I'd said I wouldn't be long."

As Duncan placed two steaming bowls of stew and a golden round of bread upon a roughhewn table, Maire hugged the blanket more tightly around herself, still shivering.

Aye, he hadn't been long, no more than a few moments and time enough for her to change out of her wet clothing and into a woolen sleeping gown the tenant's kindly wife had left upon the bed in the adjoining room. Patched and worn, the garment was nonetheless clean and soft and smelled of fresh air from hanging out to dry. Its warmth gradually stilled her chattering teeth.

The snug, plainly furnished dwelling-house was warm, too, or mayhap it was the way Duncan stared at her now that made it so. He had appeared almost disappointed to see that she had changed so quickly, and the look lingered as his gaze swept her from head to foot. Bare toes peeked beneath the blanket as her slippers were thoroughly sodden. He studied them as if he wished the whole of her was exposed, then met her eyes, a teasing smile that oddly seemed subdued coming to his lips.

"I'd hoped at least to help you out of that wet gown, but it appears you've managed well enough without me."

"Aye, I was so cold . . . but I could assist you," she said softly, her gaze falling to the water dripping from the hem of the dark cloak that he wore over his hauberk. "I've done so once before."

His smile faded, the sudden intensity in his eyes causing Maire to shiver in a manner having nothing to do with any chill. Yet he nonetheless shook his head and shrugged out of the soaked garment without her aid, regret in his voice as he hung his cloak on a bench in front of the central hearth.

"Nothing would better please me—it's what I'd planned, but now that must wait. Come. The food will warm you."

His expression had become so grim that Maire was concerned something might be amiss, her thoughts jumping to the prisoners as she moved to the table. "Duncan, what's wrong? Is it the O'Melaghlins? Have they said something to make you doubt—"

"They've said no different to me than what they told you—come, Rose, I want you to eat while it's hot."

Maire did as he bade her, taking the chair opposite him while Duncan sat too. Again he seemed so preoccupied, his mind clearly elsewhere, that her growing concern far outweighed her hunger though she took a small bite of the savory venison stew.

As he silently poured them wine into plain pewter cups, she wondered if thoughts of Gerard might be plaguing him. Duncan had said that morning when he'd come to fetch her from the tower that his discussion with his knight hadn't been pleasant, but he'd revealed little else. Did she dare press him . . . ?

"On my way back with the food, I was stopped by one of my men. He said he glimpsed riders to the south just before I rejoined you outside the settlement—he counted at least sixteen before they disappeared into the trees. Irish."

Maire stared at Duncan as he stared at her; she didn't know what to respond, but she felt she must say something, anything to break the heavy silence.

"O'Melaghlins?"

He nodded, such relief swamping Maire that he'd said nothing of suspecting anyone else that her hand shook as she attempted to raise a spoonful of stew. She saw he noticed, and she fumbled quickly for words to distract him.

"I-I feared it would be so since this morning—they don't know yet, Duncan, surely no messenger has reached them. They don't know you plan to release the prisoners. Do you think they might attack us? Are we safe here?"

"As safe as any settlement filled with armed men. That's why I can't stay. Guards must be well posted to keep watch—God's teeth, it would have been better if we'd continued on to the castle, storm or no!"

Clearly angry at himself, he rose from the table without touching food or wine and Maire made no comment upon it. In truth, the little she'd eaten had settled uneasily in her stomach for the anxiety now gnawing at her.

It hadn't been O'Melaghlins riding to the south.

And Duncan wouldn't be safe, not as long as she remained here. Jesu, Mary, and Joseph, what was she to do?

Maire rose, too, as Duncan went to throw his cloak around his shoulders; for a brief moment, he stared into the fire crackling in the hearth, his face so handsome and yet so grave. He turned abruptly to find her staring at him, and her knees felt weak at the concern so evident in his eyes.

"If you hear any sounds of battle, Rose, any at all, find a place in the bedchamber to hide. I'll come for you as soon as I can. Do you understand? Don't dare step outside—promise me."

His voice was so grim, she could only nod. But she started in surprise when he came toward her and grabbed her roughly by the shoulders.

"You must promise me, woman! Say it! By the blood of God, if anything should happen to you . . ."

His voice had grown almost hoarse before dying away, his eyes burning into hers, demanding that she answer him as if by doing so he might feel certain she would be safe.

"Aye, Duncan, I swear it. I won't leave—"

His mouth silenced her before she could finish, but already she felt as if she were choking upon her own lie. As his hands slid down her back to draw her against him, she gave no thought to the blanket pooling at her feet or that the front of her sleeping gown was made wet by his cloak.

All she knew was the incredible possession of his kiss, his lips warm and hard, his tongue thrusting deep into her mouth to claim her even as she clung to him, her fingers entwining in his damp hair. She scarcely realized when he lifted his head, she'd grown so light-headed, but the fierce emotion burning in his eyes made her heart seem to stop.

"I love you, Rose. Do not doubt it."

Maire couldn't speak, all she'd ever dreamed uttered in three words that made tears jump to her eyes, but, already, Duncan had released her. He brushed a final kiss to her cheek, and then was gone, not glancing behind him even as he disappeared out the door and left her alone.

Utterly alone. No one but she heard the words Maire could barely whisper, her throat was so tight.

"I love you, Duncan FitzWilliam. Saints help me, I love you."

She couldn't say how long she stood there, staring at the door left slightly ajar, nor did she blink when a clap of thunder so deafening rumbled across the sky that the ground seemed to shake. Only a fierce wind gusting into the dwelling-house made her stir when the flames at the hearth fanned and flared high, and Maire thought suddenly of Triona as rain began to beat upon the thatched roof.

Aye, her daring sister-in-law had several times used the cover of a heavy downpour to elude Ronan. Why couldn't she? Somehow Maire made legs grown wooden carry her to the bedchamber where she'd left her wet clothing, no time before Duncan had called out to her to say he'd returned to hang them to dry.

Numbly she tugged the sleeping gown over her head and donned again her sodden camise, blue silk gown, and slippers; it suddenly seemed fitting to her that she wore her own clothing and no Norman garb, a wrenching reminder that she could never as an O'Byrne have been accepted into Duncan's world. She settled her cloak around her shoulders, and, with a last longing look at the simply made bed she had thought tonight they would share, she turned and hurried as well as she could into the next room.

The door had blown fully open, wind and rain causing the fire in the hearth to sputter and whirl, and Maire drew her hood over her hair even as her heart had begun to slam against her breast.

She'd never felt so nervous, so wretched, fearing any moment Duncan might return to find her dressed and ready to flee. What excuse would she make to him then? She was almost to the door when a tall silhouette appeared at the threshold, and she nearly collapsed when she spied the gleam of mail.

"Ah, God, Duncan . . ." was all she managed, a scream welling in her throat when she saw blood splattered down the front of the hauberk. But a hand was clapped over her mouth so suddenly that she made only a wheezing gasp, Maire staring in disbelief as Ronan lunged into the room and pushed her against the wall.

"By God, Maire O'Byrne, will you bring the damned spawn down upon us?"

Chapter 29

Maire shook her head quickly, so stunned that she had no words to speak even if Ronan's hand weren't covering her mouth.

In the next moment she was drawn into his arms and hugged so tightly she couldn't breathe, yet as suddenly he stepped away from her and gestured that she not move. She watched wide-eyed, her heart pounding, as he ventured a glance out the door, his hand firmly upon the hilt of his sword.

Jesu, Mary, and Joseph, his sword.

She saw then the blade was bloodied, and it came to her that he must have slain or gravely injured a Norman to have disguised himself by wearing a shirt of mail. One of Duncan's knights left to stand guard at the outskirts of the settlement? It might be so; a few of Duncan's men-at-arms possessed armor, but most wore hauberks made of thick leather—

"Now, Maire, we must go!"

Startled into motion, she took his outstretched hand, the rain blowing so fiercely through the door that it stung her face no matter her hood.

Ronan wore a mailed hood, too, a good thing given his wild black mane; he appeared as much a Norman knight as any other except that the Irish sword he bore was slightly smaller and lighter than the heavier weapon Duncan wore at his belt.

Swallowing hard at the thought that such deadly swords might meet, Maire did her best to hurry as she and Ronan plunged out into the storm and his strength aided her, his grip on her hand powerful and sure. So grateful it had grown dark, she still kept her head down and did her best, too, to walk as steadily as she could, fearing at any moment someone might recognize her by the light of the scattered torches hissing and sputtering in the driving rain.

"Niall and the others await us in the field, with horses," came Ronan's low, urgent voice to spur her along. "We've only to clear that mill ahead."

Niall was near, too? A sudden crack of thunder made Maire jump, her nerves raw as she followed Ronan's gaze to the edge of the settlement, where he must have come upon the hapless knight. Guessing that he must have been hiding in that same field and seen everything when Duncan carried her into the tenant's house, she couldn't imagine how else Ronan could have found her.

That her brothers had been so close all along—saints help her. If that guard hadn't spied Ronan and her clansmen riding to the south, Duncan would have been with her, aye, they'd have been sharing a meal . . . or sharing a bed when Ronan—

She couldn't finish the thought, tears biting her eyes as much from unbearable heartache as panic that Ronan had suddenly seemed to tense beside her. She gasped when three men-at-arms came at them as if from nowhere and yet ran right past, mud and water splattering Maire in their haste. Her heart plummeted when one shouted into the night, his voice filled with alarm.

"Lord FitzWilliam, a man is down! By the mill!"

"Damn the spawn!"

At Ronan's curse, Maire had never felt so stricken, fright making her limbs feel weak beneath her. As if sensing that she was close to collapse, Ronan swept her into his arms and began to run with her past a last dwelling-house, his sharp whistle cutting the night, a signal she recognized at once for Niall.

Already she could hear more shouts behind them, but it was nothing to the vehement command that rang out from a Norman who had suddenly stepped from the dwelling-house to block their way.

"Hold there—God's blood!"

Maire cried out as she was set upon her feet so abruptly that she crumpled to her knees while Ronan pulled his sword from his belt to swing violently at his opponent. Horror filled her as she recognized Gerard de Barry, the knight dodging Ronan's blow within an instant of losing his life and drawing his own sword, the dreaded ring of weapon striking weapon piercing straight into Maire's heart.

Yet nothing could have startled her more

completely than Adele's bloodcurdling scream as the woman appeared at the open doorway, and Maire knew then that she and Ronan were lost. As if caught in a slow-moving nightmare, she glanced over her shoulder to see men running toward them brandishing torches and weapons while the frantic neighing of a horse suddenly drew her stricken gaze back to the life-and-death battle raging between Ronan and Gerard.

She could not believe her eyes to see that Niall had ridden wildly out of the darkness, and he steered his mount straight for Gerard and nearly ran him down. Only the knight's throwing himself into the mud and rolling out of the way spared him from the thrashing hooves, while Adele's frantic scream once more shattered the night.

"Maire, come on!"

She felt Ronan hauling her to her feet, but her eyes flew past him to where Gerard struggled to rise, his enraged roar striking her like a blow.

"Damn you, Black O'Byrne, you will die!"

And Maire knew he would, Duncan's men almost upon them, so many Ronan and Niall together would not be able to fight them off. So many even the rest of the O'Byrnes hiding in the dark would not be enough. With all her strength, she wrenched herself free of Ronan's arms and shoved him desperately toward Niall's horse.

"Go, Ronan! There's no time. Save yourself and Niall—please, Ronan, go!"

She'd never seen his face so ravaged, but as if he knew to do otherwise would bring certain death, he turned and vaulted onto the horse's back behind Niall, who veered the wild-eyed animal around and kicked him into a hard gallop.

"That's the man I saw riding from the meadow, I swear it!" Adele cried out, even as Gerard roared and cursed that they were getting away. Then he turned his eyes upon Maire, all of his rage directed straight at her as he came toward her, limping, and struck her so violently across the face that she was knocked to the ground.

"By the blood of God!"

Her ears ringing, as if from a great distance she'd heard Duncan's voice, then Gerard's once more as the knight shouted out fierce commands.

"Crossbowmen! Take position and cut them down—did you hear me? Cut the bastards down!"

"No . . . no, they're my brothers . . . please, no." Maire tried to raise herself from the mud but she could not. Dizziness overwhelming her, the side of her face had begun to throb. As distantly, she felt hands upon her and someone lifting her, but she could not see for the darkness swallowing her like a shroud.

Nor did she fight it, but surrendered with a broken sigh, an angry heartbeat pounding against her ear.

"Damn you, Gerard." His vehement whisper heard by no one but himself, Duncan sat beside the bed and stared down at the woman he felt he no longer knew.

She still hadn't stirred, not even when he'd

stripped her out of her wet, muddy clothing and tugged the sleeping gown over her head, then covered her to her chin with warm blankets while Gerard and Adele waited impatiently for him in the adjoining room.

They awaited him still. Duncan was not ready yet to speak to Gerard, and especially not to Adele. They'd followed him to the dwelling-house like hounds after a scent, and only his shouting orders to his men to prepare themselves for any sign of battle forced them to keep silent.

He knew full well what they wished to say. His throat tight, he lightly touched the ugly purple bruise marring Rose's cheek, and then drew his hand away.

Not Rose.

Maire. Or so Adele had claimed the rebel Black O'Byrne had called her. A great hollow ache twisting inside his gut, he didn't want to believe it was true. God's teeth, that it was not! But he had heard himself words as he'd knelt in the mud beside the woman he loved that cut him still.

No, they're my brothers . . . please, no.

Damn him for a fool, how could he not have guessed? Dropping his head to his hands, Duncan thrust his fingers into his hair and stared blindly at the dirt floor as events from the last week ran over and over through his mind.

That she'd been so frightened of him—more than any daughter of a chieftain loyal to King John would have been, no matter her clansmen had been slain.

By the blood of God, she no doubt had

remembered every terrible moment of the attack but had lied to him all along . . . lied to him about everything, her name, that she could summon no memory of her family, her home. Yet given the damning secret she bore, what else could the woman have done?

Duncan swore and thrust himself from the chair; restlessly, he began to pace a bedchamber that had grown too small to contain the emotion raging inside him. Not yet ready to face Gerard and Adele, he was grateful that the door was bolted against them.

Maire O'Byrne . . . the sister of one of the most hated rebels in Leinster. How many times had he said Black O'Byrne's name in front of her? And all the while she had known, lying to him and carrying out her ruse so skillfully that he'd even taken her to Dublin in hopes of finding her clan.

That thought made Duncan stop to stare at her lying so pale and still in the bed, his heart thundering as hard as when he'd gathered her up from the mud.

So she had tried to escape that day in the woods, wanting him to think she had drowned in the bog, his suspicion aroused then though he hadn't heeded it. And the night Adele had attempted to aid her in leaving Longford Castle—even his half sister had been played for a fool!

Yet what again, of that night in Dublin when Rose—God help him, Maire, had cried out she couldn't marry him? Now he could see that much had been the truth . . . but everything else was lies, her agreement that she would stand by him if her clansmen came to claim her, her sworn promise tonight that she wouldn't leave the dwelling-house, and he'd said he loved her—*loved her*!

Sickened, Duncan could almost not bear to look at her, for the realization that she must have been waiting for the chance to leave him all along. It was enough to make him storm from the bedchamber; he wasn't surprised when he drew the bolt and threw open the door that Adele and Gerard were waiting just outside.

"Is she awake?"

Adele's query more a demand, Duncan ignored her and brushed past both of them, but Gerard angrily caught him by the arm.

"Dammit, Duncan, we should tie the wench to a post this very night and threaten to cut her throat if Black O'Byrne doesn't give himself up. That will draw the bastard—"

"And if it doesn't?" Duncan bit off, angered and sickened as much that Gerard could have struck Maire although he knew two long years of frustrated hatred had incited him. Even now his knight's eyes were fierce with loathing, his face twisted. Duncan decided then to post guards as much to prevent Maire from trying to escape again as to protect her from Gerard. "Ease yourself, man, as well you can. There'll be nothing done this night except to watch for an attack."

He wrenched his arm free, but Gerard followed him, still limping upon a twisted ankle, and close on his knight's heels came Adele.

"Nothing done, Duncan?" she said so shrilly as to make him clench his teeth. "You've the sister of the man who murdered Robert de Barry in that room, one of your men-at-arms slain by his hand as well, and you say you'll do nothing?"

"Not this night." His voice grim, Duncan didn't turn around until he came to the outer door, and then he gestured sharply that they both leave the dwelling-house. "There will be time enough to decide the best course—and I've the O'Melaghlins to release to their clansmen first—"

"At a rebel's behest?" His expression incredulous, Gerard stared at him as if he'd gone mad. "The woman tricked you, Duncan, lied to you these past days, and still you would honor—"

"Yes, I will honor it because I want peace in West Meath and not slaughter! That much at least hasn't ceased to make sense, no matter her clan. Now go, both of you. We will talk of this tomorrow."

"So we *will* talk of it," came Gerard's terse reply as he brushed stiffly past Duncan, while Adele hurried after him out the door. Yet she stopped to pull the hood of her cloak over her hair even though the rain had dwindled to a light drizzle, her eyes sweeping Duncan with open disgust.

"See what your compassion and misguided sense of chivalry has brought you? That Irish bitch reasoned you for a fool from the very first—"

"Damn you, woman, go!"

His vehemence making Adele blanch, she spun on her heel and hurried away, half-running to catch up with Gerard while Duncan slammed the door shut with such fury that the wall shook. Yet he told himself fiercely as he strode to the hearth that he should have left the dwelling-house as well. God's teeth, why did he linger? One glance into the bedchamber made it clear Maire still lay as if dead . . .

His gut clenching, Duncan went to her side, reasoning to himself that it was only her value to him now as a prisoner that made him want to check upon her, though he knew it was as broad a lie as any he'd been told. She breathed slowly and steadily, some sound color returning to her face, and he suspected then it wouldn't be long before she opened her eyes.

He sensed, too, what she might say, her first concern no doubt for her brothers, which cut him deeply. Not that she had lied to him. Not that she had surrendered her body to him only as a means to gain some time until she could leave him—ah, God, so much deceit!

She must have known all along that the arrow which had struck the rogue Norman had come from her brother's bow. It was no wonder she'd held such concern for the O'Melaghlins, convincing him so easily to release them . . . a way to free herself as well from Longford Castle so she might have a greater chance of escape—

"Duncan . . ."

His heart lurched, and he cursed under his breath that one ragged whisper could so affect him as Maire tossed her head upon the pillow.

"Duncan, please . . . I love you . . ."

He stared at her, frozen, feeling as if time itself had stopped around him while she fell still and silent once more.

Yet somehow a moment later, he made himself move, scarcely realizing he was outside the dwelling-house until cold drizzle stung him in the face. Only then did he tell himself fiercely that those words had been a lie like everything else.

By the blood of God, a lie! Pulling his mailed hood over his head, he went to join his men.

Chapter 30

Maire shivered at the many eyes boring into her back and clutched the reins as bravely as she could, no matter her fingers trembled. And it wasn't so much the chill wind making them shake, the sky as dark and threatening that morning as the day before though it hadn't yet rained.

Saints help her, it was the ill will directed at her; she'd become the enemy now. An O'Byrne. She didn't have to look to the left or right to know that the four guards flanking her would be as grim-faced and silent as any ordered to escort a prisoner. She didn't have to see Gerard de Barry or Adele glance back at her to know that hatred filled their eyes.

Maire swallowed hard against the tears threatening to fall, her clouded gaze fixed upon Duncan riding ahead at the front of his men.

Aye, that was the worst of all. As far as she could tell, he hadn't looked at her once since she'd been brought forth from the dwelling-house by the same guards who accompanied her now. It was just as she'd feared if he ever learned the truth. He clearly hated her, too. Her anguish reached so deep and was so complete, that she could not imagine ever feeling otherwise again.

She'd awoken deep in the night to find herself alone in the bed, horror once more filling her as she wondered if Ronan and Niall had escaped with their lives. The last thing she remembered was Gerard shouting for crossbowmen to cut them down, and she'd risen shakily, her thoughts still so dazed she had imagined she might find Duncan in the next room so she might ask him about her brothers.

Instead, she had found two guards warming themselves around the central hearth and another two standing watch at the outer door, the men turning to stare at her just as she stared at them.

Cold realization had struck her then. Duncan was nowhere in sight. A harsh command by one of the guards that she shut the door and return to bed had told her, too, that everything had changed. He had allowed only that her brothers had escaped into the night, and she asked no more, the angry curses rumbling among the men enough alone to make her retreat back to the bed.

Maire turned her gaze to the distant countryside shrouded by deep mist, wondering if Ronan and Niall still were near. She sensed they were, but what could they do to help her now?

Everything had grown worse, so much worse that sleep had been an impossibility during those long tortuous hours before a guard had pounded upon the door and told her to dress. In clothing still wet from last night's rain, she shivered again, almost relieved to see the stark outline of a walled fortress looming ahead for the shelter it would offer from the gusting wind.

But what shelter lay ahead for her? A dungeon? She forced away fresh tears, willing herself not to cry. That would not help her either. Nor would reliving futilely those moments when she and Ronan had seemed so close to escaping the settlement, so close but for Gerard de Barry—

"You wretched Irish bitch. I should thank you for sparing me having to find some way to be rid of you—a task you've accomplished quite delightfully on your own."

Rid of her? Maire stared into Adele's cold blue eyes, her heart pounding and her hands growing clammy as much that the ruthless woman had fallen back to ride alongside her as at what she'd just said. Jesu, Mary, and Joseph, did Adele know of Duncan's plans for her? Mayhap that he intended to drag her to the dungeon as soon as they arrived at the castle and then leave her there to rot?

"I think the reward Duncan will win when he captures and hangs your rebel brothers will more than make a suitable wedding gift for the Norman bride I intend to help him find, don't you?"

Adele spurred her lively dappled gray forward before Maire could summon a reply, even though she truly had none. To hear what Adele had said of her brothers was horrible enough. But to think of Duncan taking another for his wife made Maire's throat constrict so painfully she doubted she could have spoken. Had he already said that he planned to do so to Adele? Could love voiced so fiercely last night have disappeared altogether? Ah, God, she was such a fool!

She could not count the lies she had told him, and even without that there was the deep-seated malice he bore toward Ronan. That she'd come so close the other day to revealing the truth about her clan made her believe now she must be mad to have hoped the barriers between them could be conquered. She had no hope left!

"Bring the prisoner forward!"

Maire paled, her gaze flying to the three O'Melaghlins before she realized with a start when one of the guards grabbed the reins from her hand that the outcry had been meant for her.

Her heart leaping to her throat, she saw that Duncan conferred ahead with a cluster of his knights near the gatehouse, where a drawbridge was being lowered. Her approach scarcely drew a glance from him. Only when the same guard yanked her mount to a stop not far from Duncan's did he finally meet her eyes, his expression so hard, so cold that she knew then he must truly hate her. Though he spoke to the man still holding the reins, his intense gaze never left her face.

"Escort her into the keep—my private quarters. See that she remains well guarded."

"Yes, my lord."

"Tell Edward de Valognes that he remains in command until I return—"

"God's breath, Baron, you've barely arrived and now you leave us?"

Maire's gaze flew to the swarthy knight who'd called down to them from the top of the gatehouse, and she saw then that a host of men-at-arms lined the battlements. Astonished anew at the numbers Duncan commanded, she started when his grim voice broke the silence.

"I've a matter of peace to discuss with the O'Melaghlin—but enough, man, I trust Lady de Londres will tell you all."

Adele's sharp intake of breath made Maire twist round in the saddle, the woman glancing in disbelief from Gerard to Duncan.

"But . . . but I thought I was to accompany you—"

"Only this far. Ennell Castle isn't as grand as Longford, but you'll find your needs ably met."

With that Duncan sharply veered his horse around while Adele could but sputter, Maire struck by a fresh stab that he hadn't spared her a further glance. Yet the O'Melaghlins—Finian, Innis, and Tynan . . . clearly Duncan still meant to release them.

Warmed no matter how indifferently he'd treated her, she felt a glimmer of hope flaring in her heart. All might not be lost. And he'd said to take her to his private quarters, nothing about a dungeon—

"Damn you, wench, you may think you've won some reprieve, but you haven't—do you hear me?"

Stricken, Maire met Gerard's burning eyes as he purposely walked his mount past hers, his face darkened with fury.

"I'll have Black O'Byrne dead at the end of my

sword before we leave this place, I swear it, and you're going to bring him to me!"

Gerard kicked his horse into a gallop and joined the rest of Duncan's men thundering away from the castle, while Maire could but stare after him, blood roaring in her ears. She was almost grateful when the guard yanked her mount once more into motion, anything to spare her from Adele's hateful gaze as well.

Any hope she'd felt so fleetingly all but dead, she knew nothing now but desperation as she thought of Ronan out there watching them, of Duncan mayhap riding into his path—Jesu help her, of Gerard's threat!—and her gaze fell to the moat as they passed over the drawbridge.

It was empty, no more than a muddy ditch.

"Aye, lord, that's the same castle—repairs made, the walls fortified, but the same."

Flann O'Faelin flat on his belly beside him, Niall on his left, Ronan's jaw clenched as Maire disappeared into the gatehouse, one Norman leading her mount by the reins while three others followed. Then went the blond woman who'd shrieked like a wild banshee last night and brought the baron's men down upon him, while the bastard he'd fought rode after Duncan FitzWilliam—by God, if only he had more clansmen with him, he'd attack now!

"Aye, almost two years ago, lord, we came by here, and you struck a man down if I recall."

"Because he raised his weapon like a damned fool and tried to spear you in the back, Flann O'Faelin. What the devil else was I to do?"

Ronan got no answer but a grunt, while Niall remained grimly silent. It was better than listening further to his younger brother blame himself about Maire. Aye, he knew all about such guilt. But a brazen, flame-haired hoyden had saved him from his own. An ache rose inside him at the days spent without seeing Triona and little Deirdre. How many more would pass now that his attempt to rescue Maire had failed?

"I'm wondering if the man you slew has anything to do with the baron," came Flann's low voice. "You said the spawn you fought recognized you, knew your name. Did he seem familiar to you?"

Ronan shook his head; he remembered more the corpses rotting in the dungeon than any of the Normans he'd made to lie facedown upon the floor while his clansmen went through the castle looking for anything of value. Yet God help him, what did any of that matter? Maire was in grave danger . . . though his gut told him that she hadn't been before.

There had been no guards posted outside the dwelling-house, and none inside, only Maire dressed and heading to the door to his surprise as if to flee. He wished they'd had time to speak, but wishing was a futile business to the circumstances they faced now. The bastards knew Maire was an O'Byrne, though he suspected that they hadn't before. Just as he'd hoped, she must have managed some ruse—

"Good God, Ronan, what are we to do? If only a section of the wall was down like before—"

"Aye, we clambered over the rubble like

goats," Flann interrupted Niall, who cursed in frustration. "The wall had been battered down thanks to King John and his army come to destroy their own kind."

"But we've no battering ram, Flann, so why even speak of it?" Niall slammed a clenched fist into the ground. "And this time the castle is overrun with Normans, not like the few we came upon two years past."

"So we watch and wait, just as before." Ronan glanced from Flann to Niall. "If Maire was attempting to flee last night, she might very well try again."

"Last night she had a chance, Ronan—no high walls to frustrate her, and you said she had no guards to prevent it. The devil take them, it's different now!"

Ronan could but stare at Niall in silent agreement. His gut tightened at the realization that the Normans might decide to threaten Maire's life as a means to capture him.

It was becoming clearer all the time that she must have fooled the spawn since she'd been abducted; the memory plagued him still of Maire outside Longford Castle throwing her arms around Duncan FitzWilliam's neck. And then last night . . . when he'd watched the baron kiss her before carrying her into the dwelling-house—by God, why was he tormenting himself? No matter to what drastic lengths Maire must have gone, all was changed, just as Niall had said.

"Aye, we watch and wait," Ronan repeated more to himself, adding under his breath like a fervent prayer, "and get as close to the castle as we can. If Maire tries again to escape, we must be ready . . ."

He said no more, already on his feet. Niall and Flann glanced at each other and then shoved themselves from the ground to follow after him.

Chapter 31

"God's breath, Duncan, the O'Melaghlins are freed, your blessed peace achieved! It's time we speak of Black O'Byrne and what's to be done with the wench—I'll wait no longer!"

Scowling, Duncan spun around at the entrance to the keep to face Gerard, having borne all that he would stomach from his knight. "*My* blessed peace? Dammit, man, the accord struck today affects all within the barony, not only me! If you weren't so consumed by the other, you might see it as well."

"So consumed?" Gerard's voice had grown quiet, almost emotionless, his eyes riveted to Duncan's face. "I thought we shared a like intent, you and I, to avenge Robert's murder. But perhaps now that has changed—"

"Nothing's changed. I wish Black O'Byrne dead as much as you." Duncan scowled even more deeply as thunder rumbled across the darkening sky, dusk falling like a heavy veil. "Enough. You see little else can be done with this day, and another storm comes."

"Let it howl and bluster! Did that keep the bastard from slaying one of your own men last night?"

Duncan didn't answer, sensing what Gerard planned to say next even as his knight's voice grew harsher.

"It's not so late we cannot act, Duncan. Give the wench over to me, and we'll see how quickly Black O'Byrne runs to save her—"

"By the blood of God, man, enough! The woman remains in my quarters until I've decided the best course—didn't I say as much last night?"

Duncan turned and strode into the keep before Gerard could answer. Knowing that his knight's furious eyes burned into his back stoked his own mounting anger. And he felt it no more acutely than his fury at himself.

Why was he delaying a decision? Tonight, tomorrow morning. A few hours would not alter the fact that the woman who awaited his judgment even now had deceived him as surely as her brothers and clansmen watched Ennell Castle. He had felt their eyes fixed upon him, too, as he approached the fortress, though he'd seen no sign of them.

His tension growing, Duncan ignored servants and his men alike as he navigated the rabbits' warren of lamplit stairways that ran between floors. Longford Castle's design was much more to his liking than this towering square keep. The place was like a maze, and he almost wished the fire set within the great hall on the uppermost floor by Walter de Lacy's men had gutted the castle so he might have had good reason to tear it down and start anew.

According to the villagers a violent thunderstorm within the bailey had doused the blaze, but nothing had saved the outbuildings, constructed entirely of wood. Yet those, too, had been rebuilt, the great hall, the roof of the keep, and the curtain wall repaired where King John's forces had broken through . . .

Duncan swore under his breath; Black O'Byrne and his men a few weeks later had gained entrance at that same point and within moments, Robert de Barry lay dead. *That* was what he should be thinking of. His anger grew so fierce that as he took the narrow steps spiraling up the tower to his private quarters three at a time, his heart began to pound.

Two guards flanked the entrance when he reached the landing, but his thunderous glance sent them into retreat down the way he'd come while Duncan considered kicking down the door. Gone was the eagerness he'd always known before, in its place as much raw pain and fury as the countless lies he had believed ran through his mind. Somehow he made himself thrust open the door, still with so much force that it slammed against the wall.

He wasn't surprised at the gasp that greeted him, Maire turning from the single window so suddenly that she nearly lost her balance and had to catch herself against a table. Her eyes were as wide and uncertain in the blazing firelight as he'd ever seen them. She stared at him even as he stared at her, neither speaking for what to Duncan seemed like endless moments.

He saw her swallow hard and it cut him that she must truly fear him now; he wondered if she thought he might strike her as Gerard had done. That she might believe him capable of such an act cut him even deeper, but what else was the woman to think at how he'd stormed into the room?

Stunned that his anger could be so easily tempered, Duncan steeled himself against her ashen pallor, steeled himself against impassioned memories that even now leapt into his mind, and shut the door hard behind him. She started, but lifted her chin not in defiance but as if bolstering her courage, her beautiful gray eyes not straying from his.

"Duncan, I—"

"Spare me any more lies, woman, there's little for us to say to each other. You are Maire O'Byrne, sister to the Wicklow rebel Black O'Byrne?"

She didn't readily answer, looking so stricken that once again, Duncan had to steel himself against the effect she had upon him. Just hearing his name upon her lips had been difficult enough—

"Aye, Ronan Black O'Byrne is my brother."

Her voice soft as a whisper, Duncan saw that she trembled, and he had to fight with all his will the sudden hunger to go to her and pull her into his arms. He saw, too, tears glistening in her eyes, one spilling down her bruised cheek stabbing him as deeply as any knife.

"Will you— Will you use me to hurt him?"

Duncan felt his throat grow tight, the anguish in her gaze, her words like a breathing, palpable thing between them. All that Gerard had suggested to draw out Black O'Byrne running through his mind, he knew in that moment he could do none of it, would do none of it—God help him, how could he allow any further harm to come to her after all she'd suffered? He loved her! Loved her still no matter the lies, the deceit. His overwhelming thought was how to protect her.

As much fresh pain as determination filling him, Duncan was not surprised that he thought, too, of Rory O'Melaghlin earlier that day reunited with his two grandsons and Finian, his harper, the proud old chieftain's face lit by such astonishment and gratitude Duncan couldn't help but be moved.

Maire had been right, no matter she'd suggested such a course as a means for her own escape. The O'Melaghlin had readily agreed to peace, even offering to join him in fighting against any rogue Normans before Duncan had even spoken of it, and vowing as well that no more cattle would be stolen from the baron of Longford's herds.

"Duncan . . . ?"

He met her eyes, her voice shaking, her face pale, and he spoke with a voice that sounded ragged to him as well. "No, woman, I'll not use you to hurt your brother. All you've done these past days, all you've said . . . I cannot blame you. You came to me against your will. It's only right that I release you."

A hush fell in the room, the only sound the logs crackling in the hearth, though Maire heard little but her heartbeat thundering in her ears.

Release her? Had Duncan truly said . . . ? Incredulous, she could but stare at him, her knees suddenly grown so weak she braced herself against the table for fear she might collapse.

He had burst into the room so furiously, she had thought the worst, aye, expected the worst, his dark eyes so filled with anger, his first words to her uttered in a voice so hard that her legs had nearly given way. She had spent tortuous hours agonizing over Gerard's threat and assuming that Duncan must surely agree with his knight. She had never imagined . . .

"Your brothers followed us here, I'm certain of it. Once you leave Ennell Castle and ride to the south, you'll not be long by yourself."

Duncan spoke as if a plan even now formed in his mind, while Maire could only nod, still dumbstruck. He'd said brothers as well, and she realized then that Duncan must have been the one to lift her from the ground after Gerard had struck her; he must have heard her pleading for both Ronan and Niall.

And he must have undressed her last night, too, Maire found herself thinking, as Duncan went to the bench in front of the hearth where she'd draped her cloak to dry.

Aye, changed her out of her wet clothing and into a sleeping gown and covered her with blankets—saints help her, why hadn't she considered that until now? Warmth flooded her when Duncan gathered up her cloak and came toward her; that he would assist her even in this small way made her tremble anew. Surely if he hated her, he wouldn't—

"Is it true, woman, that you've always loved wild roses?"

Maire met his eyes, drawing in her breath as much at his low query as that he stood so close to her to settle the cloak around her shoulders. "A-aye . . . the red ones best of all."

"Like those we saw at the ruins."

Slowly she nodded, her heart pounding, an emotion passing across his handsome face that she could not name.

"And you're fond of embroidery? You possess such skill, I thought you must be."

Maire could not speak for a moment as she searched his eyes, wondering that he would ask her such things but feeling relieved too, that she could finally share the truth.

"Aye, I did little else until I regained the use of my legs two years past—but mine is no match for your mother's, God rest her. I've never seen such fine needlework . . ."

Maire fell still at the sudden hard lump in her throat, such intense regret filling her that she'd never been able to speak so openly with him before. And he with her—Jesu, Mary, and Joseph, might he feel the same? Was that why he'd posed such questions? He seemed about to ask her something else, only to suddenly curse under his breath, his expression grown hard again.

"Come. It's time we go."

He began to move away, but Maire reached out before she even realized what she was doing and caught his arm. "Duncan, wait, I want you to know—" She faltered at the intensity in his eyes as he turned to face her but made herself rush on almost recklessly. "Your mother—she could only have been good and kind to have a son such as you. And she wasn't mad, couldn't have been mad to have made a thing so beautiful as that screen. Yet that you came by it given your half brothers—"

"They didn't steal everything from me. The needlework was secreted from the tower by a loyal servant, the screen fashioned at my mother's wish. She bade the woman to keep it safely hidden from those who might destroy it, and so the screen was, for years, until I sent for it after I won the barony. A gift to a son she swore upon her deathbed was as true a FitzWilliam as the love she'd borne for her husband—God's teeth, she might have named me a fool as well!"

Maire was startled that Duncan pulled away his arm and strode out onto the landing; his face had grown so grim that she doubted he wished to say anything more at all. Yet he watched her intently as she joined him, and she swore she saw emotion raging in his eyes that made her heart race all the harder . . . saints help her, pain so vivid that she knew then as surely as she breathed that he did not hate her.

"The steps are too many."

He said no more but swept her into his arms, Maire never more tempted to reveal what raged inside her. Yet after all that had happened, would he believe how much she loved him? And even if he did, Ronan, Niall, and the rest of her clansmen still waited outside the castle, the chasm separating her from Duncan as wide and terrible as before.

Tears bit her eyes as they descended the narrow stairway but she forced them away, telling herself, too, that just because Duncan was releasing her didn't mean his hatred for Ronan ran any less deep. And what of Gerard? What of Adele? Begorra, who was truly the fool? It was not to be! Ever since she'd seen the empty moat, she had prayed for nothing more than a way to escape the castle so she might protect Duncan, and now he was setting her free himself—

"Lord FitzWilliam!"

Maire felt Duncan tense as Edward de Valognes, the swarthy knight who'd appeared at the battlements that morning to shout down at them, came lunging up the steps.

"Rebels, my lord, we've sighted them moving toward the castle! I've crossbowmen positioned and ready to fire atop the towers, it's not too dark yet—"

"Dammit, man, I gave no such orders!"

Duncan's roar ringing in her ears, Maire found herself set abruptly upon her feet and left behind as he pushed past his knight, de Valognes glancing at her with some surprise before turning to rush after him. It seemed within an instant they were gone, the distant sound of a door slamming while Maire sank onto a step, stricken.

Crossbowmen were ready to fire? God help them, at Ronan? Niall? She started at a clap of thunder so violent that the tower around her seemed to quake, but it served to rouse her shakily to her feet and her gaze flew down the spiraling steps. Somehow she had to get to the tower battlements. Somehow . . .

She didn't think further but kept one hand pressed to the wall as she did her best to hurry, cursing that she couldn't move faster than what seemed a snail's pace when she so desperately wanted to fly. Her only comfort was that Duncan had clearly gone to amend the orders. She began to pray Ronan and Niall and her other O'Byrne clansmen would recognize their danger and retreat, that a violent downpour would send the crossbowmen running for cover, anything to avert disaster as she reached a landing and half stumbled through the door.

She was astonished to see a short passageway and another stairway leading downward, her desperation mounting because she knew the battlements lay upward. Yet there was no other route; surely Duncan had gone this way. She must have descended twenty steps when she came to another landing, Maire as breathless from exertion as confused by the long lamplit passageway that greeted her.

She could hear nothing, no commotion to guide her, yet she plunged ahead, tempted to call out for Duncan, to anyone to help her. The route to his quarters had seemed more straightforward, but she'd had the grim-faced guards then to lead the way.

She could do nothing but continue on, sensing with wretched certainty that she was lost even as she tested the nearest door, cracking it slightly. Relief swamped her when she heard someone speaking—

"I vow it, Gerard, my brothers would not fault you! That Duncan delays even now should tell you he no more intends to rid himself of that

Irish whore than he'll help you capture Black O'Byrne. He's betrayed you! He's dishonored his family. I say he should die!"

Chapter 32

Maire didn't move, couldn't move, her hand frozen to the latch as Adele's voice grew more venomous, more heated.

"Can you stomach the thought of Black O'Byrne's sister for Duncan's wife? The sister of the man who slaughtered your brother? It will happen unless something is done—you could go to his quarters now! You said you believed them together. And you must use your knife, Gerard, Duncan bears one as well. It will look as if she committed the deed, then you'll truly have her to do with as you like!"

Horrified, Maire backed away from the door, the sound of heavy footsteps moving toward her filling her with panic. Wildly she looked back the way she'd come—Jesu, Mary, and Joseph, would Gerard take that route? She must choose!

Maire lunged in the opposite direction, her heart thundering as she kept one hand braced against the wall so she wouldn't fall. She heard the door creaking open behind her, and pushed herself all the harder to reach the end of the passageway—Jesu help her!

She nearly fell in her haste to duck around the corner. Adele's low voice carried to her as Maire stood with her back pressed to the wall and fought to catch her breath.

"I'll wait for you here, my love. Think of it! Black O'Byrne will be slain this very night—Robert's death finally avenged. You must not fail!"

Sickened, Maire didn't wait to hear Gerard's vehement reply but hastened as quietly and quickly as she could through an archway and down a short dark passage. Her hands shook so badly when she reached an opposite door that she could barely lift the latch. Yet she had only to think Gerard might be close behind her and she made her fingers obey, her fear tempering her astonishment when she entered a vast room ablaze with torchlight that was clearly the great hall.

Servants were rushing to arrange long trestle tables and benches for the evening meal, and Maire called out to a kindly-looking Irishwoman near her; she wasn't surprised her voice was all but hoarse.

"Please . . . I must find Lord FitzWilliam. He's gone to the tower battlements—you must take me there!"

At the woman's nod, Maire had never known such overwhelming relief as she followed her from the great hall, ignoring curious glances thrown their way. Yet her heart sank moments later when she was faced with more spiral steps, and she feared then she would never make it to the battlements in time. Even now Duncan might be returning to where he'd left her while Gerard was headed there too—

"Miss, would you have me go after him? The climb might be too much for you—if you don't mind me saying so."

"Aye, please! Tell him I'm waiting here—oh, please, you must hurry!"

The Irishwoman didn't linger, Maire feeling an aching heaviness in her legs even as she wished desperately it was *her* climbing the tower. Only when the servingwoman had disappeared did it strike her that Duncan might not believe what she'd heard from Adele, and she sank in anguish onto a step.

"God's teeth, she's where?"

"Outside the great hall, lord, aye, and pale as can be. I came to find you as quickly as I could."

The servingwoman having shouted to be heard above the rumbling thunder, Duncan didn't wait for her to say more. With a last glance at the darkening countryside, a burst of lightning illuminating the distant line of ancient oak and birch where he sensed in his gut that the O'Byrnes had taken refuge, he brushed past Edward de Valognes, who squinted against the stinging drizzle.

"If the rebels venture closer, Baron—"

"Do nothing, not unless I tell you!"

That the strapping knight looked at him with as much puzzlement as when Duncan had roared for the crossbowmen to stand away from the battlements only made him curse under his breath; he had no time or inclination to explain things further. He ducked into the tower and charged down the steps, his mind racing that Maire hadn't waited for him where he'd left her.

He could only guess that she must have attempted to follow him, and his gut tightened that she held such concern for her brothers. By the blood of God, he would settle for half as much for himself, a quarter!

Yet he'd heard no protests when he'd said he would release her, no apologies, no explanations, the realization striking him like an ice-cold blade at how eager she must be to leave Ennell Castle. To leave him. Was there any greater fool that he still hoped some small word from her might alter the lies and deceit that had gone before?

That he'd asked her of the roses, of her embroidery, proved he was only deceiving himself as well. He'd longed for nothing more than to ask her a thousand questions, to sit down with her and talk and learn all there was to know of Maire O'Byrne and never let her go—God help him, why could he not stop tormenting himself?

His gut clenched all the harder when he spied her sitting upon the step with her back to him, her head resting almost forlornly against the wall. Yet she must have heard him coming; she twisted around, her face as ashen as the servingwoman had claimed, her lovely eyes stricken just to see him. Wondering if she feared he had changed his mind about releasing her, he took almost perverse comfort that he could arouse some emotion within her though not the one he so hungered for.

"Duncan, we must speak!"

He reached her in time to help her rise, struck

as much that she sounded so alarmed as that he could feel her trembling. But he didn't wish to speak—he wanted this wretched torment at an end! He swept her from her feet no matter she gasped in surprise, and then attempted the impossible task of not thinking that he would hold her no more after this night as he continued down the tower steps.

"Duncan, please—"

"Your accursed brothers are safe, woman, no arrows unleashed upon them. Save your words for your fond reunion."

"But Duncan—"

"Enough! Did you not hear me before? We've nothing further to speak of, you and I—nothing! I'm releasing you to your clansmen, that alone should suffice."

She had blanched, which cut him. The lithe weight of her cut him. That she was so incredibly beautiful cut him. That he would never again know the taste of her lips or feel her touch tore at him so unbearably he almost groaned aloud. Grateful the steps in this tower were as straightforward as any in the other three, he reached the bottom floor in what seemed no more than a moment's time and strode through the narrow forebuilding toward the entrance to the keep.

"Duncan, you must hear me."

She'd spoken so softly, her voice pleading with him, but he ignored her still and stepped outside into what had become a steady downpour, the bailey dark now but for scattered torches guttering and hissing. It was a short stride to the stable, and he set her down more roughly than he should have beneath the eaves of the low building while he went inside to saddle a mount.

Men-at-arms who'd sought refuge from the storm turned to stare at him, and Duncan waved away the assistance of two young stableboys who came running. He was so angry now, so wretchedly hopeless that he needed something to do, anything to keep from exploding, the emotion raging inside him had grown so fierce.

As if reading his temper, none said a word, the stable silent but for the low nickering of horses and the sharp whinny of the dun gelding he saddled for Maire. It seemed the Wicklow O'Byrnes would gain a prize animal tonight, too, for he knew he wanted a strong mount beneath her. He led the gelding from the stall, not surprised to see that Maire stood at the stable door, watching him.

Yet when he drew closer, she glanced with apprehension over her shoulder and he wondered suddenly what she might fear. Adele? Gerard? He cursed under his breath, imagining what they would have to say of his decision—by the devil, he had no time to think of them now!

"Duncan, if you'd only listen to me," came Maire's plea again as she met his eyes while he gestured sharply for her to step closer. "I must tell you something . . . of Adele and—"

"I know, woman, they'll not be pleased." He cut her off, his hands encircling her waist to lift her onto the sidesaddle.

She was wet and shaking, her teeth chattering, and he felt such an urge to seize her against him, to warm the chill from her body one last time that it was all he could do to release her. Somehow he did, forcing himself not to look at her further but focusing instead on leading her mount the short distance to the torchlit gatehouse as he wiped cold rain from his eyes.

"No, no, it's far worse! You must hear me!"

He said nothing, steeling himself against the urgent timbre of her voice even as he signaled for guards to lower the drawbridge, the loud creaking stabbing at the very heart of him.

"Duncan, they plot against you! I knew you might not believe me, but you must know—aye, Gerard intends to kill you!"

Duncan stopped cold, such fury filling him that she would concoct an incredible lie as he prepared to release her, he didn't trust himself to speak or to face her.

"I overheard them, Duncan, while I was trying to find my way to the battlements. Adele told Gerard to use his knife against you—that it would appear as if I'd been the one to slay you since you bear a knife, too, and then he could finally use me to capture my brother—"

"By the blood of God, woman, will you not cease? Enough!"

His roar echoing about the bailey, Duncan had rounded upon her but she shook her head, her expression as stricken as determined in the torchlight.

"No, Duncan, it's not enough, not until you hear all! Gerard lied to you about the O'Melaghlins, didn't he? He lives to avenge his brother, aye, his hatred has become his blood and breath and he thought you stood with him. But now he believes you've betrayed him—Adele said as much! Can you not see that he might turn his hatred upon you?"

Duncan didn't answer, couldn't answer, his grip so tight upon the gelding's bridle that it hurt. Somehow he made himself turn around even as a ragged sigh came from Maire—she must know he gave no weight at all to her words. How could he?

He didn't stop again until they reached the lowered drawbridge, the downpour become so heavy, pounding against the wood, that it sounded like a roar in his ears. Nor did he hear the enraged shout behind him; only Maire grabbing wildly to catch his hand as he released the bridle made him glance over his shoulder to see Gerard running through the mud toward them.

He felt it then, a niggling of instinct suddenly burning like fire in his gut, while Maire made as if to dismount from her horse. Cursing, he pushed her back into the saddle and he saw then, too, that she was sobbing in terror, her fingers ice-cold as they frantically clutched his.

"Duncan, draw your sword! Saints help you, he'll kill you and I love you too much—too much!"

He didn't heed her, no longer hearing the rain for the wild thundering of his heart as he shoved the reins into her hands and slapped the gelding's rump, his only thought to protect the woman he loved as fiercely. He caught a last glimpse of her face and then she was gone, horse and rider galloping into the darkness while

Duncan spun around to meet the opponent who was already upon him.

"It's Maire, Ronan, I would swear it!"

He had already spurred his horse from the cover of the trees before Niall had shouted to him, that no men-at-arms lined the battlements of the fortress convincing him further that something he'd never expected was taking place. Rain lashing at his face, he rode as hard as he could remember, incredulous to see, too, that Maire had reined in her mount not far from the castle and appeared to be turning around. Cursing, Ronan drove his heels into his stallion's heaving sides.

"By God, Maire, stay your ground. Stay your ground!"

He knew she couldn't have heard him above a deafening crash of thunder, and he made no attempt to shout again but rode all the harder, Maire's mount suddenly rearing as lightning burst across the sky. If not for that he doubted he would have caught her; she'd already ridden halfway back toward the castle.

So close to the towering battlements now that he knew he was a fair target for any crossbowmen, Ronan reached out and grabbed the gelding's bridle to steady him, but he saw at once that Maire was another matter. A blinding flash of lightning showed her face twisted with such anguish, fierce sobs shaking her, that he knew then much was not as it seemed this night.

"Help him, Ronan, please help him!"

He followed her gaze to the fortress and the fight raging on the drawbridge, heavy sword ringing against sword, Ronan's gut instincts screaming for him to do no more than grab Maire from her horse and ride back to Glenmalure as if the spawn of Satan himself were at their heels. Yet her agonized cry when one of the Normans crumpled to his knees cut him to the quick. Maire frantically slid from the saddle to attempt as best she could, slipping and stumbling, to run toward the castle.

"Saints help him, no! Ronan, please, I love him! I've never asked you for anything before!"

An arrow was flying through the air before she'd collapsed to weep helplessly. Ronan cursed under his breath as the missile found its mark, the second Norman pitching sideways into the empty moat. Dead, aye, he was certain of it, the very man he'd fought the night before, and he vehemently hoped the same for the baron of Longford who lay still upon the drawbridge. As shouts coming from the castle filled the night, Ronan had no chance to dismount before Niall reined in beside him and jumped from his horse to gather Maire into his arms.

"Please, I want to go to him! Let me go to him—ah, God, Duncan!"

Niall said nothing to her frenzied cries and Ronan couldn't, wishing to think no further of what had transpired these past days, his throat as tight as his grip on the reins. To hear her speak of loving a Norman . . .

"Lord, we must ride! Look!"

Flann O'Faelin's urgent voice spurred Ronan as much as the commotion raging on the drawbridge, and already Niall bore Maire back to his horse. Her desperate cries silenced, she still wept disconsolately but even to that Ronan closed his heart and his ears. He scarcely waited until Niall was mounted, Maire slumped in his arms, before he kicked his steed into a gallop.

"To Glenmalure, all of you, home!"

Chapter 33

"Does she speak?"

Triona closed the door quietly to Maire's bedchamber and gave Ronan a small nod, the story that had poured forth brokenly after two days of poignant silence as heartrending as any she'd known. Yet she doubted that Ronan would wish to hear it. Even now his countenance was black, and he'd looked no different since he had returned with Maire to Glenmalure.

It pained Triona so deeply that she'd failed to cheer him. Their little daughter Deirdre didn't understand in the least why her beloved papa would not smile. Triona sighed as Ronan lunged from a chair and went to stand before the central hearth, his broad back to her; she didn't attempt to go near him. It seemed he would have to reconcile his anger on his own, aye, she'd judged well that Ronan was furious with Maire.

And that made her angry, too, for poor Maire's sake. Jesu, Mary, and Joseph, as if anyone could govern the path of love! Had she imagined Ronan Black O'Byrne would one day become her husband when he'd answered her godfather's deathbed summons and come to the glen of Imaal? Oh, aye, that's why she'd aimed her bow at him and threatened to skewer him with arrows!

Triona sighed again, telling herself to mind her temper as well as her tongue though she wanted so badly to do otherwise. And there was another matter that must be attended to, so sad and wretched a task she hoped Ronan would help her to break the unhappy news to Niall. It was no wonder Maire had wanted to wait until they were home in Glenmalure before she revealed Caitlin MacMurrough's change of heart.

"By God, Triona, tell me it was all a ruse. Tell me Maire wasn't in love with that Norman spawn!"

Ronan's voice filled with as much raw anguish of his own as anger, Triona waited silently until he had turned to look at her before she spoke.

"The truth will be harsh to you—"

"I will hear it!"

Triona's heart went out to him at the pain in his eyes, but she'd seen far worse in Maire's. "It began as a ruse—all done to protect you, to protect Niall and the rest of our clan. But aye, Ronan, she fell in love with the baron, and it's a fortunate thing she came upon him and no other Norman lord."

"Fortunate? That she lies in there now, mayhap never to be the same for her misguided grief? Mayhap his vile seed growing in her belly?"

"Begorra, Ronan, if she does bear a babe

mayhap it will bring some comfort to her! She fears Lord FitzWilliam is dead—"

"He is dead! As dead to her as any accursed Norman would be whether he lives yet or not!"

Triona winced that he would shout so vehemently, and she knew Maire must have heard him. But she couldn't go to her now, determined that Ronan would hear the full story even as he stormed from the dwelling-house. It might do no good, but at least he would know it.

He would know what an honorable man Duncan FitzWilliam had proved to be, as honorable in his own right as Ronan, both of them holding to their convictions so fiercely and being in that sense, so very much alike. Oh, aye, she could just hear what Ronan would have to say about that comparison!

And there was Niall, too, the day truly promising to be a bleak one. Doing her best to bolster her spirits, she ran out the door after Ronan, her coppery curls flying. Yet even allowing herself a muttered curse failed to ease her.

"Maire, do you hear me?"

She blinked open her eyes, the oil lamp guttering beside her bed the only thing she saw, and at first she thought she had just imagined Niall's voice. But a hand upon her shoulder made her roll over, her heart thudding at how stricken Niall looked as he leaned over her, his handsome face drawn, his blue-gray eyes ravaged.

Maire knew then that Triona must have told him about Caitlin, and she sat up and threw her arms around his neck even as he sank onto the bed to hold her tightly too.

"Ah, Niall, forgive me! I wanted to tell you—but you were so happy, I couldn't. And I feared you'd ride back to Ferns and try to fight—"

"I'll not be riding to Ferns."

Niall had spoken so harshly that Maire almost didn't recognize his voice, and she pulled away to look into his eyes. Since childhood they had been so close, Niall always there to help and cheer her, yet she saw something in his gaze that she'd never seen before . . . all the boyishness, all the laughter and love of life fled, and in its place a hardness behind the pain that chilled her.

And what of her? What might Niall see in her eyes? He stared at her, too, and brushed a loose strand of midnight hair from her face with such gentleness that she knew her beloved brother hadn't changed entirely.

"Poor, sweet Maire . . . how you've suffered."

Tears stung her eyes, but she willed them away; no amount of weeping would alter the horror she'd seen upon that drawbridge . . . the savage thrust of Gerard de Barry's sword—God help her, Duncan falling to his knees. She had wanted so desperately to go to him even as she'd known Ronan would prevent it, Maire astounded still that he had unleashed one of his arrows and struck Gerard down.

"Triona told us everything, Ronan and I—Good God, you deserve some happiness more than any of us! Irish, Norman, if the man is honorable and truly loves you—"

"I don't know if Duncan loves me . . . loved me." Her throat grew so tight Maire could barely speak. "I don't know if he lives—"

"If he lives, he loves you, the man would be an accursed fool for it to be otherwise!" Niall rose from the bed and began to pace the room, his agitation mounting as he seemed to be thinking aloud. "Ronan won't be happy if I go—Ronan be damned! Did he turn Triona away when he learned of the blood she bore in her veins?"

Maire could only watch Niall with growing concern as he paced back and forth, a wildness about him, his face stricken again, and she feared then that the news Caitlin had forsaken him had not fully struck him yet, far worse depths to be known. She started when he stopped abruptly to look at her, and she saw in his tortured eyes how dearly he suffered, too.

"Do you want to know if the baron lives?"

She stared at him, dumbstruck, her heart begun to race.

"Answer me, Maire O'Byrne! Do you want to know if the man you love lives?"

"A-aye, Niall, but—"

"The devil take it then, at least I can do that much for you. Watch for me within two days."

He said no more but left the room while Maire, incredulous, sank onto the pillows. Surely he didn't intend to ride back to West Meath and Ennell Castle—would he?

She had only to think of the strange wildness she'd sensed within him to know that was exactly what Niall planned, and she knew, too, that no one, not her, not Triona or even Ronan, would be able to stop him. And his words . . . *Good God, you deserve some happiness more than any of us!* Did Niall believe that if Duncan lived, there might be some slight hope . . . ?

Maire rose from the bed, such a tumult of emotion filling her that she didn't want to lie there another moment. Begorra, she'd already done so for two days!

Her legs were shaky, but she managed well enough to reach the ornately carved chest which held all her clothing. Her hands were shaking as she threw back the lid and pulled out a gown of vibrant green silk that made her spirits soar all the more dizzily.

She changed out of her sleeping gown quickly, so light-headed and flushed she had to take a few moments to catch her breath. She donned soft slippers, too, combed her hair, astounded that her appetite had suddenly grown so fierce, her stomach growling noisily.

Triona had coaxed her to eat a wee bit of broth, but she'd taken little else, not wanting to eat, not wanting to speak until Triona had finally convinced her that she must to ease some of her grief. Yet even that hadn't helped, given what she'd heard Ronan shout from the other room about Duncan. She had wanted to do no more than keep her face turned to the wall, the ache inside her so terrible at times she'd wanted to cease breathing altogether.

Maire went to the door, as astonished that the pain seemed not so intense now, though she tried to tell herself she knew nothing yet . . . that she would be foolish to allow vain hope to overwhelm her. Ah, but if it were so! That she and Duncan might yet—

"Aye, little sister, that's much better now."

Maire gasped to find Niall waiting for her just outside her bedchamber, the tiniest familiar bit of light in his eyes as he gave her a fleeting smile, then turned and strode from the dwelling-house.

This time she couldn't keep the tears from coming. As her hope flared all the brighter, she realized he'd given her much more that day than she could ever thank him for.

"Baron . . . the O'Melaghlin has sent his own healer."

As Edward de Valognes bent low to his ear to speak to him, Duncan gritted his teeth through the pain ravaging his body and nodded. But he cursed violently in a rasping voice that didn't even sound like his own when a spare little man with owlish eyes moved to the bed and drew the bloodied bandages from his right side. Some of the linen sticking to the ugly wound had to be pulled away, the sensation stinging like fire.

"Forgive me, lord—oh, aye, clean through to the ribs, not good, not bad—"

"God's teeth, man, which is it?" Duncan gripped the side of the mattress and raised his head to see as the healer began to poke lightly and prod, Edward's usually swarthy face grown so pale the knight appeared as if he might retch. "Will I live or die?"

"You, lord? Ah, me, I'm no seer—"

"Will I live or die?"

His roar making everyone in the room stare wide-eyed, poor Clement who'd exhausted his talents in trying to help him, a pair of O'Melaghlins who'd accompanied the healer, Edward de Valognes and several other knights standing guard at the door to his quarters, Duncan ignored them all and kept his gaze riveted upon the little man who busily began to prepare an herb poultice.

"Most likely you will live, lord . . . unless the wound turns poisonous. I smell some in the flesh already, but I pray it's not too late."

At this grim news Duncan swore again and let his head sink upon the sweat-soaked pillow.

"Your own healer deserves much praise for keeping you upon God's earth this long—is he here?"

"Clement, come."

Ashen-faced, the stout friar approached the bed at Duncan's hoarse command and was immediately handed several iron rods with sharpened tips by the Irishman who appeared only a third his size.

"We must burn the wound."

"Burn it?" Clement's voice stricken, he crossed himself and glanced doubtfully at Duncan. "Lord—"

"Hear the man!" A searing wave of pain so intense struck Duncan that he once more dropped his head to the pillow while Clement blanched and nodded.

"It is a thing learned from a traveling priest who spent many years in the Holy Land," came the Irish healer's grim voice. "Set the rods in the fire—we must waste no time."

Duncan distantly heard Clement's murmured assent through a familiar blackness threatening to overwhelm him.

By the blood of God, he had felt the same before when he'd nearly died two years ago—and he did not want to die! He could not die! Maire was waiting for him, he could sense it even now. She was thinking of him just as he'd thought of little else but her, every moment of agony no matter his curses making him thank the saints in heaven he was yet alive.

"Baron, can you hear me?"

Duncan opened his eyes, Edward's face strangely blurred as the knight once more leaned close to his ear.

"Word has just been brought from Lady de Londres's guards. She threatens not to eat, my lord, not unless she's released at once—"

"Then she may starve." Such fury welled inside Duncan at the thought of Adele, at the thought of Gerard spurred to attack him at his half sister's treacherous urging, that he sensed such violent emotion alone would help him survive. He ground his teeth at another wave of pain. "Let her scream, make her threats . . . there'll be no change to my orders. She remains a prisoner."

Edward de Valognes nodded gravely and moved away, and Duncan shut his eyes against the glowing tips on the rods being brought back to the bed by Clement.

God help him, he thought no more of Gerard, struck through the heart by an Irish rebel's arrow that had saved his own life. He thought no more of Adele.

He clenched his jaw as he sensed heat drawing nearer his flesh, and thought only of Maire.

Chapter 34

"Aye, this babe will be a son for Ronan, I know it."

Maire looked up in astonishment from playing with little Deirdre. Triona's lovely green eyes were alight as she held her hands to her stomach, which still bore no sign she carried a child.

"It's a secret though, Maire. Ronan can't know, not yet. Do you promise me? I want to wait a while longer to tell him."

Maire nodded, her throat tightening at the shadow that touched Triona's face, and Maire knew Triona was thinking of the unborn child, a boy, she'd lost some six months ago. Jesu, Mary, and Joseph, had it been that long? Familiar heartache suddenly gripping her, Maire was glad to be distracted by Deirdre's antics with her wooden toys. Though she'd been back in Glenmalure two months, it was still so hard for her to believe.

Two months. And with each passing day her hope grew dimmer, even the afternoon when Niall had returned with word that Duncan was alive had become a memory more like a dream than it had truly happened.

Niall had refused to enter the stronghold, shouting what he'd discovered at the top of his lungs to clansmen guarding the stout outer gate, who'd then brought the news to Maire. They had said, too, that Niall had then ridden away, adding nothing else to give them a hint as to his destination.

Ronan hadn't been pleased about any of it: Niall riding back to West Meath, his news about Duncan, or that the younger brother he'd chosen as his Tanist and who would one day, if the need ever arose, become the chieftain of the Glenmalure O'Byrnes, had disappeared and not been heard from since.

Not pleased? Maire almost shuddered as she rolled a ball of woolen thread toward Deirdre's snow-white kitten, remembering how furious Ronan had been when a few days had passed and still Niall hadn't returned home.

He'd ridden himself to Ferns in Wexford to speak with Donal MacMurrough, the powerful chieftain as resigned as any father whose daughter had broken her troth to one man so she might marry another. And Donal had seen no sign of Niall, as much to his relief since he wanted no deadly battle fought over Caitlin. Aye, she would be wed to the MacMurrough's godson Brian by now—

"Maire?"

She met Triona's concerned gaze, that she'd remained silent no doubt leading Triona to guess her thoughts. Yet how selfish of her! She tried to summon a smile, but it was halfhearted at best. It seemed she could rarely do better.

"Forgive me, Triona, truly I'm happy for you—"

"As I wish I could be happy for you. I so hoped, for your sake, that you carried a babe, too. Have you told Ronan yet?"

Her throat growing all the tighter, Maire shook her head, the final proof she'd wanted so desperately not to see come only a week ago. Her monthly flow had arrived last month, too, but she hadn't wanted to believe then either, that she didn't carry Duncan's child.

She swallowed hard. Niall had shouted to her clansmen, too, that Duncan was gravely wounded, the villagers he'd spoken to outside Ennell Castle knowing only that a healer had come from clan O'Melaghlin. Now she had no hope of a babe, and if these two long months meant Duncan hadn't survived—saints help her! She couldn't think of it, wouldn't think of it! He had to be alive, or how else would she go on breathing?

As if sensing her despair, Triona rose from her chair and scooped up Deirdre, who began to protest until the beautiful child was placed in Maire's lap. At once chubby arms flew around her neck to hug her, and Maire inhaled the sweet scent of Deirdre's midnight curls. Triona sank to her knees beside her.

"I cannot forgive Ronan for treating you so unkindly, and I will speak of it to him tonight. Begorra, Maire, no more! Two months to lay such anger at your feet. I've held my tongue for too long and—"

"No, Triona, please. It would be far worse to bring this thing between you. Ronan's raided against Normans much of his life, our clansmen—Fiach and the others, your father, too, died at their hands. He cannot help but feel hatred for them."

"Aye, I remember a time when I feared he would hate me as well. . . ."

As Triona fell silent, Maire let Deirdre climb from her lap; the child toddled after her kitten and nearly tripped over Conn, Triona's huge wolfhound, who slept by the hearth. Yet all were startled when a loud pounding came at the door, Conn jumping up to bark, the kitten yowling and streaking into an adjoining bedchamber. Triona glanced at Maire and then rose to rush across the room, gathering up little Deirdre on the way. Maire arose too, as Triona threw open the door to a clansman whose ruddy face in the bright afternoon sun was even redder from exertion.

"Lady, the O'Byrne sent me running to tell you Niall rides across the glen."

"Niall?" Maire hastened as well as she could to reach Triona, who held out her hand, her voice filled with as much scolding as excitement.

"It's time enough he came home to us! Come, Maire, I'll help you."

Together they stepped outside Ronan and Triona's dwelling-house to find other clansmen running toward the gates, wives and laughing children. Maire felt such overwhelming relief she couldn't help being caught up in the excitement, and she found herself smiling too.

All three massive sets of gates guarding the

stronghold had been thrown open to welcome Niall. Maire was out of breath and her legs aching from hurrying by the time she and Triona reached the second. A large cluster of clansmen stood at the outer gate, and Maire could see Ronan's dark head at the front of them all, where he no doubt waited to greet Niall as much as heatedly demand where he'd been.

Yet her brothers were so close, aye, they would resolve any differences between them, Maire was certain. And mayhap one day Ronan would find it within his heart to forgive her. She knew his anger stemmed from love—

"Something's not right. Aye, everyone's grown too quiet."

Maire glanced in alarm at Triona, but it was the way her clansmen were suddenly looking at her, their expressions grave as they parted to let them pass, that made Maire's heart pound.

At the sight of Ronan's black scowl, she felt Triona squeeze her hand tightly even as Maire looked past her eldest brother to the rider who approached the stronghold.

He was alone, no knights, no men-at-arms surrounding him, his shirt of mail glinting in the sun.

Jesu, Mary, and Joseph . . . not Niall, but Duncan—

"Stand your ground, Norman, come no closer!"

Ronan's roar shattering the charged silence, Maire felt as if her knees were giving way when Duncan ignored the command and rode even closer, though he'd slowed his great bay stallion to a walk, his eyes intent upon her as much as Ronan.

"By God, FitzWilliam, I know why you've come, and you will not have her!"

"The choice is not yours, O'Byrne, but Maire's alone," came a voice as fiercely resolute as Ronan's. "If she wishes it, I will make her my bride and none will dare speak against it. King John has sanctioned our marriage—I've only just returned from England to ask his favor—"

"I care nothing for your accursed king or his favor! Leave now, or you'll die here."

Stricken by Ronan's ominous words, Maire saw a flushed-faced clansman then, pushing his way through the silent crowd bearing Ronan's sword.

"Triona . . . no." Her voice no more than a whisper, Maire glanced at her ashen-faced sister-in-law and then back to Duncan to see that he had dismounted and stood with his sword in hand.

"I have not come to fight you, O'Byrne, I owe you my life. I want only to speak with Maire. But if you raise your weapon against me—"

"I do raise it."

Ronan grabbed his sword and lunged away from them to attack even as Triona hoarsely shouted his name, but he gave no heed to her or that Deirdre had begun to cry. Like a clash of titans, Maire watched in horror as Duncan's heavier weapon met Ronan's blow, metal against metal ringing across the glen, the terrible meeting she'd so feared finally come to pass.

She could see at how Duncan fended off a

second blow that he meant only to defend himself, yet Ronan clearly intended to kill him. Within an instant, Duncan was made to fight in earnest, too. Maire felt her heart stop when Ronan barely dodged a blow that would have severed his arm, only to lunge at Duncan so violently that she could not still her desperate scream.

"Ronan, no more. I will tell him to go! I will tell him to go!"

Tears blinding her, she tried to move toward them only to find herself pulled back by the hand and Deirdre thrust suddenly into her arms. It was Triona who ran to Ronan, her cry as angry as anguished.

"Damn you, O'Byrne, I'll not have our son born to this world without a father! Do you hear me? And Maire's babe deserves a father as well—damn the both of you to break the hearts of the women who love you!"

Triona reached Ronan even as he turned around, his sword fallen to his side while Duncan, his sword lowered too, stared at Maire, his chest heaving from exertion, sweat dripping down his face. She hugged Deirdre close, the frightened child still wailing, and went to him. Duncan's gaze was so intent upon her she scarcely realized when Triona eased Deirdre from her arms. God help her, to see him again, to know he lived! Desperate to throw her arms around him, she still didn't dare, not certain of what Ronan might do.

"You bear . . . you bear a babe?"

His voice was labored and she saw, too, from

his grimace how it pained him to draw breath, Maire knowing then just how grave his wound must have been. She wanted nothing more than to tell him she carried his child, their child, but she could only shake her head.

"I wished it to be so, Duncan—"

"By God, woman, what ruse is this?"

Ronan's face was truly thunderous, but Maire saw that Triona held her ground, even lifting her chin a stubborn notch at her husband while she cradled Deirdre in her arms.

"How else was I to make you stop this madness? You've been so angry these past weeks, at Maire, at everyone, I didn't know if my news would be enough . . ."

Triona couldn't finish, her voice breaking, something Maire had rarely heard from her brazen sister-in-law. Ronan cursed under his breath, some of the tension in his shoulders clearly ebbing. He enfolded Triona and his daughter in his arms, though the dark glance he threw at Duncan told Maire the danger was far from past. His voice was harsh when he turned his gaze upon her.

"Tell him to go, as you said."

Maire heard the pain there, too, stabbing her, but she moved closer to Duncan and took his hand, her heart soaring when he enmeshed his fingers with hers. "I cannot, Ronan, I love him. I wish for nothing more than to be his wife."

"Then go, damn you! But know if you leave with this Norman, you'll be forever dead to us—"

"Ronan, no!"

Maire's heart went out to Triona as she stared at her husband in disbelief, her eyes filling with tears.

"She's your sister, Ronan, you can't pretend she doesn't live and breathe! I bear Norman blood, Deirdre, the babe in my womb yet you love—you love!"

Maire's own eyes brimming, she felt Duncan squeeze her hand, and she glanced at him, stunned that Triona's revelation hadn't seemed to surprise him. He looked no more than grim, his voice low as he drew her toward his steed.

"There's no more to be said here. Come."

A lump growing in her throat, Maire saw it was true. Ronan, his arm still around Triona's shoulders, shepherded her and Deirdre toward the gate, and their clansmen stepped aside for them, every familiar face as somber, every O'Byrne as silent.

It was all so terrible, but Maire knew she would alter nothing. She could not. Her life and love were bound together with Duncan. There was no other choice to be made.

His hands were strong and sure as he lifted her onto the saddle, his handsome face so dear, so dear. He joined her then, mounting behind her, his arms going round her to hold her close, and Maire felt her heart soar again.

If not that Ronan's back was still turned to her, though Triona faced her now, Maire couldn't have imagined a more wondrous moment. And Niall, poor Niall. Would she ever see him again? She could only hope that one day he would see how happy she was, his wish for her finally come true.

"Do you know how much I love you, Maire O'Byrne?"

She nodded at Duncan's fervent whisper against her ear—aye, she knew, she knew! He kicked his stallion into a walk to give her time to glance again at her family, and her eyes met Triona's as they moved away, truly the dearest friend she'd ever known. Maire wiped at the wetness on her face, but more came as she thought of everything Triona had done for her.

"She's a brave one, your brother's wife. I heard the story of her true family from King John—he remembers Ronan and Triona still, and not so fondly. I feared then he would refuse our marriage."

"But he did not? Truly?"

Duncan drew her closer, warming Maire even as he whispered huskily in her ear. "He did not. Truly. When I told him I would relinquish my barony to wed you, anything to have you, he thought it better for us to wed and produce as many children as we could to thin the rebel blood—"

"That's what Adele said of you—why she wanted you to have a Norman wife . . ." Maire didn't finish when she felt Duncan tense and suddenly she felt uneasy, too, just thinking of his half sister.

"She's gone, you know. Back to England. She'll not hurt you from the tower where King John sent her—and my half brothers and their vassals have been forbidden ever to set foot in Ireland or they'll join her there."

Duncan hugged her tightly, so tightly Maire had never felt more safe, or more grateful to a

Norman king. Almost to a rocky slope now which led from Glenmalure, she felt a lump rising once more when Duncan stopped their mount so she might gaze a last time upon the O'Byrne stronghold, the only home she'd ever known.

Her breath caught, glad tears filling her eyes.

Ronan stood watching them with Triona, his back no longer turned. And she could see Triona within her husband's embrace smiling too, which told Maire much—Ronan had granted her the only blessing that he could. She knew then he had forgiven her.

As Duncan pressed a fervent kiss to her brow, truly, she had never imagined a more wondrous moment.

Author's Note

Dear Reader,

It is my sincere hope that you enjoyed Maire and Duncan's story. What two courageous people could be more deserving of love, and of each other? I will miss them, I always miss my characters; the wonderful O'Byrne family is very dear to my heart. And I'm wondering . . . what's to become of Niall? I think he deserves a story, too, don't you?

If you would like to write and share your comments, please send a stamped, self-addressed envelope (long or legal-size works best) to me c/o Avon Books, Publicity Department, 1350 Avenue of the Americas, New York, New York 10019.

I enjoy hearing from you.

Until then, I've found an Irish blessing for you, and wish you the best with all my heart.

May all your skies be blue ones
May all your dreams be seen,
May all your friends be true ones

And all your joys complete—
May happiness and laughter
Fill all your days for you,
Today and ever after
May all your dreams come true.

Sincerely,

Miriam Minger